SECRET OF THE CASTLE

Published 2020, by Aionios Books, LLC, Carlsbad, CA, USA

Printed in the United States of America.

ISBN-13: 978-1-949428-09-4 (Paperback)

Library of Congress Control Number: 2020923958

SECRET OF THE CASTLE

BOOK 2
THE SILVER KINGDOM

tayla jean grossberg

AIONIOSBOOKS

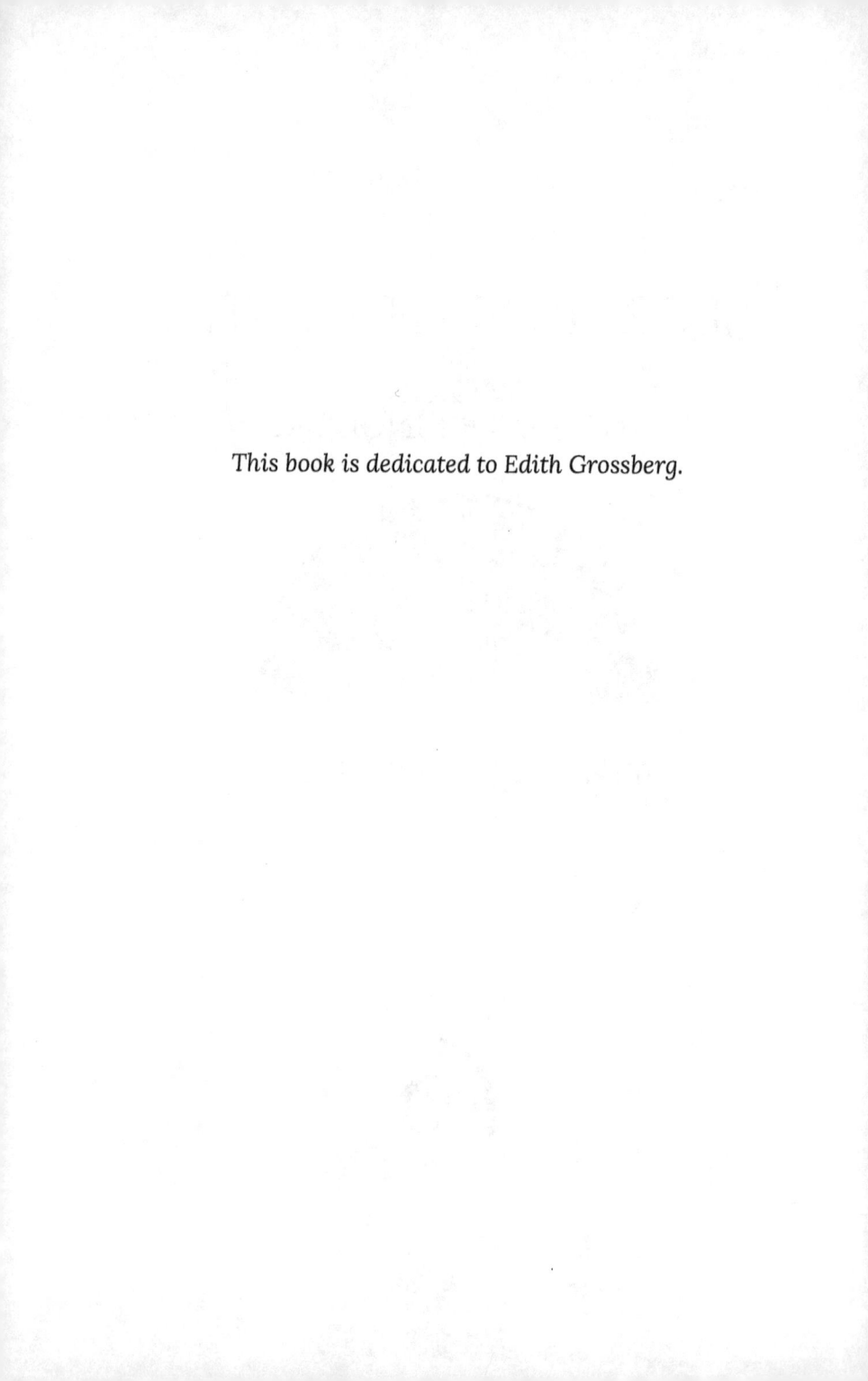

This book is dedicated to Edith Grossberg.

CHAPTER 1

I DON'T WANT them to die.

Rafe's nightmare was so real he might as well have been reliving his past. His whole childhood and cubhood played out before him. He watched himself helping his mother in the kitchen, and his father teaching him to be a wolf. He replayed many long-forgotten memories and many broken promises from years ago. He saw faces he knew he'd never see again.

Rafe knew he was dreaming when he saw his younger self with his family. He knew he had blocked out these memories—even the happy ones were painful. But the enchanted dream catcher under his pillow forced him to remember. He knew he would not wake up easily and he did not fight the spell. He just stood there, in dreamland, and watched his past go by.

In these dreams he could even see the little details, like the cold freezing the lake over. He could see his sister's beautiful dimples when he made her laugh. He could feel his front and hind legs burning from running with his family.

He relived his former happiness. He could feel the love in his heart flare up. There were moments when he recognized his old self: the warmer, kinder Rafe. The Rafe that made jokes because he enjoyed making everyone laugh. The Rafe that didn't hide behind his humor. The one who didn't smile to cover up his loneliness. That Rafe didn't exist yet. He was a kid again, and he wanted to be one forever. He wanted to go back to when life was simple, easy. He wanted to be surrounded again by people who loved him.

He wished he could stay asleep forever. He wished he could have his family with him forever. He wanted to stay right there in that moment. But that moment changed. He relived fights with his father, and the stress from experiencing it again resurfaced. He remembered how it felt to be forced into a leadership position he didn't want. He remembered running away. All those emotions took over again. Anger. Fear. Sadness. Hopelessness.

He watched his younger self fall through the cracked ice, felt the needle-like pain that crept into his heart. Then he watched himself crawl home, frozen and defeated. At this point Rafe wanted nothing more than to wake up.

2

He heard his father's voice telling him not to come back if he left again. He remembered having the urge to. And then the worst part of it all... *I don't want them to die. I don't want them to die. Please don't die.*

He found his family's corpses spread out across the mansion floor. He saw their blood splattered on the walls like paint. He didn't cry—he couldn't. He felt as though even his tears had frozen and everything inside him had turned brittle and now began to break.

"Rafe! Wake up!" Her voice was hysterical. "Rafe! I need you!"

Rafe suddenly sat up, almost head-butting Caitlin in the process. He looked around frantically. His hands shook, heart racing. He was not ready for the hysterical Caitlin he saw in front of him.

"Rafe!" she cried, throwing her arms around his neck. He didn't hug her back. His mind still hung somewhere between sleeping and waking and he also felt suffocated, but she didn't seem to notice as she clung to him.

"What is it?" He said groggily.

"I don't even know where to begin! Do you remember

I told you Brutus and Scarface disappeared down an alley?"

"Hmm?" Rafe was still thinking about his dream.

"Well I followed a cat there, and I'm not sure why." She looked around for it. It sat on the kitchen counter watching them. "That cat!" she exclaimed. "Rafe, I followed that cat!"

Rafe looked at where she was pointing. A black cat sat quietly, viewing them with boredom. Rafe recognized it as the one Maggie was petting by the pool. Caitlin reached for one of the couch pillows. She threw it violently but missed, and the cat jumped to the floor with a look of annoyance.

"Get out!" Caitlin picked up another pillow.

"Stop that," Rafe said reaching for her wrists.

"I hate being followed, hate being watched—even by a stupid cat. And that one gives me the creeps." Then Caitlin took a deep breath and dropped the pillow. She took Rafe's hand and said, "I'm sorry. I'm just so freaked out!"

She was talking so fast Rafe could hardly process everything she said. He had never seen her like this before. True, she lost control of her emotions from time to time, but this was different. "Maggie was probably feeding the cat," Rafe suggested. "That's why she is here. She just wants more food."

But Caitlin was hardly listening. "The alley leads to a secret passageway that leads to hidden rooms and tunnels under the castle. Rafe, it's where all the stolen people are being kept! The king had them kidnapped for the MOP!"

Rafe looked confused. "The what?" He pulled his hand free.

Caitlin didn't take the hint that he felt crowded. She reached for his arm. Touching him comforted her. "The Magic Obliteration Program," Caitlin said with an impatient huff. "The king found a way to erase people's memories and replace them. He does this with a device that his alchemists and healers have created. The victims of this device—Magical people—were moved to River Town so that he could see how well the experiment worked in the long-term."

"That can't be possible," Rafe said. He thought about the Blankness potion that Matilda had given him. Not even that potion was perfected.

"I'm telling you that it's true!" Caitlin said with pleading eyes. "You have to believe me!"

"Alright. So that means your family is Magic?" Rafe said. He thought about how much Gerald despised Magic. *How ironic! Magic!*

But Caitlin hadn't even thought about her family yet. After eavesdropping on everything the king had told Dylan, her thoughts raced and blurred together. "Yes," she said. "I suppose that does mean they have Magic. But they have no recollection of it."

"What about you? How come their memories were altered but yours weren't?" Rafe thought about her memory loss—that maybe she was in the MOP but it hadn't entirely affected her.

"I don't think I was part of the MOP originally," Caitlin confessed. "I don't have the identification tattoo that all the people in the MOP had. You know—the tattoo on the back of the neck just under the hairline?"

"Okay... Then what were you a part of?" Rafe asked.

She paused and blinked, eying him. *Why is he looking at me like that? Is it... disgust?* She hoped it wasn't. Tears welled in her eyes. "Rafe, I found the king and Dylan down there. I heard a lot of things that I should not have."

"Like what?"

It's okay. It's Rafe. I can tell him anything. "The king wanted a weapon, like Ears told us. To create this weapon, he experimented on unborn babies."

Rafe snarled. He was without a doubt disgusted now. Caitlin hoped he would not be disgusted with her, or what she was. She slowly told him, "I was one of those babies."

Rafe turned pale. She wondered if he would vomit. He sat unnaturally still, reminding her of a statue.

"I understand my dreams now because they were never dreams. They were memories. Rafe, I was born and raised in the tunnels under the castle!"

Rafe thought back to their encounter with Ears. She really was a perceptive witch. She had immediately guessed where he was from. He thought about what she guessed when she saw Caitlin....

"I'd say you're from the castle." Rafe had chuckled at

that. He had found her guess to be almost humorous.

"*Don't laugh,*" Ears had said. "*Just look at her. She's built like a warrior, moves and stands like one. She's clearly been trained in their ways.*"

Rafe thought about the little town that no one knew existed.

"*I'm from River Town,*" Caitlin had told Ears.

"*I have never heard of it,*" replied the witch.

"*It's in the Riverlands.*"

The witch had not believed her. "*There's no way that you are from the Riverlands. Tell me where you are really from.*"

The witch had been right. River Town wasn't a real place. Rafe started connecting the dots. "I couldn't find it on the map."

"No, it's not on any maps. The king and his entire staff kept River Town a secret," Caitlin replied. "But I don't know why they erased my memories and then sent me to River Town. All I do know is that I was trained to be a weapon." Caitlin thought about how she had poisoned Stacey, her class rival. "I was trained to be dangerous. I was trained to fight." She thought about how she had beaten up their sparring instructor during one of their training classes, and how she had fought the famous assassin Black Blade, and about her conversation with Eddy. "I was trained to kill for the king."

"Are there others like you?"

"Yes, but their bodies couldn't handle the change,

so they died.... I don't know how my memories got obliterated. I only know the king said two of his 'weapons' survived, and also that one was sent to River Town—a girl. Rafe, I'm that girl."

"And the other one?"

"He is running around inside the castle walls killing people. The king hired Dylan to hunt him and kill him."

"I trust Dylan can handle killing a monster," Rafe said.

Caitlin pulled away from him. "Rafe, he is like me. I can't remember much about him at all. But I know he was created with me. So am I a monster?"

"What? Of course not," Rafe said quickly. "I didn't mean it that way."

"Then how did you mean it?"

"I didn't think before I spoke."

"Well maybe you should have." Caitlin stood up. She felt like he had just stuck a dagger in her heart. Her world was falling, crumbling like a piece of paper. *Is everything I believe a lie? Does this mean I'm bad? Am I just a weapon? A killing machine? What did they do to me? What am I? Does the man inside the walls feel as scared as I did? Is he as lost and confused and twisted as I am? Maybe he's the only person in the world who can understand me....* Her thoughts seemed never-ending.

She realized that she didn't have a family. She never had a family. She never had anyone. Not really.

For a moment, she felt truly alone.

Then Rafe got up and pulled her to his chest. "Let's figure out what we are dealing with before we make any further assumptions."

She hugged him back, letting the feeling of safety he provided engulf her like a warm blanket. She closed her eyes. "Okay."

Caitlin felt better by the time Rafe gently released her from his embrace. She wasn't shaking anymore and her tears had dried up. Rafe had this impact on her. He could be intense, intimidating, and even a little bit dangerous and still make her feel safe. It's why she'd sought him out. He was the one person she knew who could calm her.

"How do you want to handle this?" she asked Rafe.

"I should investigate," Rafe said. "I will go down there and see what I can find."

"We should do that," Caitlin said with a smile, emphasizing the first word.

"Caitlin, I don't want to put you in any danger."

"But we are stronger as a team. Besides, if I'm the king's other... weapon, then I should be able to handle it."

"We're not even sure what you are...." Rafe tried to keep his voice kind so that she wouldn't flip out again.

"I clearly have Magic blood. That's why I got sick when that wild dog bit me."

"But you didn't die. And you healed yourself. If a shifter got infected by the disease, he would go crazy and there would be no cure."

"That's because I'm not completely Magical. I'm not a shifter," she said, voicing what she knew he was smart enough to have already figured out. Then she added, "The disease was created by the healers in the castle by accident. The king said Campbell was responsible for the mistakes. I'm assuming he is the one behind all this."

"Then why would the king kill Campbell?"

"I don't think the king was very interested in any of Campbell's projects," Caitlin conjectured. "He never even saw one of his weapons–children, like me, who were injected with blood from Magical creatures–and he didn't show any interest in the disease."

"Then why would he let Campbell go so far?"

"I think the king liked the idea of having even more power, so he gave Campbell a lot of leeway to see what Campbell could do, what he could accomplish. But when Campbell kept making mistakes and became too much of a liability, the king disposed of him," Caitlin said.

"But now that Campbell is dead, shouldn't he be shutting everything down? Who else will run it for him?"

"I don't know," Caitlin said. "All I know is that he wants Dylan to kill the other weapon."

"Do you think we should let him?" Rafe asked. "Look, I understand that you feel, well, a connection with this... weapon."

"Is it possible to stop Dylan from killing him? If Dylan is as good as I've heard, then I don't think I can stop him."

Rafe snorted confidently. "Maybe not... But we can." Dylan was a good hunter, but Rafe was also a good fighter. It would be interesting to see who would win in combat. Something inside Rafe wanted to see—wanted to hurt the man who killed so many of his kind.

"I don't know how to find him...." Caitlin said. "There are so many tunnels and passageways and rooms. He could be in any of them."

"We'll find him," Rafe assured her. "And we'll help him." Rafe said these words to calm Caitlin down, but he wasn't sure if even he believed them himself. He had no idea what kind of monster the king's men had created.

Chapter 2

MAGGIE WAS ON a class outing: a tour of Sky Castle. She wore her best dress, the one that Rafe had bought her. Her hair was braided and some strands had pulled free and fell around her face. Although she looked like the other girls, she wasn't one of them. She wasn't raised the way they were nor taught their ways.

None were mean, but they weren't kind either. Daisy had told her that it might take her time to make friends. She didn't mind being alone. She had a great imagination to keep her busy. And if she felt lonely, she could always play with Rafe and Caitlin. With the two of them in her life, what more did she need?

The outing was everything Maggie had wanted, and her guide, one of the teachers, taught them about the history of Sky Castle as they toured it. They walked as a group clustered together. The teacher was speaking but Maggie wasn't listening. She was daydreaming. She was imagining herself as a princess with fine clothes and jewelry. She saw all her adoring fans and heard them call her name, cheering for her as she walked past, nodding at them and smiling regally, not too widely and with her mouth closed.

Maggie was enjoying herself. She sometimes fell behind to admire a painting or the décor, but the teacher usually noticed and called her back. There was simply so much to admire. The palace was so big, all they'd get to see was a fraction of it.

As they walked through the ballroom and dining halls, Maggie saw herself dancing with handsome young lords all night, with the light from the chandeliers making her eyes sparkle and her gown glitter. She fantasized daintily eating petite morsels from elegant platters in the castle's elegant halls.

The tour group walked on, and Maggie stopped at the sight of a passageway. She thought she'd heard a faint growl emanating from it. She wasn't scared, not after everything she had seen and survived. What's the worst that could happen? She stood there and listened for a moment. The class group disappeared into another room. The teacher was still talking. Maggie took one step into the passageway. She put her ear against the stone wall.

Something was breathing behind it.

"Hello. Do you need some help?" Maggie asked innocently.

There was no answer.

She took a step back from the wall and looked around. To her left was a small hole in the stones, big enough for her to peek through.

"Meow!"

The cat made Maggie jump. It rushed over to her. It sounded irritated and brushed against Maggie's legs. Maggie tried to walk toward the opening but the cat kept blocking her way. So she lifted it and put it behind her.

"I'm trying to reach the hole!" she told the cat.

The cat hissed at her. Maggie paid no heed. She put her eye against the hole, then caught her breath. An eye was staring back at her! It was bloodshot and yellow. Its skin was unnaturally pale. It was breathing raggedly.

The cat jumped against Maggie's legs and this time she moved backward. At the same time, the creature slammed its fists against the wall. The stones shuddered and rumbled. Maggie froze. The cat pawed her leg. This time Maggie heeded its warning and ran and ran without looking back. The cat kept up effortlessly. Then Maggie realized that she was lost. She had run throughout the castle without any idea of how to get back to her group.

At least she got away from the monster. She could no longer hear it and could no longer see the dark passageway with its rumbling stone wall. She looked behind her with a shudder. She bent down and pet the cat in thanks. It rubbed its head against Maggie's palm and then started walking purposefully down an adjacent hallway. Maggie hesitated and then followed it to a door that was slightly ajar. The cat pushed through effortlessly but Maggie stopped at the threshold.

I shouldn't trespass! she thought. So she stuck her head through the doorway and peeked inside. The room contained a huge canopy bed with dark purple curtains, silk sheets in an assortment of rich jewel tones, and big, fluffy pillows. Lavish curtains covered the large windows and intricate tapestries covered the walls.

Maggie couldn't resist. She meekly stepped inside. Thick wool carpets and plush rugs covered the floors and muffled her soft footsteps.

Her mouth gaped at the full splendor laid before her. The room was filled with paintings of landscapes, portraits of obviously important people she didn't know, jewelry boxes of all shapes and sizes, and clothes in every color for every occasion.

Exotic plants graced the walls by the windows and vases of flowers adorned the tables and shelves. *Oh, how pretty!* she said to herself as she clasped her hands over her gaping mouth. She walked up to each and closed her eyes as she smelled flower after flower, ferns, herbs, and—then she gave a quick gasp. On the canopy bed, hidden behind its half-drawn curtains, sat a lady, cross-legged and surrounded by a mound of pillows and three dogs. She was reading a book that looked large in her slender fingers.

The cat jumped onto the bed and the lady looked up to see Maggie.

The cat jumped back down, hissed at the dogs, and ran from the room.

Should I run too?

Maggie wasn't supposed to be there, but at the same time, she couldn't take her eyes off the beautiful lady. She was wearing pink corset that hugged her body as though it was part of her skin. Her long blond hair fell to her waist.

"Hello," the beautiful lady said in the warmest voice Maggie had ever heard.

Maggie couldn't answer.

The lady closed the book and swung her legs to the other side of the bed. "Are you lost?"

Maggie gulped and nodded. The normally talkative girl was at a loss for words.

"My name is Evelyn," the beautiful lady said, walking over to Maggie. "If you tell me where you need to go, I will gladly help you find your way back."

"Are you a lady?" Maggie blurted out.

"Why yes, I'm a duchess. My name is Lady Evelyn," she replied with a smile.

"You're so pretty," Maggie said with admiration.

Lady Evelyn laughed and Maggie looked up at her wide-eyed. Her laugh was as gentle as a songbird's and Maggie forgot all about the creature she'd seen behind the wall.

"I think I've heard your name before," Maggie said.

16

"Do you own the school?"

"Yes, I do. I love teaching and I love children."

"But I wasn't accepted. I go to another school," Maggie said.

"That's odd," Evelyn replied. "My school is designed for children like you."

"Children like me?" Maggie wrinkled her brow in confusion.

"Special children," Evelyn winked but didn't elaborate. Instead she asked Maggie questions and listened intently. She looked truly interested as Maggie talked about how badly she wanted to become a lady, about the life she'd been leading, about her family, and on and on.

"Can you teach me to be like you?" Maggie asked Lady Evelyn when she finally ran out of words.

I wish I could, Lady Evelyn thought. I could take this precious little girl and raise her myself, but the sweet thing already has parents. "Alas, I cannot, although I wish I could," she confessed.

Maggie's shoulders drooped in disappointment.

"I'll tell you a secret though."

Maggie perked up.

"Will you promise to keep it just between us? A lady's promise?"

Maggie nodded eagerly.

"A lady always keeps her hopes up!" Evelyn chirped.

Maggie repeated her words optimistically: "A lady always keeps her hopes up!"

"Come then, let's get you back to your group." Lady Evelyn rose from the bed and took Maggie by the hand.

Once they reached the school group, the teacher rushed over to them. "Maggie! I've been worried sick! Where have you been?"

"I'm sorry," Lady Evelyn replied. "Please don't scold her. It was my fault. I didn't mean to keep her so long."

The teacher was in no position to question the duchess. She broke her gaze and looked down at Maggie. "It's alright. I'm just glad you are back."

"Will I see you again?" Maggie asked, looking up at Lady Evelyn.

"That depends. Remember our secret?" Lady Evelyn asked.

Maggie nodded with a big smile.

As she watched the little girl disappear with the tour, Lady Evelyn wondered if she could contact her parents to ask them if Maggie could help her with some errands in the castle. She liked the sweet little girl so much. She wished she had one of her own.

Upon returning to her chambers, Lady Evelyn was surprised to hear someone call out from behind her.

"You're not planning on stealing one of those children, are you?" the silken voice drawled.

Lady Evelyn didn't have to turn around to know who it was. She knew that voice all too well. But she turned around cautiously anyway.

"Whatever gave you that idea, Katherine?"

The king's advisor had snuck up behind her. It disturbed Evelyn how easily she could appear out of nowhere without a sound.

"I'm talking about children that disappear too often these days," Lady Katherine countered back.

Lady Evelyn knew that children were disappearing all around the Silver Kingdom. It was truly horrific. No one knew where they were being taken or by whom. "Are you suggesting what I think you are?" Lady Evelyn tried to stand up as tall as possible but never managed to completely hide her fear from the most powerful woman in the kingdom.

Katherine met her petrified eyes and smiled as if it was a game. "I heard that several children from your school have disappeared."

Evelyn's face went blank: Katherine had struck a nerve. Evelyn couldn't answer her back even if she wanted to.

No response.

"I recall that when you came to the castle you told me you wanted a big family," Lady Katherine pressed.

"I'm not stealing other people's children," Evelyn protested.

"I believe that," Lady Katherine cooed, speaking to Lady Evelyn as if she knew everything but enjoyed taunting her anyway. "You're too smart to steal someone else's child."

"I don't know what you mean."

"I mean you know a child could never be made into your own." Katherine sighed dramatically. "Oh, how young and ambitious you once were! I remember the first time I saw you. You were cradling someone else's baby. You've always had a love for children."

Lady Evelyn nodded cautiously.

"And then there was the first time you laid eyes on Duke Patterson...."

Lady Evelyn remembered that day very well. From the moment she saw him she fell in love. She wanted him all to herself in a big house filled with children.

"It's a shame you've not produced an heir for him," Lady Katherine continued. There was no sympathy in her voice. "Maybe you are too busy focusing on other people's children at the school instead of focusing on having your own. Or maybe, they are a distraction from the truth."

"How long have you known?!" Lady Evelyn interjected, her voice wavering. Lady Evelyn hadn't even told her own husband. Tears welled up in her big blue eyes.

"I've known ever since you got married," Lady Katherine said. "You did not conceive on your honeymoon or any time thereafter. It's obvious."

20

Evelyn looked down in shame. She hated Katherine more than she'd thought possible but was too scared to stand up against her. Saying the wrong thing to the king's right hand could result in beheading.

"Stay away from that new girl," Lady Katherine said. "She'll never be yours."

There was something almost threatening in Lady Katherine's voice. Then she smiled spitefully and walked away.

Evelyn felt empty. What the king's right hand had said was true. She would never have a child.

CHAPTER 3

HE WAS A good son, a strong warrior, a brilliant fighter, and an intelligent man. He had always done everything his father asked of him without defiance. He took pride in becoming the man he was today and followed in his father's footsteps, yet he often thought about leaving his trade. He'd never thought it wrong. He killed the bad guys, saved the innocent, but the king's experiments with children and helpless adults somehow felt wrong.

Dylan felt muddled. He didn't think he should interfere—it's not like he could stop the king—and he himself had killed hundreds of Magical kids and adults. So why did he feel so guilty now? It's not like the king had asked him to help with the MOP. His Highness simply wanted him to kill another monster, one created by the healers and alchemists—a monster that took innocent lives.

What would his father do? Surely not defy the king. No one would be foolish enough to do that. Besides, a good son would do what his father told him.

Kill the beast.

Dylan wasn't sure what he was up against. The king didn't describe his failed weapon. He only said it was good at fighting and very dangerous. But Dylan wasn't scared. He had his bow and arrows on his back. He had one sword in his left hand and a torch in his right. *How hard could handling it be, just one-on-one? This creature can't be totally crazy. It's not attacking blindly or it would have attacked the patronizers by now. It must be choosing its victims—choosing fights it can win and not thrashing around needlessly. Would it see me as a target? Or would it realize my sword can kill it and decide to avoid an encounter?*

Dylan let his thoughts roam as he searched through the tunnels for the monster. Some portions of the tunnels had more sunlight than others, so he was able to see without help from his torch. But some areas were so dark that he could only see five to ten feet ahead. Some walls were covered with green moss while others smelled of mold and decay. Some tunnels were littered with bones and others were crawling with rats.

Dylan walked on and on until he was lost, but he'd been lost before. Although he had a map of the tunnels, it was hard to read by torchlight, especially while he held his sword.

He kept wandering and much time passed. At first, every little sound made him jump and sometimes it was so quiet he wondered if he'd imagined the sounds he'd thought he'd heard. He stopped after a while and let out an exasperated sigh. There were too many tunnels. It was hopeless. He was never going to find the beast, but he wondered if he could set a trap for it somehow. Then he smelled something rotten. The stench was so bad he covered his nose with his arm. He walked toward it. A corpse. The body was mutilated so badly Dylan couldn't tell if it was male or female. It had been down in the tunnels for a while. His strong stomach kept him from puking.

How many has this monster killed? I must find it soon.

He started walking back the way he came. He walked past the patronizers. They made him jump. Their soulless bodies stood there like they were dead. He couldn't tell if their eyes were on him because their hoods hung low over their faces. It was strange to think that they were once normal humans, like him.

What would happen if people knew what was going on down here? Would they riot? Or would they support the king?

He walked past the door that had imprisoned so many men, women, and children. *Do they count as human?* They were shifters and monsters. *They deserved to die.* But he would want them to die quickly. There was no need to make them suffer. Not all the creatures he'd hunted had died quickly. He had tortured some until they told him where to find their families.

But why do I feel this way? he thought. *What more is there to do here?*

Dylan started exiting the tunnels when something stopped him. It was a sound he had never heard before. No word could describe it except hell. "What is that?" he asked the patronizer.

It didn't answer him. It just stood there without responding.

"Do you know what that is?" Dylan asked the other patronizer.

It also stood unresponsive and Dylan wondered if they could speak. They were experiments gone wrong. Dylan shuddered at the thought of them once being people like him, like his aunt Lillian, like his father.

What did they do to deserve this?

As Dylan walked away from the emotionless creatures, he knew there was no saving them. There was nothing left to save. No heart. No soul. No humanity. But he could save other people who lived in the castle, if only he could find the creature—that failed weapon. He headed toward the sound—a banging against the walls, a rattling of chains.

His pace slowed as he approached. His grip on his sword tightened. Then he leaped forward, swinging the torch toward the sound. The creature didn't move away from the flame like he had expected. Instead, it jumped toward it! But its chains held it back and it screamed.

Dylan staggered backward. He was shocked. It wasn't the king's weapon. It was the sort of creature he had only read about in storybooks. It had a horse's body with huge, sharp iron hooves. It was enormous and monstrous. Its teeth were long and sharp and like none Dylan had ever seen, too many for it to close its mouth properly. It licked its lips. Blood dripped from them. The beast had been starved, and its ribs were nearly piercing through its skin. Its red eyes looked at Dylan with famished hatred as it struggled against its chains.

"You're a hell horse."

Of course, the creature didn't respond. It was the deadliest being in the Silver Kingdom. It hated every living thing except its own kind, to which it was fiercely loyal. And even though it was tied up, Dylan was scared.

I run toward what I fear.

He unsheathed his sword shakily. The hell horse didn't flinch.

Should I kill it? Is it part of the experiments?

These animals were known for having uncontrollable tempers. Given the chance, it would rip Dylan to shreds. Dylan looked more closely at its body. There were no more muscles. *What does it eat and drink?* It looked like everyone had forgotten about it long ago. Or they just didn't care. It was too weak to pull free.

Dylan wondered if its friends were too far away for it to call them. Usually hell horses stayed together and fought together. They had a special mental connection. A hell horse was supposed to be able to call its herd unless it didn't belong to one.

"Are you a lone stallion?" Dylan asked it.

The creature lunged forward. Dylan looked at it in pity and lowered his sword. He could put the animal out of its misery. Killing it would be a mercy and he would try to be quick. He raised his sword again and eyed its neck, just above the collar. Dylan swung.

The horse had perfect timing. Instead of slashing head from body, Dylan's blade connected with metal, severing the beast's chain in two.

Dylan's eyes widened in fear, like those of a deer about to be shot, and for a moment, he could swear the animal was smiling. Then the hell horse lunged at him.

Dylan blocked but his blade broke into shards between the beast's teeth, causing him to lose his balance and fall to the ground. But instead of attacking Dylan, the horse bolted away, stomping on and dislocating his right shoulder with an iron hoof.

Dylan screamed in pain as he watched the hell horse dash down the tunnel. He had just unleashed the kingdom's most dangerous creature into the castle, among many innocent people. *What have I done?*

His grip loosened on the hilt, letting what remained of his blade to clatter to the ground. He pulled himself to his feet. Then he clenched his jaw, took a deep breath in, followed by a long breath out—and slammed his right shoulder hard into a wall. He staggered dizzily and almost fell but managed to maintain his balance. Dylan then took several slow, deep breaths and slowly rolled his shoulder to the front, the back, up, and down, then rotated it, testing it. *Fixed it*, he grunted softly to himself.

He readied his bow and clutched an arrow in his hand. How fortunate he was a good shot. How fortunate he knew how to fix a dislocated shoulder. How fortunate that the horse's hoof only struck a glancing blow; otherwise his shoulder would have been completely mangled and useless.

He rushed after the hell horse, hoping it wouldn't cause a catastrophe. *I have to stop it before it hurts anyone. I have to.*

CHAPTER 4

"I HAVE TO tell you something," Rafe said, looking intently at Caitlin.

The sun had already set and they were both in her bedroom. They had just returned from a fruitless search for the monster that the king had created–the weapon that was her counterpart. Soft candlelight set Caitlin's hair aglow and caught the amber specks in her green eyes. She had been so open and honest with him that it was only right he returned the favor. Trust and communication were a two-way street and he had hidden himself from her for far too long. It wasn't an easy confession, but it was time.

"What is it?" she asked, a worried expression creeping across her face.

"Do you remember when we were at Matilda's house and you left before I did?"

She nodded and Rafe hesitated nervously. She sensed his anxiety and became nervous in response.

"She gave me something," Rafe said, choosing his words carefully. He didn't want Caitlin to feel betrayed and he knew she was temperamental—the slightest misstatement or an unfortunate turn of phrase could upset her.

"What did she give you?" Caitlin prompted when he didn't immediately continue.

Rafe stuck his hand into his pocket and pulled out a tiny vial. He handed it to Caitlin.

"I don't know what this is," she said, studying the bottle.

"It's a potion called Blankness," Rafe slowly described. "It's used to give and take memories."

Caitlin recalled him asking Ears if it was possible someone had used a potion to make her forget her past. "Why would she give this to you?" Caitlin inched away from Rafe and her expression changed from one of trust to caution.

"I think you already know the answer."

"You were going to use it on me?" Disbelief choked her throat and tears welled up in her eyes. "Why?"

"It was just a precaution," Rafe said. "I wasn't absolutely sure I could trust you back then. You know my secret. I had to be safe."

"Safe?... Trust?... And what about me? Did you ever think about me?"

"Of course I did."

"So what do you call this?" She shook the bottle in his face.

"But I never used it. And I trust you now." Rafe stepped forward, repeating himself with a well-meaning gesture. "I trust you, Caitlin."

She cried.

To Rafe it was the most damaging sound in the world. His heart broke. "I am so sorry." He stepped closer to hug her but she pushed him away. It was the first time she had ever pushed him away.

"I learned long ago that secrets and lies are necessary because the truth is hard to handle." Rafe's thoughts raced beyond his words but dared not mention them. *I should have just disposed of the bottle and never mentioned it. All of this could have been prevented.*

Her emotions and temper took over. "You're sorry?... SORRY?!" she screamed at him. "Do you think the people who stole my memories are also sorry?"

"Don't compare me to them," Rafe growled.

"But you wanted to do the exact same thing!" she screamed. "Lies... secrets... it's not right! Imagine what this could have done to me—to us. It's not right to mess with someone's mind! It's not right to lie to them —and definitely not right to change who they are!"

"I wasn't going to change you," Rafe said.

"Then what were you going to do?"

"It would have made you forget me, if needed," Rafe confessed.

31

Caitlin wanted to hit him. She wanted to badly. She had never felt more betrayed. "I've been open with you about everything. Yet you've kept things from me, especially this...." She turned away from him for a moment to wipe tears from her face, and then slowly turned back.

A damaging silence took hold before she spoke.

"You know what, Rafe? I'll never forget you.... but I'm not sure I'll ever forgive you."

"Caitlin..."

"Leave me. Please."

"I—"

"Get out! Now, Rafe!" she screamed.

And with a heavy heart, Rafe turned to leave. He could understand how she felt. He was the one person she trusted. The one person she relied on. The one person she told everything to. He should have told her sooner or not at all. In his heart he knew she could forgive him with time. Doubt ate away at his mind but he thought she would have to forgive him; otherwise he couldn't tell her what he needed to most. I don't want to lose you, he repeated the thought over and over in his mind.

He stopped to linger at the doorway and then his shoulders heaved before he turned back to look at her. Their eyes met. But she did not stop him, did not go to him.

And then, "I love you," he said.

But this was not the time. She broke eye contact

and turned her head away. She heard the door click softly shut. He was gone.

That night Caitlin cried herself to sleep.

Later that night, Caitlin dreamed. She saw herself as a sixteen-year-old, the same age she was now. She was seated chained to the stone floor of a prison cell.

In the adjoining cell lay a body that looked almost human. His nails had metal tips that could easily rip open someone's throat. His eyes were unnaturally red and yellow and his teeth unnaturally sharp.

"I can't control my body," he told Caitlin. "I shift and lose control."

"I don't know what to tell you, Divan," Caitlin said. There was little hope left in her heart. Every day she felt more dead than alive. Every day it was harder to open her eyes but she wouldn't give up as long as her heart was beating.

"How do you do it?" Divan asked. "Stay so healthy? And calm?"

Caitlin was in fact healthy compared to Divan. "Calm?" she asked. "Didn't you see what happened last time I tried to escape?" She had tried to escape several times but every time she tried, she got caught by the patronizers. She had killed many of them and planned on killing the rest. She'd ripped them to shreds along with the healers. She was surprised she hadn't been executed yet.

"You're calm most of the time," he said.

"My thoughts aren't." She was always thinking of a way out. She wanted to get out alive. She wanted to get as far away from this place as possible. She hated these dark tunnels and dreary rooms.

"Mine aren't either," Divan said. "I'm changing a lot—but I don't know into what."

Caitlin didn't say anything to that. She didn't even know what she was or what she would eventually become. She was not scared of herself but everyone else seemed to be.

"I don't think we're ever getting out of here," Divan said sadly.

"I refuse to think like that," Caitlin said.

"They should be coming to get you soon," Divan said. "For more tests. Always more tests. More potions. More needles..." He rubbed at the angry bruises and purple streaks on the insides of his arms, moaning softly.

"Let them come," Caitlin said as she slowly lay down on her side. She closed her eyes even though she was not tired. She heard their footsteps long before they arrived at her cell. Then she heard the key turn in the lock and the cell door swing open.

She was ready for them.

They walked in, their hulking presence almost filling her cell. Patronizers—two of them. They were very strong and fast. She had fought them before and it wasn't easy. Fighting them was the only way out of here and the idea of hurting them made Caitlin excited.

The first patronizer bent down to unlock the chain anchored to the wall. Caitlin felt it come loose. Then as it leaned forward to pick her up, she swung her legs around and kicked its legs out from under it. The patronizer fell backward, banging its head against the cell bars. If it was human it might have cracked its skull. Caitlin did not focus on it or waste time. She immediately tried to bolt but the other patronizer was blocking her exit.

Divan reached through the bars for the patronizer that was closer to him. He grabbed its head—it was strong—and twisted it. Caitlin heard it snap.

The other showed no remorse for its dead friend. It tried to slam the gate shut but Caitlin stopped it with her shoulder. She'd worry about the pain later.

The patronizer at the gate had one hand made of daggers. Caitlin knew it was lethal, but it held the keys to her cell in its other hand, a bony thing missing skin. If she could get out without having to get them, she would. She tried knocking it off its feet by bracing herself against the gate and kicking with all her might.

I can't even come close! So she re-evaluated and re-engaged.

She sprang off her back foot trying to run fast past

the patronizer, but the chains clasped to her wrists dragged too heavily behind her. The patronizer stepped on them, yanking her backward. She turned around to face it and manipulated the chain so it would twist around the patronizer's legs, but it mirrored her every step.

She wondered if it expected her to surrender or if it even thought that far ahead. She pulled the chain again, and at that moment, the patronizer lifted its foot. She fell backward and groaned. Then the patronizer was next to her in a flash. It kicked her in the stomach and knocked the breath from her body and then stepped on her chains, pinning her once again.

"The keys!" Divan called.

She reached for them. The patronizer's dagger-fingers slashed at her, but she snatched the keys just in time for her hand not to get sliced off and tossed the keys to Divan. He caught them and unlocked his shackles.

Caitlin squirmed away as far as her shackles would let her go. The patronizer leaned in, its putrid, hot breath washing over her face, and slowly brought its dagger-fingers to her neck. She stopped squirming and looked into those emotionless yellow eyes. She knew he would not feel guilty if he killed her.

Then Divan threw a rock from his cell that hit the patronizer on the head, throwing it off balance. Caitlin tried to wriggle free and was almost out from under the patronizer when it yanked her hair violently with its bony hand. She couldn't pull free. It slashed at her throat with its other hand but missed and cut her hair instead. She fell forward and tried to crawl away. But it grabbed the chain and pulled her back. She screamed and kicked but its steel legs hardly felt the impact. It pulled its dagger-loaded hand back to strike. Caitlin flinched. *I'm going to die.*

Then Divan, who had used the keys to open his own cell, threw his chains around its neck and pulled the patronizer off Caitlin. She got to her feet, ready to run. Divan pulled the patronizer into his cell and shoved it down onto the floor. Once it fell, Divan dropped his shackles and slammed the door shut, locking it as fast as he could.

The patronizer looked at him from where it lay on the ground, its expression placid. Not tired. Not panting like him.

Divan rushed over and unlocked Caitlin's shackles, freeing her from the heavy, dangling chain.

"Thank you for helping me," Caitlin said, rubbing at her raw wrists.

"No, thank *you*," he said.

Caitlin got to her feet and dusted herself off. She looked at her hair that lay all over the floor and was thankful it wasn't her blood.

"Well, are you coming?" she asked.

Divan nodded.

Together they made their way through the tunnels, searching for the nearest exit

Lady Evelyn sat on her bed and stared out in front of her. Her eyes were red from crying and her nose was stuffy. Lady Evelyn was a strong woman, which meant that she didn't cry often. Even her closest friends never saw her cry.

"Darling?" her husband said as he mindfully opened the door. Duke Riley Patterson held a bouquet of colorful flowers in his hand. They were beautiful and smelled sweet. He always spoiled her with the finest wines or the most fragrant flowers. There was nothing in the world he would deny her. So his smile faded at the sight of her wiping tears from her cheeks. He sat down next to her on the bed and gently took her hand in his. "What's the matter?"

Evelyn knew he was a caring man and she never doubted his love for her. He supported her and helped her with everything. Their marriage was famed to be one of the best in the Silver Kingdom.

"I have to tell you the truth," she said. She shifted her weight on the silk sheets and struggled to look into his husband's worried eyes.

"Alright," he said. He was as calm as ever. He always knew how to handle every situation, whether personal or professional, and was able to instill confidence and trust in those around him.

Lady Evelyn gathered herself to tell him something that was very difficult to say.... "I didn't know this before we were married," she sniffled. "But I can't have any children."

The duke's face turned pale. He held her hand tightly and looked at her as if the news she told him did not change anything. He titled her chin up so she could look into his eyes. She met his gaze.

"Would you like to consult a healer about this?" he asked her gently. He was always gentle. Her feelings and needs were always his top priority.

"I have seen them all," she confessed. "They all say the same thing to me. I will never ever have a child.... You will never have an heir."

"It's alright," he tried to soothe her.

"No, it's not, Riley," she said. She wiped her nose with her hand and then quickly wiped her hand on the bed linen as her cheeks turned even redder and more tears fell.

The duke didn't look shocked at all, not even surprised.

"It doesn't look like this news has come as a shock to you," she blinked up at him.

"It's not a surprise," he said calmly.

"Really? You've known all along?"

"Until now I had only guessed," he said.

"But why did you not say anything?"

"I was waiting for you to tell me," he said, cupping her cheek in his hand.

She leaned against his hand and squeezed her eyes shut, her breaths slowly becoming less ragged. "I'm sorry I waited so long to tell you. I have been clinging on to hope for so long. I thought a miracle would happen."

"It's alright."

"It really isn't," she sobbed, shaking violently. "Why can't I do the one thing a woman is supposed to do? Why am I broken?"

"You're not broken!" he objected. "Don't ever say that!"

"I understand if you want to leave me for another," she continued. "You need an heir."

"Ludicrous!" he moved closer to her and pulled her into his arms. She closed her eyes and leaned into him. "You're the woman I love. I will never leave you."

"But what will the people say? They will start talking if we don't have children in the next few years."

"What does it matter?" he stroked her hair from her face and kissed the tip of her nose. "We're in no hurry to have children. If you wish, continue to consult healers and maybe one of them might figure something out in time."

"And if they can't?"

Riley thought for a moment. "How do you feel about adoption?"

CHAPTER 5

BLACK BLADE WALKED into the Wilde family's new house. There was no need to break in as the door was unlocked. *Why don't people lock their doors? They were making this too easy.*

He walked from the front door right into the living room. The house was small and cozy, quiet and empty —but messy. Shoes were lying around and there were breadcrumbs on the table. The house did not have paintings or drawings on the walls as the family had not had a lot of time to decorate.

Black Blade looked around and wondered where the wolf was. The wolf would fight him. And where were the parents? If they saw him, they'd probably start screaming like their little girl probably would— she was also not home. Then his eyes came to rest on Caitlin Wilde. She was sleeping peacefully on the couch in the middle of the room. The couch Caitlin slept on was big and looked comfortable. Behind her, on the kitchen table, was a black cat. The cat watched him as if he was a mouse and growled softly.

Black Blade paid it no attention. *It's just a harmless cat.* He could easily throw a dagger her way and kill her if he wanted to. But he never killed animals. He loved them too much to ever hurt them. Like his horse, his best friend in the whole wide world.

Caitlin's eyes fluttered and then she squirmed and groaned. Black Blade immediately fixed his attention on her, and for a moment, he expected that she would wake up. When she did not but kept groaning softly and thrashing around, he realized she was having a nightmare and he grinned.

Should he kill her now while she was sleeping? Black Blade had never killed anyone in their sleep before. It wasn't a matter of honor. He also enjoyed a good fight and killing someone who was asleep would take much of the fun out of the job.

But why would he kill her now? The old man was dead, so technically the job no longer existed. He was not going to get paid. *Do I even want to kill her?*

He thought back to how she made him feel the last time he attempted to assassinate her and failed. She humiliated him. She made him look like a joke. If she lived, she would be a constant reminder that he had failed to kill her. That he couldn't kill her.

Black Blade made a decision. *Well, there's a first time for everything.* He pulled his dagger from its sheath.

You deserve death after damaging my reputation. I'll do it quickly so you don't wake up from your dream. You'll die inside your nightmare and that, that will have to be fun enough for me. He allowed himself a quiet little chuckle. He crept toward her silently.

The black cat watched his movements and then jumped off the kitchen counter and hopped up onto the side of the couch. She locked eyes with Black Blade before she jumped on Caitlin's face. Caitlin woke with a fright and sat up. The cat jumped to the floor and ran away.

"What the—" Caitlin's hands first flew to her face and then up to shield her head while still allowing her to see her surroundings, to see Black Blade. There was a moment when the two of them just stared at each other.

Caitlin was the first to react. She flipped over the back of the couch at the same time that Black Blade sent his knife flying. It plunged into a pillow. Caitlin was behind the couch now, using it to shield her body.

"Come now, girlie-girl," Black Blade said. "Don't make this any harder than it should be."

"Did you seriously just ask me to give up?" she asked and peeked out from the side of the couch. She couldn't see him.

"I did," he said. "Sorry, did I not make it clear enough?"

"No, you did, but I'm not surrendering or dying, so forget it."

Again, she peeked out from the side of the couch.

43

He threw a second dagger. She saw it just in time to dart under cover again. It missed and she heard it scrape the floor.

"Please kindly step away from the couch," he said clearly. "I'd like to get a clear shot you."

"Fat chance, Blunder Blade. You'll have to come and get me," Caitlin smiled. She realized that wasn't scared at all.

"Don't mind if I do, wild girlie-girl." Chuckling at his bad pun, he advanced to the side of the couch where her head had stuck out moments earlier. Caitlin retreated to the other side. She then got to her feet and reached for the vase closest to her. She flung it at him, hitting him squarely in the chest. He screamed out in surprise and anger.

"Cheeky chit!" Black Blade brushed cut flowers and stems off before throwing another dagger.

Caitlin shifted her shoulder backward and it missed. She taunted him with smirk. "Is the great Blunder Blade almost out of daggers?"

"Guess again, girlie!" he screamed, running toward her with one in each hand.

He slashed at her. She ducked and grabbed his wrist. She twisted, but he was stronger and twisted free. He slashed at her with his other hand. She leaped backward, missing the blade by inches.

She threw her fist at him and connected with his nose. Blood spurted out. He stumbled backward but soon regained his bearings. Unfortunately, he then lost control of his emotions and ran straight at her with one of his hands cocked back, clearly telegraphing his intent. He swung wildly, but she saw and was faster, easily side-stepping him. She watched him slam face-first into a wall.

"I hope my wall's okay!"

"That's it!" He shook off the insult and injury and then turned to face her. He was in his element now and having a ball.

She punched again but this time he was ready for it. He grabbed her arm and twisted hard. She cried out in pain, unable to pull free. He hit the side of her head with his free hand. She slammed an elbow into his side and his grip loosened. She pulled free and bent down to retrieve his daggers. He smashed his knee into her face. She stumbled backward and tripped over something—a shoe?—falling on her back flat onto a delicate side table. The wood split from the force of her fall and the vase resting on it shattered. She could feel the rough wood tear through her skin as the table buckled with her to the floor. She reached for a narrow, loose board and threw it dagger-style at Black Blade as he dove for one of his dropped knives. Its jagged edge ripped at his hand but the wound wasn't severe enough to stop him.

Caitlin rolled over and got to her feet. She hit Black Blade again but he blocked well. She lost balance and fell forward. He flipped her over his hip, slamming her to the ground again. She reached for the wood piece that she had thrown at him. It wasn't a very good weapon since it didn't have a proper grip. She felt splinters of wood dig painfully into her fingers and palm. Black Blade had his knife again.

"Why didn't you bring your swords?" she asked mockingly after recalling that Black Blade had lost them in his last encounter with her.

"I don't need them to kill you," he sneered.

"Why do you want to kill me?" she asked. "Don't you know Nicolas Campbell is dead?"

"I know," he said, throwing the dagger but just missing her.

It was the perfect feint. She dodged to the side he intended, and he rammed into her. She fell backward against the wall. She swung her board at him again, but he ducked and got inside her reach, grabbing her hand.

"Then why... do you," she struggled against his grip between words, "...want me dead?"

"To prove that I can kill you.... Any last words?"

"Go to hell."

He ripped the board from her hand and buried it into her shoulder. She screamed in agony.

Dylan ran knowing he would probably not catch up with the hell horse. It sprinted past a patronizer who did not so much as bat an eye. Patronizers were ordered to guard the MOP and the scope of their responsibilities did not extend beyond that.

The hell horse accidently collided with another patronizer, raising its front legs high and stomping down hard. The trampled patronizer lay still.

As Dylan ran past it, he wondered if it could feel any pain. Like zombies, the other patronizers stared blankly. They didn't flinch as the hell horse galloped past them and did not check to see if their fellow guard was alright.

The hell horse wanted out. It would do anything. It felt angry and bloodthirsty, claustrophobic and trapped. It would find an exit one way or another. It galloped and galloped, then reached a dead end. Rays of sunlight shone through cracks in the tunnel walls. The hell horse pawed the ground and charged straight for a wall without slowing. The wall shattered against its body and stones flew left and right.

Dylan could hear people screaming as the beast emerged from the tunnels like a demon from hell. He could only imagine their horror.

He followed the demon horse through the hole in the wall and watched it storm through clusters of people, watched it sink its teeth into an unlucky man, lifting him up and throwing him to the side. The man screamed in agony as bone and flesh ripped from his shoulder. The starving beast crunched with desperate satisfaction. Dylan steadied his aim but—too late—the horse was gone, disappearing almost immediately from sight. Dylan couldn't tell which direction it had run. He looked right then left. There were too many alleys, too many twisted passageways. Dylan's worry set in deeper. *It'll kill so many people on its way out of the castle.*

He ran after it. The king's guards had already begun gathering to defend the people—some by horse, others by foot. But they were all scared stiff. They knew they didn't stand a chance.

Dylan heard people screaming and hooves clattering and ran in the direction of all the commotion, down one alley and around a corner. He arrived in time to see the hell horse look hungrily at a set of guards. A low rumble escaped its mouth. He thought the horse would attack them immediately, but it stopped instead to study the guards.

Just how smart is that hellish creature? Dylan wondered. But his train of thought was interrupted when something very strange and unexpected happened.

The hell horse looked away from the guards and pricked up its ears as if hearing something that Dylan could not. Suddenly, the beast took off.

CHAPTER 6

"ONE DAY I am going to be as beautiful as Lady Evelyn," Maggie told Rafe.

He had gone to her school to walk her back home. He hadn't asked Caitlin to come with him. He felt that leaving her alone was better than being rejected. He knew that she wouldn't want to walk with him.

I love you.

Why had he said that? Out of all the things he could have said he'd picked the worst three words possible. Usually he was so smooth and good with his words. He never got tongue-tied and always said the right thing. What was it about Caitlin that made him tell her the truth and blurt things out?

He had ruined everything. She hated him now. How long would it take her to forgive him? Would she ever look at him the same way? Would she ever trust him again?

"I am going to talk like her," Maggie said and then spoke in a softer and kinder voice. "And walk like her." She walked a little faster. "And be like her!"

Rafe wasn't listening to Maggie like he always did. Usually he gave her his full attention, but now his thoughts were running wild. Maggie held his hand but he was almost not aware of it. He wondered if Caitlin was still at home. She must be. Where else would she go?

"Rafe!" Maggie shook his hand. "Are you even listening to me?"

"Huh? Sure," he said and forced a smile onto his face.

Luckily Maggie was too young to realize that he was only pretending to listen to her. He wanted to give her all his attention but couldn't. He was too busy feeling sorry for himself.

"Lady Evelyn might need my help in the castle," she said very excitedly. "How amazing would it be if I could help her?"

What would Rafe say to Caitlin when he saw her again? How was he going to look her in the eye? How was he going to fix this? There had to be a way to make up for it.

Someone screamed and Rafe looked up just in time to see a hell horse rushing toward them. It was unlike anything he had ever seen. It was monstrous and dangerous and deadly and scarier than any hunter Rafe had ever encountered. Its bloodthirsty mouth was gaping open to reveal teeth that were as long and sharp as a hundred swords. Its hooves sounded on the cobblestone like a bell being rung to signal death, or an attack on the castle. For a moment Rafe's knees felt weak. Then he remembered that Maggie was by his side and that he needed to protect her.

The hell horse sped toward them like an arrow. Rafe knew it wasn't going to swerve out of the way to run around them. He also knew they wouldn't be able to get out of the way fast enough.

As the hell horse drew closer, Rafe focused on its too many teeth that were too close together in its large mouth. He didn't want a chunk of flesh ripped out of him.

Little Maggie clung to his arm, frozen from the shock. Rafe saw that the hell horse was going to trample her. He didn't stop to think—he shifted.

There was no way his human body would survive being trampled by a hell horse, but his wolf body might. He threw himself on top of Maggie and shifted as he did so. He protected her with his own flesh. He tucked his head in and covered the child's frail body. The hell horse ran over him and kept right on going, apparently in a hurry to get somewhere.

Rafe rolled off of Maggie. He was hurt and saw that despite her crying she was alive and not injured. She was just scared. He stumbled away from her when she wanted to touch him. He didn't want people to see that she was with a shifter. He didn't want her to be executed for associating with Magic.

Rafe stared after the hell horse. It was running toward their house. Rafe shook his head and decided that it must be a coincidence. *Why would it be running there?*

The king's guards had just arrived. They were running after the hell horse but stopped when they saw Rafe. Some froze when they saw him and stared in disbelief. "Shifter!" he heard some cry. Others drew their weapons.

Rafe knew he couldn't shift back into his human form. They had already seen him and he could not fight as well in his human body. But he also didn't want to fight them because he would kill them if he did. All of them feared him anyway.

Then a man rushed toward them. This was surprising because everyone else was trying to get away from him. It took Rafe a moment to realize that it was Gerald. He scooped Maggie up in his arms. Then he looked at Rafe with fear and distrust. "Get away!" he yelled. He was shaking and Rafe admired his courage to stand so close to his wolf form.

"Dad! It's alright!" Maggie said.

But Gerald wasn't listening. He was only thinking about how he could keep his little girl safe. He could never understand that Rafe wasn't going to harm her.

An arrow came flying toward Rafe but luckily missed.

Rafe quickly scanned his surroundings. Where could he go? He was trapped in Sky Castle. Eventually they would find him and kill him.

But he needed to try. Try to live. He would put up a fight. He wasn't sure how but he was sure that he would not survive if he just stood there. So he sprinted after the hell horse.

Caitlin kicked and kicked at his knee.

Black Blade screamed and grabbed a handful of hair. He slammed her head against the wall, and she cried out in pain.

"I'm going to kill you."

She looked angrier than scared and hissed at him as a snake would.

Did anything scare this girl?

He pulled her hair again and threw her at the front door. She hit it face first, making it swing open. Her momentum carried her out the door and slammed her to the ground where she let out a painful cough and started crawling away from him. She was slow, and he would easily get to her.

He confidently picked up his dagger and walked toward her, kicking her in her back. She fell onto her face again. Then he grabbed her hair, pulling her head back so that he could expose her throat.

In that moment, Caitlin regretted nothing more than her last minutes with Rafe. She had been so mean to him. She had hurt his feelings and had sent him away.

The dagger neared her throat.

If she hadn't reacted so badly to his confession, he might have been here to protect her. He would have saved her the way he always did.

She felt cold metal press against her throat.

He had told her he loved her. He had said the three most powerful words in the world. Now she would never be able to say them back.

She closed her eyes.

But instead of feeling the dagger slice her throat, she heard Black Blade scream. Her eyes snapped open in time to see the hell horse sink its teeth into his side. It pulled him off and away from Caitlin and threw him to the side like a doll.

The hell horse looked at Caitlin, as if to see if she was alright, and then it looked at Black Blade hungrily. Black Blade was clutching what was left of his side. It was a disgusting sight. His body was shaking from shock. He was missing some ribs, and blood was everywhere.

And Caitlin was thrilled to see this. "Any last words?" she sneered. She felt no sympathy for the fallen assassin.

"I'll see you in hell, girlie," he said.

The hell horse rushed down on him again and chomped his head off in one clean bite. The sound of his skull cracking between its massive jaws and teeth was music to Caitlin's ears.

The hell horse swallowed and chomped and swallowed some more. It stood still, its sides going in and out as it breathed heavily. And then it looked down at her.

Caitlin sat up to meet its gaze but didn't stand. She was not scared. Not even a little bit. The hell horse started walking toward her, Black Blade's blood dripping from its mouth. She didn't move. She didn't run. She didn't flinch.

People all around her were running away. Only a few stayed to watch in amazement as the hell horse bent its head down and breathed in her scent. She reached out and touched its forehead. She felt its warm breath on her face. Blood dripped from its teeth onto her lap. It was the blood of the enemy.

"You saved me," she found herself saying. "And I know why."

The hell horse nudged her fondly.

"We're the same, you and I, aren't we?" she said to him as understanding suddenly dawned on her. "Your blood runs through my veins. It all makes sense now. My dreams, my memories... They gave me Magical blood —your blood. It was your blood they pumped into me, with their needles and tubes. I am part hell horse. And that's why you came to me. That's why you saved me."

He nudged her again and she put her other hand

on his cheek. "Your blood in my veins—I have your temper. I have your fighting spirit.... And you heard me crying out for help in my mind, didn't you?"

The creature nuzzled her. Hell horses have a fierce loyalty and a special connection to their kind.

Then everyone showed up. The king's guards had their swords drawn, ready to fight.

Dylan stood between them. He had a bow and arrows with him. He was staring at Caitlin. He couldn't believe what he saw.

And then Caitlin's worst nightmare came true. She saw Rafe, in wolf form, running toward her, with a handful of guards chasing him.

The hell horse forgot about Caitlin and ran toward Dylan and the guards while Rafe ran toward Caitlin.

The hell horse knocked several guards over. One slashed it with his sword and in return the hell horse ripped his arm off. The blood sprayed onto Dylan.

"Rafe! Get out of here!" she said as the wolf reached her. "He won't hurt me!"

The hell horse saw the big wolf by Caitlin and mistook Rafe for an enemy. It rushed toward Rafe.

"No!" Caitlin screamed. She tried to push her way between them but both were much bigger than her.

Rafe wasn't listening. He shoved her to the side and the hell horse smashed into him. He cried out as he was knocked over.

The hell horse bit at Rafe but missed, its teeth sinking into ground instead. Rafe tried to move away from Caitlin so that the hell horse would follow him and not her.

Dylan drew his bow back and released an arrow. It sank into the hell horse's side. But injuring it was a mistake because the pain sent the hell horse into a blind rage.

It kicked out and struck Rafe with its big iron hoof. He fell and Caitlin's heart fell alongside him. She knew he was hurt.

Then the hell horse charged toward Dylan and the other soldiers, ripping them apart easily. Limbs flew through the air like hail and blood spattered everywhere like rain. The hell horse made killing them look like a sport.

But Caitlin registered none of that. She saw only one thing. The wolf was still down. His face was pressed against the ground and he did not move.

The hell horse knocked Dylan over and killed another soldier. Then it turned toward him and for the first time in a long time Dylan was truly scared. This hell horse could bite his sword into pieces and devour him within minutes.

I run toward what I fear.

But he couldn't run. He couldn't even get to his feet. Any moment now this creature would jump on him and rip him apart with those teeth.

Then Caitlin moved into action. She threw herself on top of Dylan. "No!" she cried, shielding him from the hell horse.

It looked at her in confusion. She motioned for it to run, to get out and away. The castle wasn't a safe place for it. Their eyes locked and she knew it understood. She also knew that it wasn't its nature to leave a herd member behind—to leave her behind.

Dylan scrambled away from Caitlin. He nocked an arrow into his bow.

Rafe managed to get to his feet but was shaking violently. He placed his weight on three legs. Caitlin saw the hell horse had hurt his fourth. How could he run away with only three?

One of the guards came toward Rafe, swinging a sword. Rafe bit his arm. They heard the bone crack and the guard cried out. Rafe didn't mean to bite that hard but he wasn't going to let the man kill him. The moment the sword dropped to the ground, Rafe let him go.

Dylan drew his arrow back, and Caitlin rushed to move in front of it.

Too slow.

Dylan released.

Rafe cried out in pain and sank to the ground.

CHAPTER 7

CAITLIN FELT SOMETHING inside of her break when Rafe didn't move. He lay there limply and she pushed the thought that he was dead aside. He was just hurt —he would be fine!

Her anger-filled eyes found Dylan. She was blinded with rage. She didn't care if there was remorse in his heart. He had hurt her Rafe. She would kill him.

Caitlin moved around the hell horse and rammed into Dylan. She forgot that moments ago she had protected him. He was bigger and stronger than her, but she threw her full body weight on him and he fell over.

Dylan wasn't even sure what was happening. He knew that Caitlin had attacked him and that he'd fallen and dropped his bow. He watched her uncontrolled rage spark the hell horse's rage. He was riveted by the sight of the fearsome horse as it tore through the guards like they were paper people. He watched in horror as it bit a man, shaking him until his back broke and his body hung limply. He watched as peasants screamed and cried and fled, some hiding in their homes while others simply running as far away as possible.

Although it was skinny from starvation, the hell horse was still strong. Dylan watched as a guard hit it with a stone. The hell horse reacted immediately and rushed to him. The guard ran to the nearest house and made it to the door. He slammed the door shut to keep the hell horse out—*as if that would help*, thought Dylan. The hell horse smashed through the door and trampled over the guard, breaking his bones before eating him alive.

Meanwhile, Caitlin had straddled Dylan and was raining her fists down on him, screaming at him, when he finally snapped back to himself. He raised his muscled arms up and blocked her blows. He pushed her off, but she was back on him in a flash. She was much stronger than he thought she would be. He tried to grab her hair, but she was moving too much.

"Caitlin, stop!" he said.

But she wasn't listening. She reached over and grabbed one of the arrows that had fallen from his quiver.

"Caitlin, I killed a monster. Despite what you think, he's not your friend. He's not a good man."

"He's a better man than you will ever be!" Caitlin cried, swinging the arrow tip down to his throat.

Dylan caught her wrist. If any other woman was on top of him, he would be able to twist her arm away easily. But Caitlin was unnaturally strong. She used both hands and her weight to push the arrow down. It tickled his neck.

Dylan had never seen anyone this angry before. He met her eyes. They were as red as the hell horse's— which was now running out of the house, unstoppable and fighting blindly. It kicked and sent a guard flying through a window. It reared and then came down hard on the earth. The ground shuddered and started cracking beneath its iron hooves.

Dylan brought his attention back to Caitlin. The arrow was now pushing against his neck, and he thought that she really would kill him. "Hey, I'm not the bad guy," he protested.

"You really don't see it, do you?" she sneered. "You've become the very thing you've hated and tried to destroy. You're a monster!"

"If you want to talk about monsters, maybe you should look at yourself for a change," Dylan said.

Their eyes locked and Caitlin's expression changed. The hardness went away and she became more human. She looked down and saw that the arrow was drawing blood. Caitlin stopped pushing it into his neck. Her heart felt heavy. She imagined her family's shocked expressions if they were to see her like this. They probably wouldn't even recognize her.

She let go of the arrow. She could feel Dylan's chest heave with every breath he took.

He looked at her with surprise. "For a moment there I thought you would kill me." His voice was surprisingly calm.

"I thought so too," she said. All her anger had disappeared.

Caitlin looked away from him and to where Rafe lay. He was human once again and his blood pooled around him. She almost cried out and got off Dylan so she could run to Rafe.

The hell horse reared and slammed its hooves down onto a man already lying on the ground. The cobblestones shook and then cracked, and Caitlin lost her balance. They were actually standing on a floor that formed the ceiling of an underground space. She had managed to take a step before the earth completely gave way. The hell horse, several guards, and Caitlin, all plummeted down into darkness.

Caitlin hit the ground hard and lost consciousness.

She began to dream but the dream was different from those she'd had before. Despite not having a dream catcher to help her remember everything clearly, this dream was still vivid.

She was with Divan. They had left their cells in a hurry and were moving through the tunnels. Although they had grown up in the castle, they didn't know all the tunnels very well, only the ones that they had been exposed to. They didn't know how to get out.

"Do you have any idea which way you went last time?" Divan asked her.

"I don't," she confessed. The last time she had tried to escape she had run blindly. Most of the tunnels looked the same. She had gotten lost like a small child in a dark forest. She had tried to get out as fast as she could and hadn't thought twice about all the noise she was making. So despite her speed, they had easily located her and cornered her.

"We need to be quiet," she said. "It's alright if we move slowly as long as we don't get caught."

"That's fine with me because it's really dark and if I move fast, I might trip over something," Divan confessed.

Patronizers never carried torches around the dark tunnels. Caitlin didn't know what kind of eyesight they had but she knew they could see well in the dark. Luckily, she could too. Her eyes adjusted very easily and the dark didn't bother her much.

Divan had always been uncomfortable in the dark. Not being able to see scared him and drove him crazy. This was a huge problem since he lived in the dark tunnels. He didn't have hell horse blood like she did.

"I don't think they meant for us to become this," Divan told her.

"Become what?"

"Their enemies," Divan said. "I think they created us to be their allies."

"And then we became unruly because we're not brainless zombies," Caitlin said. "We want out."

"We'll get out," Divan said. He didn't sound very hopeful but he wasn't being negative either. He was smart enough to know that despair would only get them caught.

Caitlin grabbed him and pushed him against the wall.

"What is it?!"

Her hands clasped over his mouth so that he couldn't make any more noise. He touched her arm but didn't push her away. Then he heard the footsteps and understood that more patronizers were walking toward their cells.

"How many are there?" Divan asked when she took her hand away.

"Three," Caitlin said. "Let's go."

They headed in the opposite direction as the patronizers quickened their pace. Caitlin was on the lookout. She held Divan's hand as the tunnels got darker. He couldn't see a thing. He was slowing her down. She stopped suddenly and he walked into her.

"What?"

"Divan, walk backward slowly," she whispered.

Far ahead of them, in the tunnel, stood a patronizer. Its face was looking the other way, so it hadn't seen them yet.

"Walk backward," Caitlin whispered again with greater urgency. Divan did so, as did she, but her eyes remained fixed on the patronizer in front of them, until Divan suddenly stopped. She didn't think they'd walk right into a patronizer standing behind them.

"Argh!" Divan cried out in agony.

Caitlin spun around and watched the patronizer sink its dagger-like fingers into Divan's shoulder.

"Run!" he told her.

Caitlin didn't think twice. She felt no loyalty toward Divan, and if necessary, she would leave him there. She sprinted forward.

The patronizer at the end of the tunnel had seen them and approached. She was boxed in on both ends. *I have to get past them!*

She was close to the patronizer in front of her. She kicked upward, striking it in the face, using the rest of her momentum to flip backward and land back on her feet.

The patronizer looked disoriented for a split-second. Then it attacked. It swung its arms toward her and she ducked.

Divan was forced to his knees. He was bleeding and whimpering in pain. He didn't want to move because then the daggers would only sink in deeper.

Caitlin blocked a blow from the patronizer. It swung

a second punch and she moved. Its hand went through the stone wall. She threw her weight onto its out-stretched arm. If it was human, its arm would have broken, but its arm was made of steel instead of bone.

The patronizer pulled its arm back. Caitlin ducked and then punched it in the stomach. This only made her fists hurt. She cried out in frustration.

"Run!" Divan told her again.

She could hear more patronizers coming. They would soon be outnumbered and overpowered.

She bent down and grabbed a rock. She hit the patronizer several times in the face with it. This was much more effective than her fist could ever be. The patronizer stumbled back, its arms flailing. She hit it again, striking its dagger-like hand. It came apart. Then she kicked the patronizer and it fell backward. She looked down at the dagger hand that she had just severed from its body.

"Caitlin!" Divan called. "Help me out..."

She couldn't free him from the blades that stuck into his flesh. It simply wasn't possible. Even if she got the patronizer's fingers out of him, he would be too badly injured to escape, and she saw that there were several patronizers coming up behind him now. He wasn't worth dying for. Not when her freedom was in hand.

She turned and started running.

"*Help me out...*"

Caitlin realized too late what he meant. He wasn't

asking her to save him. He was begging her to help him out of an impossible situation. To help him out of his misery. To kill him.

And she didn't do it. She missed her chance.

CHAPTER 8

CAITLIN AWOKE TO a crunching sound. She became aware of the pain in her shoulder. There was a wood shard stuck in it. Her head hurt even more and she touched it softly.

She was lying face down on the cold hard ground. She flipped over, careful not to jar her shoulder. High above her she could see the light. That's where everyone was fighting. That's where the earth gave way.

How long had she been down here? It couldn't have been that long, or the guards would have come to get her—unless they thought she was dead or trapped with no way out.

She sat up and closed her eyes, waiting for the world to stop spinning. Then she opened her eyes again and wished she had something for the pain. She would have gulped down the gross tea that Matilda had made without complaining if she had any.

She looked to her right where the hell horse was having a feast. All of the soldiers that had fallen through the floor with them had died and the hell horse was devouring them.

Caitlin tried not to gag. The hell horse heard her, looked up, saw she was awake, hurt but not too badly. So it dug back into the man's rib cage to get at the nutrient-rich organ meat, crunching through the bones that got in the way.

Caitlin didn't look up into the light so that she wouldn't be blinded in the darkness of the room. Slowly she got to her feet. Her body felt numb. She took two shaky steps toward the hell horse. It flattened its ears against its skull in warning. Blood dripped from its open mouth.

"Relax," she told him. "I'm not going to take your food."

The room was big and full of dust and cobwebs. There were some broken and moldy tables and chairs. It looked a lot like a classroom and felt familiar. Caitlin started walking toward the door. Its handle was broken and rusted. She walked through it and found herself back in the tunnels.

The hell horse whinnied after her, desperate to not be left behind. This sound sent shivers down her spine. She didn't want anyone to hear it and come after them.

"Come on then and be quiet!" she whispered.

It gulped down another chunk of the guard that lay at its feet and then it followed Caitlin. Hell horses were herd animals and this one had been alone for far too long. Caitlin was sure he wasn't going to attack her, but she didn't trust him either. He was still a wild animal.

Caitlin's hand went to her neck. The necklace Maggie had given her was still there. She clutched it like her life depended on it and worried about her little sister.

Maggie was crying.

"They took Rafe!" she cried to Gerald. They had seen the guards pick up Rafe's limp body and had watched them carry Rafe to the throne room. "We have to stop them!"

Gerald was dragging Maggie home. Her hand was in his and he had to grip it tightly or she would break free. She was resisting and pulling against him, but her attempts were futile.

"Maggie..." Gerald said. How could he possibly explain to a six-year-old that one of the people she loved was a monster? How could he tell her that Rafe can't ever come back to their home? That he can't ever play games with her again.

"We have to help him!" she cried.

"We can't help him," Gerald said with a heavy heart. He had had no idea that Rafe was a shifter. The shock was still settling in. The very creature he hated had been living in his house. The creature that killed his kind had fallen in love with his eldest daughter. The creature Gerald wanted dead had saved his family many times.

Gerald thought how fast Rafe shifted out in the open. He could still see Rafe's clothes tearing as the change took place. He had done that to protect Maggie. He had thrown his body on top of hers when he could just have run away and saved himself.

"But he would have helped us if the guards had taken us!" Maggie cried.

Gerald thought about the countless times Rafe had helped them. He thought about how good Rafe had been to them. Would Rafe still have shifted in front of all those people if Maggie hadn't been in danger and he had been alone? Gerald didn't think he would have. He would have jumped out of the way or been trampled in his human form. He shifted so that he could protect Maggie. He exposed himself for her.

"They are taking him to the king," Gerald told her. "There is nothing we can do."

Gerald remembered how hopeless and scared he had felt when he was tied to the stake back in River Town. He didn't deserve that, just like Rafe didn't deserve this.

Yes, Gerald felt betrayed by and even scared of Rafe.

But he didn't want to see him dead. Rafe was different from the other shifters. He wasn't all bad.

"They are going to kill him!" Maggie cried, tugging at his hand. "We can't let them!"

"So what would you have me do?!" Gerald didn't intend to raise his voice to his younger daughter. He never screamed at his children or his wife. But at this moment his heart was also hurting.

"Go save him! Go ask the king to spare him! Tell the king he is part of our family!" The little girl's body was shaking violently as she cried. Her eyes were blood-red and swollen and her cheeks were pink. Her nose was running and her tears kept rolling.

Gerald managed to get himself under control. He spoke kinder now. "If we tell the king that he is part of our family, we will all be killed."

"It's not fair!" She pulled against her father again.

"I know, Maggie." Gerald said.

They reached their home where Daisy was already waiting for them. She had come home early after she had heard about a hell horse being set free. It came as a shock when she saw their broken table and broken door.

She didn't know what had happened or what she could do to help. It seemed like all she could do was wait for her family to come back and hope they all came back alive and well.

She stood in the doorway and opened her arms when she saw Maggie. Gerald let go of his daughter's hand and Maggie ran to her mother's warm embrace. Daisy closed her eyes as she held her daughter tight. Maggie was alive. Maggie wasn't hurt. But she was crying.

Gerald's heart ached. He knew Caitlin was not home. He had no idea where she was but he knew she would die trying to save Rafe. He just hoped that she would be alright in the end.

What could he do to make the situation better? He would do anything to keep his daughters safe and happy. But this situation was out of his control. As he watched his daughter sob, he felt his heart break.

Daisy started crying as Maggie told her what happened. She held onto her little girl, comforting her, as she realized that there was nothing more she could do. If Rafe was being taken to the king, no one would care about what a peasant thought or wanted.

"Can we go to the king now?" Maggie asked her mother with pleading eyes. "Let's at least try!"

"No, Maggie..." Daisy's voice was barely audible. This was hard for her as well. "There is nothing we can do." She met Gerald's eyes. She immediately realized that Caitlin wasn't with him. She couldn't help but wonder in what sort of danger her older daughter was in now. She wondered if Caitlin would interfere with Rafe's execution. Caitlin was crazy enough to do that.

"So we will do nothing?!" Maggie screamed. It was very unusual for the six-year-old to be acting this way. Caitlin was always the defiant one. Maggie was never unruly or hotheaded.

"Maggie," Gerald said, "that's enough."

Daisy understood the child's pain. Her whole world was falling apart. She was too young to understand that they couldn't fix it. She would have to learn to live with the pain of losing Rafe.

Maggie glared at her father and then at her mother. She stomped her foot hard on the ground in anger. "Fine. I will find someone who will help me!" Then she turned and ran from her parents.

CHAPTER 9

LADY EVELYN PATTERSON was walking back from the school. Today she had taught her children how to make a yellow-blue flower grow. It was a flower that was often used in healing potions. It was a rare flower and it wasn't the right season for it to grow. So the children found it a bit challenging when she gave each of them a seed, some soil, and a pot and showed them how to make the plant grow. Most of them succeeded.

They were having a good day until the news of the hell horse reached them. All of her students were scared and school was dismissed so they could go back to their families.

Lady Evelyn wondered where the horse had come from as she walked quickly to her room. She arrived, pushed the door open, and was surprised to find someone waiting for her.

"Where were you?!" Maggie cried. She was sitting on the bed, crying. Lady Evelyn's three dogs were around her for comfort. The soothing smell of herbs and flowers filled the air.

"Maggie?" Evelyn asked in surprise. "What are you doing here? You should be at home!"

"I didn't know who else to go to!" Maggie said. She jumped off the bed. Her sudden movement startled the dogs and they began to bark at her. She rushed into Lady Evelyn's arms. The duchess smelled of mint and her embrace was warm and soft. Maggie leaned against her and let her tears flow.

"What's the matter, child?" Evelyn asked, stroking her hair.

"You're powerful, aren't you? You're a duchess, right? So people listen to you...."

"I suppose," Evelyn said. "Why?"

"I need someone to help my friend." It took all her courage to tell Lady Evelyn. She had promised Rafe that she would always keep his secret, but they were going to kill him! So it didn't matter if she told....

"Who is your friend?" Lady Evelyn asked.

"Rafe Grey," Maggie said. "He is a shifter."

Evelyn looked more surprised than horrified. She didn't freak out like Maggie expected. Maggie spoke quickly, her words tumbling over each other. "But don't be scared of him," she put her hand on Evelyn's arm. "He is a really good wolf. He has saved my life many times. But the king wants to kill him."

Evelyn had heard about the wolf that had shifted and had ripped a guard's arm off. Everyone spoke about him as a vicious beast that deserved to die. They spoke as if he had come to the castle to eat their children and rip their lives apart.

Any other lady would have sent Maggie away after hearing her request. No other lady would risk her life for a child that she hardly knew. Any other lady would want nothing to do with Magic.

But Evelyn wasn't any other lady. "I'll see what I can do," she said. "But in order for me to help him, I need you to leave. Go home and be a good girl."

Maggie nodded. "Thank you!" She hugged Evelyn one last time and then left the room in a hurry.

Evelyn stood still for a moment and then she closed the door and locked it. If the king had Rafe, then they would be in the throne room. Rafe's fate would be decided there. She already knew they would sentence him to death.

How could she help him? She had no trade in the throne room, so she couldn't just show up. Her husband the duke was working so she couldn't run to him for help.

Lady Evelyn decided to take a chance. She moved the rug that lay by her bed. Under it was a trapdoor. She lifted the wood door and climbed down the stairs into the tunnels. She intended to go through the tunnels to reach the throne room.

She walked quickly and confidently through the

dark. She had used these tunnels many times before and knew her way around. She had even made herself a map. She stayed away from the areas where the red-caped creatures, the patronizers, stood guard. She didn't know what the king was doing in those locked rooms—and she didn't want to know.

If the king knew her secret, he would kill her. She always thought Lady Katherine would figure it out. She was a frightfully smart woman who knew every-thing. She knew everything except that Evelyn was a witch. If she knew that, Evelyn wouldn't be alive today.

Lady Evelyn took one of the torches from the wall. She snapped her fingers and it burst into flames. Just like most people, witches couldn't see in the dark.

Although she owed the shifter nothing, she hated seeing one of her kind get murdered. And the sweet little girl had asked so nicely. Evelyn was flattered that the child had run to her for help. She did not want to let her down. What would she tell her if Rafe got executed?

She heard a sound behind her and spun around. She held the torch out so that she could see. She saw nothing except stone walls and darkness. She must be imagining things.

Lady Evelyn turned around again and continued walking. Then she heard a growling sound that made her turn around one more time.

"Hello?" she called.

There was no answer, but she could sense that she

was not alone. So she started running. In all the time she had spent exploring these tunnels, she had never encountered another being except for the ones with the red capes. She could hear footsteps behind her. Something was chasing her!

She couldn't run very fast in her high-heels, and her corset was suffocating her. Whatever was chasing her was fast! She felt a claw rake across her back. She cried out and fell forward. The creature continued slashing through her skin.

She screamed again and then she remembered that no one would come to save her, not in these tunnels.

CHAPTER 10

CAITLIN HEARD THE scream. It echoed through the tunnel walls. The hell horse snorted and oriented toward the piercing sound.

Caitlin froze for a split second and then found herself running in the direction of the scream. She never wanted to be a hero and the last time she checked she wasn't very good at saving people either. But she charged to the rescue anyway.

It wasn't long before she saw a torch swinging violently from side to side. The lady who was swinging it wore an elegant gown and ridiculously impractical heels. She was not dressed for running around dark and dirty tunnels. Caitlin wondered what she was doing down here—how she'd managed to run into the creature now attacking her.

It was barely human. Its skin was a sickly pale white as if it had never been in the sun before. Its blue veins bulged and throbbed. Its teeth were pointed and dripping with saliva. Its body was lean but still muscled. Its hair was tangled and matted with dirt. Its eyes were yellow.

"Hey!" Caitlin called to get its attention.

The monster was crazy. It was out of control. It slashed at the lady's dress and ripped pieces of fabric off.

Caitlin thought she would have to fight. But the hell horse pushed past her. It shoved her aside against the wall and that hurt her bleeding shoulder even more.

"Get out of the way!" Caitlin yelled and the lady in the ball gown did just that.

The hell horse, looking fierce with its mouth open, baring all its sharp teeth, ran toward the creature. But the creature showed no fear. Caitlin wondered if it was beyond any human emotion.

It wasn't beyond pain. The creature cried out as the hell horse slammed into it. Its screams were disturbingly human.

Caitlin couldn't let the hell horse kill the creature. She rushed forward and threw her arms around the hell horse's neck. It turned to bite her—it thought she was stealing its food. She moved out of its way just in time as its jaws snapped at a mouthful of air. She was relieved that it didn't rip her apart.

"Stop it!" she told the horse firmly.

It snorted its annoyance but didn't bite her again.

Caitlin watched as the creature crawled deeper into the tunnel, watched it stand up on two legs–like a human. "Divan?!" Caitlin called.

The creature recognized the name that had once been his. He had become crazed during the years spent in isolation in the dark tunnels. After Caitlin had left, he had no one–no friends to talk to, to laugh with, to share with–and so he had regressed into a savage beast.

That name didn't mean much to him now. He locked his yellow eyes with Caitlin's green ones. Then he ran deeper into the tunnel and disappeared from sight.

Caitlin turned to the woman in the beautiful gown. The lady pressed herself against the wall and looked at Caitlin with wide eyes. She was bleeding and she held the torch out toward Caitlin. Caitlin wondered if she was doing it as a warning.

"You don't have to be scared of me," Caitlin told her.

The woman was beautiful. She had long blond hair that fell over her shoulders. Her blue eyes went to the hell horse. It licked its lips.

"Don't mind him," Caitlin said. "He listens to me–most of the time."

The lady made a squeaking sound and Caitlin wondered if she would faint. She looked terribly pale.

"Why isn't he attacking you?" the lady asked.

"I guess we are friends," Caitlin said.

"Hell horses only befriend their own kind."

"I'm special."

The lady took a step back that made Caitlin think she would run. She hoped that if this happened the hell horse wouldn't follow.

"I'm also... special," the lady said. She reached out and touched Caitlin's wounded shoulder.

Caitlin considered pulling away but she thought any sudden movement might startle the hell horse and she didn't want that to happen. She soon felt her shoulder grow warm. When Evelyn pulled her hand away, the shard of wood in Caitlin's shoulder came away too. Her wound was completely healed.

"How did you—?" Caitlin started and then the realization hit her. "You are a witch."

"Yes, and who and what are you?" the lady asked. "You can't be non-Magic if you have a hell horse as a companion."

"I am part hell horse, believe it or not," Caitlin said without hesitation. She didn't think the lady witch would believe her but she didn't seem shocked or scared. She wasn't sure why she chose to tell the truth either, but she felt as if this lady witch knew how to keep a secret. "My name is Caitlin Wilde."

"Wilde?" the lady repeated. "Do you have a younger sister called Maggie Wilde?"

"Yes. How did you know?" Caitlin put a hand on the hell horse's chest when it took a step forward. It stopped when she gently pushed against it.

"I'm Evelyn Patterson. I met your sister when she was touring the castle with a school group."

"Lady Evelyn?!" Caitlin exclaimed. "You own the school. Not the one Maggie's going to but the other one."

"Yes."

"But how are you a witch? How have you not been burned for your Magic?"

Her laugh was like the sound of little ringing bells, clear and musical. "No witch is dumb enough to get caught and burned!"

"So I've heard," Caitlin mumbled.

The hell horse stomped its hooves. It was getting impatient. Luckily, it was not attacking Lady Evelyn. It didn't view her as a friend but accepted that she wasn't a threat.

"Let's walk," Caitlin suggested.

The hell horse pushed past them and led the way. Caitlin didn't think it knew where it was going. Lady Evelyn was very cautious around it. "What are you planning on doing with him?" she asked.

"I don't know," Caitlin confessed.

"He shouldn't stay in the castle," Lady Evelyn told her gently. Her eyes followed the hell horse. "It's not safe for him or the people."

"Then where do I take him?"

"I don't know where," she said. "But I do know how to get him out."

"Let's do it then," Caitlin said.

"Now?" Evelyn sounded a bit taken aback.

"Yes. I have a friend that needs my help. The hell horse will only complicate it. He's following me around everywhere and he has to go."

"He won't let you go easily. You are his companion and he is attached to you," Evelyn warned. "Who is it that you want to help? The wolf?"

"How did you know?"

"Maggie told me. She's the reason I am down in these tunnels. I wanted to see if I can go below the throne room and hear what they decide to do with him."

"Can you take me with you?"

"Sure."

"How do you know the tunnels so well?"

Evelyn stumbled over a rock but caught herself. The torchlight flickered and their shadows danced against the tunnel walls.

"I have spent a long time exploring them. When I came to Sky Castle, I knew I wanted to open a school for Magic kids. But I needed a way to get everyone out in case we got caught. These tunnels are perfect. They lead all over the castle, no one ever uses them, and they provide hidden passageways into and out of the castle."

Caitlin thought about the school. It was the school that rejected Maggie and many other kids. It all made sense now. Maggie was rejected because Maggie herself didn't know that she had Magic and they didn't want to tell her. The non-Magic kids weren't allowed in either, no matter how smart they were.

"It's amazing that you have managed to pull this off! All of this Magic right under the king's nose!"

"It's the most obvious place," Evelyn said. "So he would never suspect it."

There was a light at the end of the tunnel. The stones started turning to sheer rock and the ground became browner.

"Are we in a cave?" Caitlin asked.

Evelyn nodded. "This leads to the side of the Whispering Mountains."

The hell horse was behind Caitlin. It had taken a different turn but when it realized that it had been separated from Caitlin it turned around and found her again—like she knew it would.

"I think you might need to stand back," Caitlin told Evelyn.

"You don't have to ask twice."

Evelyn flattened herself against the wall so that the hell horse could walk past. Its eyes lingered on her but it didn't attack. Caitlin let the hell horse walk toward the light. It was cautious at first because it hadn't seen sunlight in many years. It stopped and waited for her to follow.

"I can't come," she told it.

It turned around and faced her. The cave was wide enough for it to turn around easily. It tilted its head to the side. Its ears drooped and its eyes widened. Its confused expression almost made it look cute, like a puppy begging to be adopted. Of course, the cuteness faded when Caitlin glanced at its long fangs.

"Please leave," Caitlin said.

The hell horse didn't understand. It sensed that she wanted it to go. But why would she want that? They were a herd. Herds don't separate.

It walked toward Caitlin as if to persuade her to leave with it. She knew she had to get it to go. So she clapped her hands together loudly but it didn't spook. "Go!" she yelled.

It whinnied at her. The sound shook its skinny body as if calling her to follow or begging her to let it stay. Caitlin's heart ached. She realized she didn't want it to go. Her instincts told her that they were safer together.

But she had to save Rafe. If the hell horse came with her, everything would be chaotic. And it couldn't stay in the castle with her and her family. This was no place for a hell horse.

Caitlin didn't want to do this, but she didn't know how else to get it to leave. She picked up a rock and threw it at the horse. But it didn't flinch.

"Leave!" she cried.

It stared at her in confusion.

She picked up another rock. This time it hit flat in the chest. But her throw was too soft. The horse tossed its head from side to side and walked backward. It was baffled when she threw another one, hitting hard on its shoulder.

The hell horse turned and ran toward the light. It ran out of the tunnel and the sunlight hit its dull coat. Once outside, it stopped and looked back at her.

Caitlin tore her eyes away from it and forced herself to turn around and walk deeper into the tunnel. She reached Lady Evelyn.

"He might come back for you," the lady witch said.

Caitlin's heart felt heavy as she heard it cry for her.

CHAPTER 11

EVELYN DREW A rough map in the sand and showed Caitlin the layout of the castle. Caitlin tried to memorize as much as possible. She was a fast learner but there were so many tunnels that she got confused.

After studying the map in the sand, the two of them walked deeper into the tunnels. It was cold down there. Evelyn held the torch close to her so that she wouldn't shiver.

"Now that I've shown you the map," Evelyn said, "can you tell me what I will find if I go that way?"

"The patronizers," Caitlin said.

"How do you know what they are called?" Evelyn asked. "Do you know what they do down here?"

"I'd rather not talk about it," Caitlin said. She didn't want to explain to Evelyn what the king was doing to Magic folk. That would only complicate things and upset the duchess. She could tell that Evelyn was courageous, but she still had a soft heart.

Caitlin tried to take the lead and get them to the throne room. She made one wrong turn and Evelyn corrected her. Finally, they reached the big room that they were looking for. It was the shape of the throne room but had no furnishings. They couldn't see through its ceiling but they could hear what was going on above them.

"Bring him in," the king commanded.

The throne room's big heavy doors swung open. Rafe had shackles around his feet and wrists. Someone had given him pants to wear. The pants weren't given to him to spare him the embarrassment of walking around nude; it was done so that he would be presented to the king in a proper way. He had a guard on either side of him holding him upright. His head was hanging and he had an arrow in his chest. He'd lost a lot of blood and looked drowsy. He didn't look like he would pick a fight.

The guards dragged him into the room and dropped him, on his knees, in front of the king. Rafe's breathing was deep and heavy as he forced himself to look up. The king was glaring down at him. His lips formed a snarl and his fists were clenched on the throne's armrest.

On the king's right, Lady Katherine Black was sitting on her jewelled chair. Rafe had never seen her before. She was as intimidating as he had heard. Her dark eyes looked all-knowingly down at him. Her lips were pressed together in a fine line. He expected her to look happier. He expected her to enjoy this more. Wasn't that what sadistic people did?

Rafe coughed and took a ragged breath. He frowned, sniffed the air, and caught a strange scent. Was it what he thought it was?

Rafe didn't have time to dwell on the scent because the king started speaking. His voice seemed to bounce off the walls and make everyone jump. "So you are the wolf?"

Rafe didn't say anything but met the king's gaze and refused to break it. There was no point in denying it when he had been caught shifting in plain sight.

"What brings you to the castle?" the king asked.

"I came to huff and puff and blow your castle down," Rafe responded with a smile.

One of the guards sniggered and got elbowed by his friend. The king didn't smile. Rafe wondered if he was smart enough to get the joke.

"Why would a shifter be dumb enough to come to Sky Castle?" the king asked. "You do know that you came to the most dangerous place in the kingdom for your kind?"

"I came to seek an audience with his excellence," Rafe said. He had to play his cards right. He didn't have anything to gamble with besides his life and lies.

"What for?" the king sat up a little straighter, curious.

"I was going to offer you my services," Rafe said. He tried to ignore the guards snickering. "I hear you sometimes hire us Magic folk to work for you in exchange for our lives."

Now the king laughed. "I've never done that and you will be no exception."

It had been a long shot but at least Rafe gained a very important piece of knowledge. The king never hired any Magic folk. So Brutus and Scarface weren't working for him. Had Campbell kept the king in the dark? "It's your loss, Your Highness," Rafe said with a smirk.

"You're a funny one," the king said, although he wasn't laughing. "You should have gone to work for the circus."

"I'm over-qualified," Rafe stated.

"Of course you are," the king said sarcastically. "But it doesn't matter because you're going to die today."

"I was afraid you'd say that," Rafe coughed up some blood. He knew he shouldn't taunt the king.

"Is there a favorite way you'd like to die?" the king asked.

"How kind of you to ask," Rafe said. "Quick and painless would be acceptable."

"Alright." For the first time the king smiled. Then

he turned his attention to his guards. "I want this man stoned—slowly and painfully."

Rafe grunted. The guard nodded. He thought that he would be dragged from the throne room again. To his surprise, Lady Katherine spoke up.

"Your Highness, I must object," she said in her silken voice. "Since I have taken over Campbell's work, we have made immense progress with MOP."

The king's full attention was on her.

"I would like to use this man as one of our test subjects."

"Nothing good has come from those experiments," the king said peevishly. "All of my weapons are dead, except the one running amok and killing people. My little fabricated town was destroyed too."

"And we have Campbell to blame for that," Katherine told the king in a placating voice. "Now that I am in control, I can assure you that NOTHING will go wrong."

Rafe looked at Katherine. She was confident and self-assured. He shuddered to think that she was running the experiments now. He didn't think it was possible for him to hate her more then he already did.

He glared at them and wished that they would just kill him now. He would rather die than be turned into a monster or be brainwashed. *Brainwashed. What if they erased his memories? What if they did to him what they did to Caitlin? If I don't remember anything, would I still be the same person?* Rafe began to shiver uncontrollably. He understood now how Caitlin had felt when he'd told her that he had the Blankness potion. He understood why she had felt so betrayed.

"Alright, Katherine. You shall have your shifter to play with," the king said. "Call the patronizers so that they can take him below—but it may be temporary. Some of tunnels have caved in or are in disrepair and too costly to fix. So I will order those sealed soon."

CHAPTER 12

DYLAN HAD TO find and kill the hell horse before it hurt any more innocent people. Truthfully, Dylan didn't know if he would be able to kill it. He had never seen a creature rip men apart the way it did. It also had this burning rage and starvation made it even more bloodthirsty. The hell horse had turned into a vengeful, killing creature as a result of being brutalized for so many years. Locking it up alone, without food, in the depths of the tunnels was not only cruel but also unwise. It was an accident waiting to happen.

Dylan wondered if Caitlin survived that fall when the ground under their feet had caved in. Most humans wouldn't have, but Caitlin was different. She was much more powerful and had a strong will to live. He was betting that she had made it.

Dylan scurried through the tunnels like a rat. He

heard the patronizers coming before he saw them. Four of them were walking in the direction of the throne room. He decided to beat them there.

"Someone is coming," Caitlin said to Evelyn. She could hear much better than the witch. "You should leave."

"What about you?" the witch asked.

"I'm going to go after Rafe," she said. "I have a pretty good idea where they are taking him."

"If you get caught you will be executed," the witch said.

"I won't get caught," Caitlin said confidently. "Try to get out of the tunnels as fast as possible. You don't want the monster down here to eat you."

"Alright," Evelyn said. "Best of luck."

"Thank you so much for all of your help," Caitlin said solemnly. "I won't forget it." She reached out and touched Evelyn's arm.

Evelyn smiled and then she walked away, the torch-light leaving with her. She took the torch with her so that she would not stumble in the dark. She headed toward the tunnel that had a hidden door by her school.

It wasn't the closest but it was convenient because she knew the way well.

Caitlin watched as the torchlight dimmed and then was extinguished as Evelyn turned a corner. It took Caitlin's eyes a moment to adjust to the darkness. She could see the stairs that led up to the throne room where Rafe was.

If she went up there, she would be revealing herself. She wouldn't stand a chance against all the guards, would she? She was the king's weapon, but she didn't know what her limits were. She did not remember all of her training.

Suddenly a hand clasped around her mouth and muffled her scream, interrupting her thoughts. Strong arms pulled her behind a wall. She felt her back press against the cold stone and instinctively her arms went up to defend herself. She looked into familiar blue eyes and the need to fight dissipated.

Dylan put a finger over his lips to indicate that she should be quiet. Then he removed his hand from her mouth. He was leaning over her and she looked up at him. Her chest was heaving from the adrenalin.

She listened and heard the patronizers. She couldn't see them from where she was standing and they couldn't see her. They were coming closer.

"What are you doing here?" she whispered to Dylan.

"Where else would I be?" he responded.

He was standing too close and it was making her uncomfortable. It was not the same pleasant butterfly feelings when Rafe was around. This was a feeling she wanted to go away. Why didn't he move? There was no reason for him to be standing on top of her!

The patronizers opened the secret hatch under the throne. The sound made Caitlin jump. She listened to them climbing up the stairs.

"Shhh," Dylan said and his fingers touched her lips. "You don't want them to see you."

"And what if they see you?" Caitlin asked. She pressed against the stone wall as if she could become a part of it.

"The king gave me permission to roam the tunnels. They won't harm me," Dylan explained.

"They are going to hurt Rafe," she said glaring at him. "Like *you* hurt Rafe."

Dylan could see the flare in her eyes. Her temper was ready to catch fire. He hoped it wouldn't. She nearly killed him the last time and he didn't know if she could stop herself again.

He didn't want to argue with her right now. So he stayed silent as the patronizers carried Rafe down the stairs and away in the tunnels. He had to push Caitlin against the wall or she would have jumped out to rescue the shifter.

"You are no good to him dead," Dylan said. The patronizers were out of earshot now.

"What does it matter to you?" Caitlin replied.

Dylan let her push him away. She stepped away from the wall and glared at him. He didn't know how to tell her that a witch had told him about her and predicted that she would need his help. How could he tell her that he had been asked to save her?

"You kill monsters, right?" she asked him but didn't wait for an answer. "Well then, you should be killing me."

Dylan remembered how Ears had told him that Caitlin would find out what had happened to her here in the castle. He had a feeling she had already found out. "Why do you say that?" he asked.

"Because I'm one. I'm a monster, an abomination." She studied him as she spoke. Her voice was placid, and she did not sound as if she hated herself. She was testing him. "I was created here, in the castle, by the king, to be his weapon. He filled my veins with Magic blood."

"With hell horse blood," Dylan realized. He recalled how the hell horse had looked at Caitlin, like she was one of its own. "Where is the hell horse?"

"He has left the castle," she said.

"You should too," Dylan said. "It's not safe here."

"I'm not leaving without Rafe," she said stubbornly, crossing her arms. "You can't make me."

"I need to get you out of here," Dylan said. He tried not to stare at her angry green eyes which seemed to catch every speck of light in the dark tunnel.

He also cared about all the lives that were in this castle. He feared what would happen if Caitlin were to get angry and lose her temper. Looking at her now he realized that if the wolf died it would tip her over the edge.

"You don't need to do anything," she snarled. "You're not doing this because you're a good person. You only want to help me because you are trying to compensate for all of the lives you have taken. You're just trying to relieve yourself of all that guilt. You are no better than a common murderer."

"I've only killed those that deserved it."

"Who are you to decide that?" she asked.

"I'm someone who cares about people's lives," he said firmly.

She laughed. "You have no respect for life! Just because Magic folk are different doesn't mean they don't have lives. They think and breathe and feel just like you do. They have a conscience."

Magic blood flowed through her veins. If he hated them, then he should hate her. But he didn't. His eyes gently swept over her and he resisted the urge to put a caring hand on her arm.

"I don't expect you to understand," he said.

"Don't expect me to listen to you then," she said. She tried to push past him but he grabbed her wrist and shoved her against the wall. He'd drawn his dagger and was pointing it at her throat. He didn't want to kill her. He didn't want to hurt her either. But she was making it very hard not to.

If she was as dangerous as Ears had said maybe she would be better off dead. How was he going to save her if she was so unruly? "Why are you smiling?" he growled.

"You're not going to do it," she said.

"Don't be so sure about that." He looked into her eyes, aware of her close scrutiny and that made him uncomfortable. But he couldn't look away. He tried to appear confident, although he had never felt so unsure in his life about anything.

"You couldn't do it before," she said, relaxing her muscles and releasing his eyes from hers. Then quite unexpectedly, she smiled. When he had pushed her against the wall, a memory resurfaced.

"What are you talking about?" he asked, his dagger still pointing at her throat.

"You couldn't kill me ten years ago...."

"I don't know what you're talking about."

"You were just a kid," Caitlin said. "You found me lying on the ground. In that battlefield along with all the corpses, remember? You raised that sword that was too big for you, but then lowered it. You couldn't strike me then and you won't do it now." She paused remembering and then added with a smile, "You're one of the good guys, pure of heart, Dylan Archer."

His eyes widened, remembering the little golden-haired girl he had found among the corpses of humans and shifters. The one he had let go. The one he couldn't kill despite his uncle's deathbed command. "It was you..." he mumbled but didn't release her.

"Yes," she shrugged. "I escaped the castle as a kid. I

was scared and I found your uncle's men fighting against the shifters. The violence made me lose control. I killed all of them. Humans and shifters, all." Caitlin didn't know how she had just remembered all that, but that day came flooding back to her with a jolt.

Dylan closed his eyes and breathed in, her scent and those long-ago memories making his head spin. "I should have killed you when I had the chance." Dylan pushed the dagger closer to her neck. He had loved his uncle and she had killed him. That man didn't deserve to die.

"I wish you had," she confessed. "The patronizers found me shortly afterward and dragged me back here. Oh, the things they did to me..."

Dylan looked at her and for the first time he felt true pity. She didn't get to choose who she was. She was made. She was manipulated and hurt and forced to be this killer. Like the way he was who he was because of his dad.

"So what are you waiting for? Do it," Caitlin pressed. "Kill me."

Dylan didn't. He couldn't bring himself to cut her throat. He found himself lowering the dagger just like he'd lowered his sword ten years ago.

Then Divan attacked him.

CHAPTER 13

DYLAN FELT A claw sink into the arm that held the dagger, yanking his arm away from Caitlin's throat. His blood spattered onto her shoulder and chest and he fell toward the creature. He struck out blindly with his left hand but missed.

The creature released his arm and moved to strike his face. Dylan swung his dagger toward it, ignoring the bulging pain in his arm.

"No!" Caitlin cried, grabbing his bleeding arm right before the dagger could cut the monster that was Divan. The creature capitalized on the reprieve and shoved Dylan who stumbled backward into Caitlin, knocking her to the floor. Then he regained his balance and started fighting.

"Don't hurt him!" Caitlin cried.

Dylan wasn't sure who she was talking to. The creature didn't look like it understood. It was strong for such a skinny thing. It looked like it had once been a human. But now it had lost its mind. Its body had been changed, mangled and contorted by all the experiments.

Dylan's dagger raked its chest. The cut wasn't very deep but still drew blood. The creature retreated a few steps.

"Divan!" Caitlin cried. The creature paid her no attention. It didn't respond to its name. "You don't have to fight us!"

Dylan realized with a shock that this was the king's weapon that had escaped and had been living in the walls. It stayed away from the areas designated as MOP in fear that a patronizer would kill it. This was the creature that had been killing innocent people. *It must be killed!*

He advanced and drew his sword. The creature was faster than he thought it would be. He danced around it and swung his sword violently. He missed every time.

"Dylan! Stop! He's like me!" Caitlin cried.

But the thing was nothing like her. There was nothing human about it. Its bulging eyes were only searching for its next victim.

Dylan swung again. He missed again, his sword striking one of the pillars that held up the roof. The creature jumped on him and knocked him to the ground.

Dylan lost his sword and grabbed the creature's chest to hold him away.

The creature was on top of Dylan and snarling and growling like an animal, clawing at his neck–Dylan was glad he didn't slice open an artery. Its mouth was open, trying to bite him as saliva dripped onto his face.

Caitlin was behind it in an instant. She wrapped her arm around its throat and leaned back. The creature threw its head back and tried to smash it into her face. But she kept her face wedged into the side of its neck and tightened her grip so it couldn't breathe. The creature fell backward and landed on top of her, intent on crushing her in the fall or loosening her choke hold on its neck. But she held on as it continued to squirm on top of her.

Dylan reached for his sword. At the same time, the creature slammed its elbow into Caitlin's side and her grip slackened. The creature pulled free and jumped onto Dylan, smacking the sword out of his hands.

Then the creature started scratching again. It fought more like a cat than a human. Caitlin went for it again but this time it was ready for her. It kicked her and she fell against the wall. Dylan ducked down as it charged him again. Then he started swinging punches. He landed a left hook into its jaw. The creature roared and jumped on top of him. He grabbed it by the chest, pushed it back, and started punching. It held up its arms but they were too skinny to block Dylan's fists.

"Dylan!" Caitlin cried. "Don't!"

The creature's face was covered in blood. Dylan stopped punching as it sank to the ground where it groveled and moaned.

"Get away from him!" She pushed Dylan to the side. Then she knelt down beside the creature. He was shaking now. She made slow, small motions so that she didn't scare him. "Divan," she said but he didn't respond. "Divan, can you hear me?"

He was nodding. His head was still down but he was undeniably nodding.

"He's gone, Caitlin." Dylan said. "We should put him out of his misery."

"He can be saved," Caitlin said. She looked at the broken and abused creature and saw herself. They had wronged him. They had made him this way. He didn't deserve this.

"He can't be saved!" Dylan got irritated.

"He has as much of a right to live as we do!" she argued.

"That's not true!" Dylan said. "He has killed many innocent people."

"It was because of his circumstances! Just look at him! He's going crazy down here."

"He is already crazy," Dylan argued. "Look at him, Caitlin. He is gone."

Caitlin reached out to touch the monster that was and still could be Divan, but it shied away. It was whispering again. It sat down with its knees pulled to its chest and its arms wrapped around them. It moaned as it rocked itself like a lost child.

"Divan, do you recognize me?" Caitlin asked.

Divan wasn't looking at her and continued to mumble. She couldn't make out any words.

Caitlin could see better than most in the dark but she could not see perfectly. Dylan found a torch and lit it. Divan instantly shied away from the light.

"Your side!" Caitlin exclaimed. Divan's side was torn open. Bones protruded through the broken skin. Her old friend was bleeding out. Dylan didn't do that. "Did the hell horse hurt you?" she whispered to the monster that was once Divan.

"He's suffering," Dylan said gently. "There's no healer who would risk helping him."

Then out of the darkness and barely audible came: "You... left... me."

"What?" Caitlin said. "What did you say?"

"You... left me," Divan said louder but still hesitantly as if unused to speaking. Then the young man that was the monster looked into the young woman's eyes and repeated clearly, "You left me and I was alone."

She saw the broken boy who had grown up with her. She saw the closest thing she had to a friend when she was a child. Memories of all the suffering they had endured together came rushing back. "I'm so sorry..." she said but knew no apology would ever make up for it.

"Did you... get out?" he coughed out.

She nodded.

"What was it like?" he asked with big eyes. "What is it like outside this place?"

"Let me show you," she offered.

He was calming down and slowly his humanity was returning. He was hesitant but he let her wrap an arm around him and help him walk through the tunnels.

Dylan handed her a dagger. "I trust you'll do what's right," he whispered, eying Divan. Then he left them. He didn't have a place or a part in their story. He would tell a guard to tell the king that he'd completed his task and killed the abomination.

Caitlin didn't watch Dylan go. She walked with Divan until they reached the cave entrance that Evelyn had shown her.

"Is the light hurting your eyes?" she asked him.

He was shielding them with one hand. "It's fine," he said. Then he sat down in the cave entrance and in the sunlight. He smiled for the first time in a long time and he looked truly at peace.

"Thank you," he told Caitlin as he closed his eyes. Blood dripped from his side. His face was purple from the bruises and his lip was cracked. His teeth were yellow and crooked.

"We need to do something about your wounds." She reached out to touch him but he pulled away.

"No."

"We have to do something," she said.

"Then make them pay for what they did to us," Divan opened his eyes. "Hurt them."

Caitlin sat down next to Divan. He was in a lot of pain. He was suffering. His breathing was shallow and labored. It sounded like he was struggling to pull the air into his lungs.

In her hands she held the dagger that Dylan had given her. She gripped it tightly. She didn't want to use it, but he was already dying.

"Caitlin," Divan said. "I must ask you one last favor."

"Yes?"

"Help me out."

Caitlin blinked back tears and gripped the dagger. She knew what she had to do.

CHAPTER 14

LILLIAN AND LIAM Archer rode up Whispering Mountain. Lillian, as always, was the one talking. She could talk about anything and everything. Liam wondered if his sister was ever serious or if she would ever shut up. As her younger brother, he loved her dearly but he didn't want to be around her so much. They had a very successful hunt out west and arrived at Sky Castle much sooner than expected.

Lillian was amazed at its beauty when they arrived. She had been very excited to come here and see Sky Castle herself. She was almost as excited about the castle as she was to see Dylan. Liam didn't speak much but when he did, he told her about the brave and fearless hunter his son had become. Lillian had no doubt that Dylan was a powerful warrior. He had always been destined for greatness.

Lillian and Dylan had a close relationship ever since Dylan was a baby. He loved her to bits. She played with him when he was a child and then taught him how to make weapons when he was older. She was his best friend, but she was also like a mother to him.

Their relationship was also tense. Liam never truly forgave Lillian for letting his wife Mary die. Of course, he didn't believe his sister let his wife die intentionally. Lillian probably did everything in her power to save Mary when the shifters attacked. But Lillian was still the last person to spend time with his wife.

Maybe he envied her for spending the last hours of Mary's life with her. Maybe he lived in regret and wished he had stayed home with Mary so that she would have been safe with him. Maybe then he could have protected Mary and she would still be alive today.

But maybe Lillian didn't try hard enough to save Mary. She had the opportunity as well as the skill to save her. Liam believed this deep down, and even if he never voiced it aloud, the thought slowly but surely wormed its way to the core of their relationship over the years.

The horses were dripping with sweat by the time they entered the castle. Lillian was very observant. She looked around at the people's houses, the other buildings, and the children. They passed a school—Evelyn's School. It wasn't a very big building and she wondered how many kids were enrolled there.

"Do you ever regret not sending Dylan to school?" she asked Liam. Lillian never liked school. No one there was competition enough for her. Her priorities were not in the classroom. But her school years still played a big part in shaping who she was today. She always wondered if Dylan had felt left out or now felt as if he had missed something. That boy wanted nothing more than to please his father. So he never complained and never asked about school again when his father said he wanted to teach Dylan himself. He was very bright. He learned quickly and eventually bested his father.

"Homeschooling is school," Liam replied bluntly.

But his words fell on deaf ears. Lillian often couldn't be bothered to listen to what other people had to say, even to replies to her questions. Her focus was always on the next thing she wanted to say, or on something else. This time her attention had wandered away from the topic of discussion....

A girl stood in front of the school. Her mother came running up, late to fetch her.

"Where were you?" Lillian heard the little girl ask her mother.

"I got caught up with something," her mother confessed.

"A hell horse tears the castle up and you are too busy to come and get me?" Lillian's eyes narrowed at the child's response.

"I'm sorry," her mother said. Then she changed the subject. "What is that?"

"It's a yellow-blue flower," her daughter smiled. "Lady Evelyn asked us to keep them in the class, but I just had to show you."

Lillian squinted her eyes to study the beautiful flower. Yellow-blues weren't in season. It wasn't a crime to have that flower, but it was rather odd. It was usually used for medicine.

"What are you staring at?" Liam asked his distracted sister.

"I'll be right back," Lillian said.

She rode her horse over to the mother and daughter. The mother looked up at her with big eyes and Lillian knew she was intimidated. *Good.* She knew what Lillian was. "Do you mind if I see that flower, my dear?" Lillian asked.

The little girl clung to the potted plant until her mother told her to hand it over. Lillian held it up and turned it to examine its leaves, stem, and flower. Nothing about it seemed different.

"It's a strange time to be growing these yellow-blue flowers," she stated and handed it back.

"I think the teacher had the flowers brought to the

castle for a lesson," the mother said.

Lillian nodded. She knew something was wrong but couldn't put her finger on what. Was the little girl shaking?

"Lillian!" Liam called.

She turned her horse around and rode back to him. The little girl stared after her and the mother just looked at the flower.

"Why are you scaring the kid?" he asked.

"I was just looking at the flower," she said.

"Did you find anything different about it?"

"Not yet." She looked back at the school and decided that she needed to investigate it later.

Liam led the way to the stables where they both dismounted, and he asked a stable boy to unsaddle and clean their horses. Liam said he would come back and pay the boy once the task was completed.

"That horse," Liam said, pointing to a horse in the stable. "Her name is Jasmine."

Lillian's eyes widened. "She is Black Blade's horse! Are you sure?"

"I'm positive."

"What would the assassin be doing here?"

"I don't know. I think we should find out," Liam said. "But we should find Dylan first."

They walked to the inn where Dylan was staying. Upon arrival, they saw that Dylan wasn't in his room. Liam surveyed the place. His son was a perfectionist and everything inside his room was clean and in order.

Dylan showed up shortly after they did. He opened the door, which he hadn't locked when he'd left, and was surprised to see his aunt and father there.

"Dylan!" they exclaimed.

He looked a mess. His blond hair was tangled and he smelled of sweat. His clothes were torn and stained with mud and blood. And he had a nasty claw mark on his arm.

"What happened to you?" Lillian asked. "Let's clean up that arm!"

"That's the healing herb cabinet." Dylan pointed.

Aunt Lillian opened it and scratched around. It didn't take her long to find the herbs she needed. She filled a bowl with water and found a clean cloth for washing the wound.

"It looks like you have a story to tell," Liam said.

"It's been a crazy day," Dylan admitted.

"Our days are always crazy," Aunt Lillian pointed out as she started cleaning Dylan's arm. He tried not to flinch.

"Crazier than normal," Dylan said. "There was a hell horse in the castle today."

"WHAT?" Lillian and Liam said simultaneously.

"I guess that kid was telling the truth. I heard a little girl tell her mother that earlier," Lillian explained. "But it was so unbelievable that I thought I had heard wrong."

"At least it's gone now," Dylan sighed.

"You fought a hell horse? That's incredible..." Liam said.

"It killed a lot of the king's guards," Dylan said bitterly. He didn't mention that he was the one who accidently set the hell horse loose. He could not tell his father and aunt that it was he who messed up so badly. They would be so disappointed in him and he would end up feeling even worse about himself.

"Where did it come from?" Lillian asked.

Dylan hesitated. "I don't know," he lied.

His aunt locked eyes with him. He didn't flinch and tried to look innocent. He was only following orders from the king. If he told them about where the hell horse had come from, he would have to tell them about the tunnels that the king had asked him to keep secret. The king didn't have any tolerance for people who disobeyed.

"Have you been fighting any other monsters?" Lillian asked.

Dylan thought about Divan. He was sure Caitlin had killed him by now. Then he thought about the wolf. If he told his family about Rafe, they would hunt him unless the king had already killed him. He decided it was better not to say anything. "No," he lied again.

Aunt Lillian wrapped a bandage around his disinfected arm—and none too gently. She knew him very well. She had known him all his life. She knew when he was lying.

She looked at Liam. She knew her brother didn't see what she saw in her nephew because he trusted his son implicitly. But Lillian's experience had taught her that no one could or should be trusted. Not completely. Not even family. She wondered how long Dylan Archer had been keeping secrets.

CHAPTER 15

HIS EXISTENCE WAS a secret. No one knew about Divan and no one would miss him. He didn't have a family and the closest thing he had to a friend was Caitlin. She sat next to his body and held his hand long after she had watched the light leave his eyes.

She wanted to bury him but there wasn't time. She had to search for Rafe. They had taken him from her and she had to get him back.

"Then make them pay for what they did to us."

They had ruined Caitlin's and countless other kid's lives before they were even born. They had wronged them. They had broken them.

"Hurt them."

Caitlin got to her feet. Her blood was boiling. She didn't want to think about what they were doing to

Rafe. If he was dead, she would kill them. She would kill them all.

She picked up the dagger that Dylan had given her and eyed the dried blood staining the blade a dark brown so it reflected nothing. Just as well. She didn't want to know how she looked.

"I will come back for you," she promised Divan's corpse. He deserved a proper burial.

She walked into the tunnel and away from the light. Her expression was angry and her stride was fast and confident. She was set on getting revenge.

She would take Rafe back. He would be just fine. She would get there in time and kill them all.

Maybe it was because Lady Evelyn had drawn her a map, or maybe her memories were returning, because she didn't struggle to find the doors that led to the MOP.

She knew the patronizers were there. She had killed them before when she had tried to escape. She could do it again.

As she approached the MOP quarters, she saw that she was right: four patronizers stood guard in front of the door. Without a doubt there would be even more behind it.

Caitlin smiled when they spotted her. Revenge would be bittersweet. She felt no fear. She had one thing on her mind, and that was to kill. She gripped the dagger as she walked toward the patronizers. She had one tiny dagger. They had blades built into their arms.

How did I kill them before? she thought, and then it came to her. If she stabbed it in the brain, it would stop following orders but it wouldn't die. It would only stop attacking her. But she didn't want them to stay alive.

Burn them. She smiled. She could burn them until there was no flesh left to keep their bodies together. She would burn them until all that remained were piles of red-hot metal.

Caitlin glanced at the torches along the walls. One was burning by the entrance. This meant that someone else was here—someone other than the patronizers that could see in the dark.

Two of the patronizers had swords as arms, no hands or fingers. They attacked first. Caitlin spun to her left as they both slashed at her. Both missed. She twirled back and stuck her dagger into the side of one patronizer's head. It immediately stopped moving—like a bird lying in its nest after the sun went down.

The other one slashed its long blade at her. Caitlin ducked and spied another patronizer behind her. This one had daggers for fingers. She grabbed the patronizer behind her by the wrist and pulled it forward—and impaled it on the other patronizer's long blade.

Caitlin reached for the torch on the wall just as the third patronizer shot the daggers from its fingers. They narrowly missed Caitlin's hand, clanked harmlessly against the stone wall, and clattered to the floor. Caitlin swooped down to grab one, feeling its weight and perfect balance in her grip. She spun around and threw it. The dagger hit the patronizer right between the eyes.

The patronizer with the long blades for arms managed to pry the impaled patronizer off its blade and discarded the limp corpse to the floor. It advanced toward Caitlin, swinging its blades in wide deadly arcs. Caitlin grabbed the torch from the wall and used it to block the blows. Neither showed fear or pain.

They fought like this, inching their way along the wall. Each attack and parry brought them closer and closer to an unlit torch. Because Caitlin had a plan and it was now within reach. She grabbed the unlit torch and judged from its heft that it was full of oil, as she'd hoped it would be. She flicked it toward the attacking patronizer, splashing it in oil. Then she touched her lit torch to its arm. It ignited and stumbled around blindly until it bumped into the patronizer that Caitlin had immobilized, igniting its cloak, and then causing them both to fall to the ground. Both were now burning. But one patronizer tried to roll to extinguish the flames. Caitlin sent her dagger through his head and watched the flames finish him.

Caitlin took what remained of the oil and doused the bodies of the other two dead patronizers. She smiled as the flames consumed them all. Pieces of metal fell to the ground as the flesh holding it together burned. The smell of burning meat would have made most people sick. To Caitlin it smelled like victory.

She took another unlit torch that was filled with oil in one hand and held the burning torch in her other hand. She kicked the door once and it flew open to reveal more patronizers. Caitlin was too angry to think about the fact that she was outnumbered. She was too fueled with rage to be scared.

She was ready to fight.

There was a time she thought that the patronizers were very powerful. They were so tall—at least seven feet tall. The steel in their bones made them unnaturally strong. They were abnormally fast too. In the past, Caitlin would rather have run than fight them.

But this was the present.

Now she wanted them dead. She started moving faster than any of them could. She was stronger and better than they were. She blocked or dodged every blow.

She set them on fire one by one. It was a shame that they didn't scream. She would have liked to have heard that.

She wiped the sweat from her brow and looked at all of the bodies around her. She felt nothing. She wondered if they remembered her from when she was a child. They'd held her a prisoner for so many years.

She proceeded into the tunnels. She had an idea that the children were being kept somewhere to her right. That area was cleaner and had more rooms. She didn't go to them.

She went to her left. That's where the experiments were being conducted. That's where Rafe would be.

As Caitlin moved toward where she knew Rafe would be, memories long forgotten came flooding back. This was where she was trained as a kid. That door led to the training room. That other door led to the poisons laboratory where she'd tricked her classmate into drinking the wrong liquid. Unlike the other tunnels in the castle, these the tunnels in the MOP sector were like an underground building, completely finished with polished walls and floors and furniture. Torches here lit every nook and corner, casting gleaming reflections off the ceilings.

She reached a big room with shimmering walls. Inside it looked like a healer's room. Rafe was sitting upright on a bed with his back turned to her.

"Rafe!" she exclaimed. She dropped her two torches and ran to him.

He looked up and was surprised. He didn't look bad at all. He was clean and his wounds were treated. He wasn't chained to the bed like she thought he would have been. He looked like a guest and not a prisoner.

"Caitlin!" he said.

She ran into his arms. He wrapped them around her and held her close. She breathed him in and closed her eyes. For a moment, the world around them faded away. It was just the two of them that mattered.

"You found me," his voice was soft and grateful.

"Of course I did," she said. Then she pulled free.

"Come on! We have to get you out of here."

"Wait," Rafe said.

Meow.

Caitlin heard the black cat before Rafe pointed to her. "Caitlin, it's her! She's a shifter."

Confused, Caitlin turned around and looked at the black cat. She was sitting on the table and looking at them. Then she jumped from the counter and shifted into a woman.

Caitlin gasped.

"It's nice to see you again," Lady Katherine Black purred.

CHAPTER 16

CAITLIN GAPED AT her. Her jaw actually dropped. She closed her mouth and opened it again but no sound came out. *How was this possible? Lady Katherine Black, the king's right hand and advisor, is a shifter!*

"Allow me to explain," Lady Katherine said as calm as ever.

"How are you a shifter?" Caitlin managed to get out. She eyed the torch which she had dropped when she'd hugged Rafe, and then shook her head. If she wanted to hurt Lady Katherine, she probably wouldn't need it to defend against a house cat.

"I was born this way," Katherine said.

"You know the scent I've been getting that's odd? The one I couldn't place? It's her. It's because she is like me," Rafe said. "I would never have guessed."

"No one ever does," Katherine smiled brilliantly. Her

cunning eyes studied Caitlin as if she expected her to start fighting. Katherine stood with her fingers laced together in front of her. She was way too calm.

"Does the king know?" Caitlin asked.

"Of course not!" Lady Katherine said with a low laugh. "You are now the only two people in this world who know my secret."

"I still don't understand..." Caitlin said. "How did a shifter become the king's right hand?" She looked to Rafe. He was as curious as she was. This secret of Katherine's was both marvelous and treacherous.

"I've helped him achieve many of his goals," Katherine said. "I've convinced him that we see eye to eye and that we feel the same way about Magic."

"Brilliant," Rafe said. "He would never expect to have a shifter right under his nose. But why do it?"

"Because someone has to take the initiative to keep our kind alive," she said. "And I can only do it from a position of power."

"But all Magic folk hate you," Rafe said. "You've killed many of us."

"Lives of Magic folk have been sacrificed but not in vain. Their sacrifice allowed one of us—me—to gain the king's trust. It's alright if they hate me. I'm more focused on the survival of our race than being liked, or even keeping an insignificant number of Magical peasants alive."

"But there aren't that many of us left. So many have been killed—or 'sacrificed' as you call it."

"You'd be surprised how many have survived, and under the king's nose," Katherine laughed. "There is even a school for young witches right here in the castle. Lady Evelyn doesn't know my secret so I never called her out on hers. But I've made a valiant attempt to help that school survive and to keep the Magic a secret." Katherine respected what Evelyn did but she still disliked her. She disliked her because Evelyn thought she had outsmarted Katherine. She thought Katherine had no idea that she was teaching Magic at her school. This is why Katherine often taunted and bullied her.

"What she's saying is true," Caitlin told Rafe. "I've met Lady Evelyn. She is a witch."

"Is this the Lady Evelyn Patterson that Maggie speaks so highly of?"

Caitlin nodded.

"It's a shame that Maggie's memories were oblit-erated," Katherine said. "She would have been a fine witch if she went to that school."

"She has no idea that she has Magic. None of them do," Caitlin said.

"It's best to keep it that way," Katherine said. "They are safer like this."

"Their safety is all that matters," Caitlin agreed.

"Tell us about this place," Rafe asked.

"These tunnels were built long ago by the witches and wizards and sorcerers who built the castle. They are the perfect place to keep secrets. The king wanted a weapon to fight the Magic folk, so Mr Campbell started making one. All of his attempts failed except for you." Her eyes fixed on Caitlin.

Her gaze was so intense that Caitlin almost took a step back. She put a hand on Rafe's leg to steady herself. "And why didn't I fail?"

"I think it was because your mind got obliterated. You don't remember all of your past and so you have stayed mentally sane."

"Why did they obliterate me?" Caitlin asked.

"They didn't. At least, not completely." Katherine paused. "Have you started to remember your past? I watched you tear apart the patronizers. If you remember how to fight, then you should remember more."

"I am slowly starting to remember," Caitlin admitted. "What's triggering my memories? Why do I remember now when I couldn't for so long?"

"Did something traumatic happen? Traumatic experiences can bring back the past."

"Divan died," she said and then added: "The king's other weapon."

"I'm sorry to hear that," Katherine said. "If his death triggered memories, I am sure that if you have another traumatic experience all of your lost memories will come back. Being back here will also bring more memories to the surface.... But I don't think you will go crazy. After being obliterated, your way of thinking has changed. I think you are now strong enough to handle everything that has happened."

Caitlin nodded. "I was scared of the past for a long time and a part of me still doesn't want to remember. But I do think I will be able to handle it."

"So, tell me how you got obliterated," Katherine requested with a straight face.

"I did it to myself," Caitlin said without thinking. Her recall was sudden and surprised her. "I was running away and I realized that there was no way out. So I found the obliteration machine. It's big and cage-like and it was easy to operate. So I did it to myself."

Katherine nodded and then she continued the story. "Campbell found you and tried to plant new memories into your brain. But your mind was too strong to accept them. That's why you never had any memories of your childhood with the Wilde family and of growing up in River Town. Campbell didn't realize that his memory implants hadn't worked. He told the king that your mind had been obliterated and that you were to be sent away to test its effectiveness."

"Wow..." Caitlin breathed.

"Campbell set himself up as the leader of River Town. He wanted to keep a close watch over the MOP subjects to make sure that all the villagers' memories stayed lost and that you were no longer dangerous. Unfortunately, the disease he had created got out of control and killed everyone."

"And so he came back to the castle."

"He did and then I found out what he was doing down here. It was all very simple really. All I had to do was wait for him to make a mistake, which of course he did, and I just used that to nudge him to the executioner's block. I knew he wanted you dead and that's why I warned you."

"Thank you for that!" Caitlin was truly grateful.

"So are you going to shut this place down?" Rafe asked. He hadn't spoken much but he had listened attentively to everything that Katherine and Caitlin had said.

"MOP should work on anyone—Magic and non-Magic folk alike. If the Wilde family still doesn't remember, then it means the obliteration machine has been perfected," Katherine said, sidestepping his question.

"But why did the king want to create it in the first place?" Rafe asked. "Why would he look for a peaceful solution for controlling Magic folk?" Then the realization hit him, and he was able to answer his own question: "So he could use it on other kings. He can brainwash anyone to do what he wants them to do and give him anything he wants.... Why have you not stopped this?"

"By making Magic people forget who they are, their lives won't be in danger anymore. They get to live," Katherine said.

"Stealing people's memories isn't right," Caitlin objected.

"It's not. But my ultimate goal is the survival of my race."

"And how's that been going?" Rafe asked skeptically.

"It has been going well, to be honest. Even better now that you are here." Katherine looked confident as always.

"What do you mean?" Caitlin asked.

"Do you remember when you were bitten by that wild dog? You were ill but then you healed yourself?"

"How could I forget?"

"Well, Healer Dan believes that the answers to making a cure are in your blood." Katherine kept her voice level, but her smile showed how excited she was.

"Really?"

"Yes. He was about to do some tests on you, but you ran away."

"I didn't know," Caitlin said. If she had known that she could help cure Craybies she wouldn't have run away from the healer.

"Well, you know now." Katherine walked to her. "Caitlin, I know you aren't a shifter, but please help us. This disease is going to kill us all. It's gotten out of control."

"What would you like me to do?"

"I'll call Healer Dan immediately to draw some blood," Katherine said. "You just have to let him. It's that simple."

"Are we prisoners?" Rafe asked abruptly.

"No," Katherine said after a short pause. "You can leave if you want to. I'll tell the king you died when we experimented on you. Just make sure that no one who knows you sees you—and tells me."

Rafe nodded and Katherine left to fetch the healer.

CHAPTER 17

CAITLIN TOOK A deep breath. Lady Katherine had given her a lot to process—but later.

She now turned to Rafe. Seeing him so healthy and strong made her feel relieved and happy. He most certainly didn't look like a hell horse had kicked him. His arrow wound was hidden under his shirt so she could not see how bad it was. Caitlin wondered if he was still in any pain. *He hides his pain well*, she thought as she touched his cheek. "Did they hurt you?"

"No," he said, taking her hand. He gave it a reassuring squeeze. "They healed me."

She observed him. He was wearing a black shirt which was torn and dirty. She lifted it up so that she could see his chest. There was a tiny scar where the arrow had hit him. But there was no blood or bruising that she could see. She touched it and he didn't flinch. It didn't hurt anymore.

He cupped his hand against her cheek. His hands were so much bigger than hers. Then his fingers were in her hair and she looked up into his beautiful gray eyes. "I really am fine," he assured her. "You, on the other hand, look terrible."

"I've been fighting," she shrugged.

"Lady Katherine said you killed the patronizers."

Was that caution she heard in his voice? She studied him and tried to figure out what he was thinking. He didn't look scared. Caitlin was still looking into his eyes but she remained silent. What was there to say?

"How many did you kill?" he asked.

"I think about twenty-five," she said. She paused to think. "There were four guarding the door that I killed first. When I entered, I was focused on fighting, not counting them. It was hard to keep track of how many there were.... But I'd guess there were twenty-one inside, maybe a bit more."

His brows shot up and his lips parted slightly but he had nothing to say. She did not understand his reaction. Killing the patronizers was not a bad thing, was it?

"I think there are still plenty more," she added quickly and wondered if her words were reassuring or frightful.

"How did you manage that?" Rafe asked. "Those things are strong!"

"All my training suddenly came back to me. It was easy then," she said. "I've fought them before, but I have never killed so many at once. It's like my anger makes me extra powerful."

Rafe found it scary and amazing and he was glad that Caitlin had come back for him. She wouldn't leave him behind, just like he would never leave her behind either. He looked at her and felt his throat tighten. Her hair was a mess and her face was dirty. Her clothes were torn and covered in blood, much like his. She was beautiful.

"I'm sorry about Divan," Rafe said gently. She flinched when he said the failed weapon's name. "I know you wanted to save him."

"He couldn't be saved," she said. "You should have seen him.... You could see that his body struggled to grow with the Magic that was in his blood. His mind couldn't handle what had been done to him. He was alone and isolated and had gone crazy down here."

"That's very sad," Rafe said. He felt truly sorry for Divan. What they did to him was wrong. But if he was as bad as Caitlin said, then it was better that he was gone.

"Rafe, what if I'm like him?" Caitlin looked down as she asked this. It's something she'd been wondering about for a while now. The thought scared her. She didn't want to be a monster.

"You're nothing like him," Rafe said reassuringly.

She knew Rafe believed that, but she wasn't fully

convinced. They were born in the same place and they were trained in the same way, with the same style of fighting. What made them different? "The hell horse," Caitlin realized. "It attacked him. It wouldn't have attacked him if we shared the same blood."

Rafe's storm-cloud eyes looked at her gently as she tried to convince herself that she would never be like that. Caitlin did not want to lose her mind and she did not want to end up alone. She was still holding onto Rafe.

"You are different from him," he assured her.

She still didn't look convinced. Rafe knew her well enough to tell from the way she kept looking down that her mind was busy and she didn't know how to put her thoughts to words.

"Tell me what's bothering you?" Rafe asked her.

She swallowed before answering. "What if I am the bad guy?"

"You're not," Rafe said firmly.

She didn't want to be the bad guy. She didn't want to be the good guy either. She just wanted to be invisible. Life would be so much easier if she was invisible to everyone except her family and Rafe.

Then Caitlin realized that in many people's eyes Rafe was a bad guy. Many people had a false perception of who he was. She thought about how much Dylan and other hunters would want him dead. And Dylan knew his secret.

"Rafe, I don't know what to do," she said. "We came

to the castle for answers and now we have them. And your secret is revealed. You can't stay."

Their eyes met and Rafe said nothing. She could tell that his heart was aching. He did not want to leave.

"I can't stay," he repeated sadly.

"Then I will leave with you," she said and leaned against him. "I can't let you go on your own."

"What about your family?" Rafe asked.

"I will explain to them that I need to do what's best for me."

Rafe was also selfish, although he knew he should not be. He didn't want to say goodbye to Caitlin. In such a short period of time she had become so important to him. It was hard to picture his future without her in it. And she *wanted* to leave with him.... The idea of running away with her was exhilarating.

"We can't leave right away," Rafe said. "I want to check out the MOP first. I want to see if Lady Katherine would really shut it down."

"Why wouldn't she?"

"You mean 'why hasn't she', don't you?" he said. "It's been over a week since Campbell was executed but everything down here is still moving forward. Something is not right. I don't think she is telling us everything."

"You don't trust her."

"I trust that she is the kind of woman who takes care of herself first."

"I agree." Caitlin also believed that self-preservation was important, but she didn't dare say it out loud. Rafe always placed others first. He wasn't as selfish as she was and so he wouldn't share her views. She didn't want to say anything to lessen his feelings for her.

"How trustworthy can she possibly be? Her whole life is a lie," Rafe pointed out.

"I don't think she means us any harm," Caitlin said. "She warned me that Campbell wanted me dead. And as a cat, she saved me when Black Blade was going to kill me in my sleep."

"But she needs you. She said it herself. She needs your blood."

"Alright," Caitlin said. "So why save *you*? Why tell the king the lie that she needs you as an experiment? She's clearly not going to use you."

"We don't know that. We don't know what she is capable of."

"She just left us here, Rafe. We can walk right out of the place if we want to."

"Maybe that's because she's scared that if she tried to force us to stay, you'll get angry and rip her face off."

"She doesn't know what I'm capable of."

"Neither do you." He saw the resistance in her eyes and moved closer. He let his feet hang off the bed. She leaned closer to him and embraced the feeling of safety that he provided.

"You're a good person, Caitlin," he said.

"You too," she said. "Rafe, I'm sorry for freaking out when you told me about the Blankness potion."

"No apology is necessary."

"Yes, it is. I overreacted. It was a sensitive subject because my memories had already been erased. I thought it was an unforgivable thing to do—to steal someone's memories. But now I realize that I did it to myself. It was easier to forget than to live with the pain of all those horrible memories. I don't even want to remember everything that they did to me. I think it would change me. I might just turn out to be the weapon they wanted."

"You won't—you are better than that," Rafe said. "And I'll never take away your memories or anyone else's."

"Neither will I," she said. "I promise."

Rafe wrapped an arm around her waist and pulled her close. Her hands were on his chest where she could feel his heart beating. He leaned in slowly. His lips were soft....

The kiss ended when they heard Healer Dan walking toward them. He was as handsome as when she had last seen him, only he wasn't smiling this time. Lady Katherine was at his side.

"Hello again," he said to Caitlin. She nodded in greeting.

Rafe studied the trembling man and realized that he was making the healer nervous. "I'm not going to hurt you," Rafe assured Healer Dan with a grin. He did enjoy intimidating people. "Especially not when you are helping my kind get better."

Healer Dan said nothing in response, just averted his eyes. He looked at Caitlin and asked, "Can I please draw some blood? I would like to start working right away."

"Sure," she said.

He motioned for her to sit down on a chair. She did as he asked and flinched when the thin glass needle entered her skin. She didn't like needles.

Lady Katherine watched as the healer drew a cup of blood. He took a lot and she knew that he would use it wisely.

"How is my blood going to help?" Caitlin asked.

"As far as we know, Craybies is carried in a shifter's blood. If the infected shifter's body fluids were to come in contact with another shifter's blood, the disease would be passed on. So if an infected shifter were to bite another shifter, its saliva would carry the disease into the healthy shifter's blood."

"Alright, I understand that part. But how would my blood help?"

"I believe that I can use your blood to create a cure. I believe that your blood contains special healing humors that fight and overcome the disease. Like so many little soldiers," Healer Dan said, pausing to display a smug smile at his own cleverness. "But I need to isolate those humors and reproduce them. Then the healing humors would have to be injected directly into the bloodstream of the infected individual to be effective."

"How soon will you have this ready?" Katherine asked.

"I think I will be able to do it quickly. I believe these healing humors are capable of reproducing when placed in contact with the disease. This would explain why the king's weapon had healed herself so quickly," he said, preening even more. "So, maybe no more than a few hours."

Caitlin's jaw tightened. Her memories of Healer Dan were few. But what existed was brutal. She recalled how he tied her to that table and how he experimented on her. She hated him. He saw her as a lab rat and not a human being. He was nice to her ever since she came back to the castle, but that wasn't enough for her to forgive him. Caitlin didn't forgive.

Caitlin looked at Lady Katherine. The lady trusted them with her biggest secret. She was risking everything to develop a cure. She couldn't be all bad. Caitlin didn't trust her fully, but she did believe her.

CHAPTER 18

IT WAS GETTING dark.

If the Archers were a normal family, they would have sat together and talked and made dinner. But they weren't a normal family and they always had work to do.

"I want to go and check out Evelyn's School," Lillian told Liam and Dylan.

"This isn't still about the flower, is it?" Liam groaned.

"What flower?" Dylan asked.

"I saw a little girl there with a yellow-blue flower today," Lillian told him enthusiastically.

"And?" Dylan sounded bored.

"And it's not the season for it to bloom."

Dylan laughed. "If you want a flower, I'll buy you one at the market tomorrow."

She glared at him.

"Alright!" Dylan smiled. "But the school is closed. We can go tomorrow."

"Where's the fun in that?" she asked. "I'm sneaking in tonight. Are you coming?"

"I'm not," Liam said. "You are wasting your time."

"I have a hunch that something is going on in there," Lillian said.

Dylan knew she wasn't going to change her mind. Lillian loved investigating even if there was nothing to investigate. "Fine, I'll go with you," he said. He made a point to sound reluctant and uninterested. "But I want to eat and clean myself up first."

"I'll do the same," Liam said. "Then I will go to the king and tell him how successful our hunting was."

"Great," Lillian said. "Hurry up then."

Dylan felt much better and ready for the night once he had eaten and washed himself. He got his weapons ready at Lillian's insistence. "It's going to look very suspicious if we go into a school carrying swords," he told his aunt.

"It's nighttime," Lillian said. "There's no one there to see us."

They parted from Liam and then left the inn and started walking toward Evelyn's School. It wasn't that far to walk. Dylan knew where it was. He had walked by it several times but had never seen anything suspicious about it. "I can't believe you are taking me to school. I thought you were supposed to be the cool aunt," he joked, trying to lighten her intense mood.

"I am the cool aunt," she told him with a smile. "Going to a school should be an adventure for you."

"It would have been if I was younger," he told her.

There was no sadness in his voice, but Lillian felt a pang of guilt in her heart. He had not grown up like a normal boy and she was beginning to wonder if that was a bad thing. "Would you have liked to have gone to school?"

"It doesn't really matter now," Dylan said. He didn't meet her eyes because he did not want her to see the regret. Yes, he had wanted to go to school but there was no point in saying that now and making his aunt unhappy. He also didn't want to linger on the past. It's not like they could go back and change things.

"It's never too late to join a university," Lillian told him.

"But then I'd have to quit hunting," Dylan said.

"No, you don't," she objected. "You could easily hunt part-time."

"What do you think Dad would say to that?"

"I think you're old enough to make your own decisions. Your dad doesn't have a say in the matter." She studied him and puzzled over what he wanted from life.

"You're probably right," he said, and again he didn't look at her.

"I'm always right," she pointed out. "Your mom would be proud if you went to study."

Dylan tensed. "Do you think so?"

Lillian nodded. "Oh yes! She was an academic after all. She always excelled in school and studied hard like a healer should. She liked saving people's lives. Kind of like you."

Dylan did not agree with his aunt's statement. His mom had been a healer and therefore she was nothing like him. She didn't kill; she spared lives. Dylan couldn't remember much about her, but he always remembered that she was very kind. "Please tell me more."

"About your mother?" Lillian asked.

"Yes. She died when I was really young. I can't remember much about her. Dad never mentions her, and I never wanted to ask because everyone always gets tense when I do."

"Well... she was a good woman," Lillian said. "She had a passion for people and always tried to help everyone. She met your father when she finished her studies and started working as a healer. He had gone hunting and got his stomach ripped open by a shifter. His hunting partner rushed him to the healer's house. She saved his life that day."

Dylan could picture his dad bleeding and hurt in the healer's house. It's usually where hunters ended up—there or in the graveyard.

"He called me and told me he loved her and that he would marry her. I thought it was just the drugs making him talk crazy. Then he did it. He married her."

"I didn't know their story," Dylan said.

"Well now you do," Lillian said.

"How did she feel about him hunting?" Dylan asked. For a moment, he thought Lillian was a bit tense, but that moment passed.

"Mary knew what she married into."

"Did she ever ask him to quit?" Dylan asked.

Lillian paused again. To be quiet was uncommon for her. Dylan knew it was hard for her to talk about Mary. She had loved Mary as if they were sisters and she missed her every day. Dylan didn't want to bring painful memories back but at the same time he wanted to hear about his mother. The stories made him feel closer to her.

"She did," Lillian said reluctantly. "I think it was only because she got tired and worried every time your dad stayed out late or came home bloodied. She didn't always realize just how important his work was."

Dylan could imagine how difficult a relationship like that must be. He wondered if his mother would have wanted him to live the life he was living. If she was alive, would she be proud of the warrior he had become, or scared because he lived such a dangerous life?

"And let me guess," Dylan said. "Dad didn't want to quit."

"He didn't for a long time," Lillian said. "And then you were born and things changed."

"Oh yeah?" She had all of Dylan's attention.

146

"Many kids are born and raised into hunting families. Your father understood this, but your mother didn't. She didn't want you to ever be in danger. I think Liam considered giving up his trade for his family and that wasn't right. By doing that he would only have been giving up his other family—his hunting family. He knew it was wrong but he loved your mother and considered doing what she wanted him to do. If only she could have understood how important hunting is."

"Maybe she was just scared."

"Or blind," Lillian said. "She didn't always realize how dangerous these beasts were. She didn't understand that they were monsters. She didn't understand that they could look and act like us and pretend to be our friends one day and then slash our throats the very next day."

Dylan swallowed hard and then braced himself to ask Lillian something that he had wanted to ask for years. "Aunt Lillian, you were the last person with my mom when she died..."

Lillian bit the inside of her cheek. "That's right," she said tightly.

"My dad never speaks about it. He only says she was killed by a monster."

"That's right," she said again.

"Please tell me what happened." He knew he was taking a big chance. He didn't think his aunt would tell him. She'd never healed from the loss of Mary.

"Dylan, it was years ago...."

"Please," he said again. "I have a right to know."

She was quiet for a bit and Dylan thought she would remain silent.

"Your father heard about shifters in Southpaw and moved there with the intention of killing them. As a healer, Mary got work there easily. You were just a kid then. It happened one day when your dad was out. I was visiting and spent most of my time playing with you. She told me about the new friends she had made. That was the day you were at the childminder's house. Remember? Where all the village kids went when their parents were out working during the day? She got off work early and decided to speak with her new friends before she picked you up. Little did she know what they truly were—shifters. The moment these so-called 'friends' of hers had her alone and away from people, they—" Lillian choked up and she had to pull herself together before continuing. "They tore her apart limb for limb. And then they devoured her. I went to look for her when she didn't come home. I found only her bones and her clothes—the bits of her they couldn't consume and didn't have time to hide before I'd gotten there."

Dylan couldn't speak. His chest felt tight.

"And then I slaughtered them," Lillian said. "All of them."

Her eyes were cold and loveless. Dylan had never seen this sad and broken side of Lillian. He thought she was done speaking, but the memories were overwhelming.

"If only she had listened to me," Lillian said. "I told her how bad shifters were! I told her they were heartless killers. I warned her. I tried my best, Dylan. I swear I did everything I could."

Dylan stopped walking and pulled her into a hug. "It's alright, Aunt Lillian."

"She died the day that she would have spent with me," Lillian said against his chest. "She died when I was supposed to take care of her while your father was hunting. He couldn't forgive me back then and he never will."

Dylan squeezed a little tighter. "I think he blames himself more than anyone."

Lillian hugged Dylan back. "You have her kind heart, boy," she whispered.

He let her go and was relieved that she wasn't crying. If she cried, he would also want to cry and that just wasn't acceptable. He was stronger than that.

They reached the school. It was quiet and a fence surrounded it. Lillian and Dylan knew no one would stop them and no one would question them. People stayed clear of hunters and left them alone to do whatever they needed to do.

The two of them climbed over the fence easily and walked to the front doors. Dylan had a small, slender strip of iron that he used to unlock the front door.

A man walking by the school stopped when he saw

them. Lillian stared at him. He realized that they were hunters and hurriedly continued on his way.

Dylan walked into the school first. Lillian followed. It was dark and looked just like any other school. The halls were empty and quiet, its floors swept free of litter and debris. The bins where the students kept their personal belongings were empty and the class-room doors were closed.

At first, they stayed together. They entered the first classroom. It was filled with yellow-blue flowers planted in tidy rows of uniform pots.

"This is odd," Lillian said. "All of these are very healthy and blooming! They aren't in season."

Dylan picked up some of the books that were on the teacher's table and studied them. "These are perfectly normal books. They are all about the medic-inal uses of plants, including that yellow-blue flower."

Lillian didn't double-check the books. She trusted Dylan to know when something was off. She looked around the classroom but nothing else struck her as strange or out of place.

They moved on and found the dining hall. The tables were spotless, and it was deadly quiet. Dylan wondered at which table he would have sat if he had gone to school. He was smart, but he didn't look like a nerd. He was athletic, but not a jock. Would he have been popular? Probably not. People would most likely have thought he was a freak when they found out he was a hunter. No one would dare look for trouble with him, but no one would befriend him either. He would have sat alone, probably at a table in a secluded corner.

"Are you falling asleep over there?" Lillian interrupted his thoughts.

"Well, you did bring me to the most boring place in the castle," he said. "Are we done now? Have you seen everything?"

"Almost," she said as she walked out of the dining hall.

Dylan sighed loudly and then followed at her heels, thinking it was a wild goose chase. But Lillian didn't give up easily. He wandered through the halls patiently and then he found the headmistress's office. The door read "Headmistress Evelyn Patterson." Dylan pushed it open.

At first it looked normal. There was a desk with papers on top of it. There was a bookshelf, stationery, and a potted plant. Dylan walked to the desk and he picked up the sheet of paper that was lying on top. It was a roster of the children who attended the school.

He was about to leave when something caught his eye on the floor behind the desk. One of the stone tiles looked like it was loose and sticking up. He walked toward it and bent down. The stones used to pave the floor were very big. He used his fingers and was amazed that the stone moved when he pushed it. He pushed it a little more. It revealed an opening.

Dylan remembered the king telling him that the tunnels had more than one secret entrance. He could immediately see that this was one of them. He started pushing the tile back into place.

"Dylan, are you in here?" Lillian was at the door. The desk was blocking her view so she couldn't see Dylan or the gaping hole in the floor.

"Yes!" Dylan said quickly and jumped up.

"Did you find anything?"

"No," he said sheepishly.

"But I thought I heard something moving?"

"I bumped into the desk," Dylan said, rubbing his hip exaggeratedly.

"That's odd," she looked into his eyes. "You aren't clumsy."

He shrugged and made sure that he didn't look down. The entrance wasn't closed all the way. He decided to stay calm as he walked toward her. "I'm just tired."

"You can go back to the house," she said. "I can check the last few classrooms myself."

Dylan knew that she would become suspicious if he didn't leave now. So he left.

Lillian left too and walked down the hall. Then she stopped and turned to watch Dylan leave the building. Once he was out of sight she went back into the head-mistress's office.

Lillian knew whenever Dylan hid something from her. As he'd done just now. She walked to where he had been standing and looked around and down. She found the stone and moved it. "Now, what do I have here?" she said to the darkness.

CHAPTER 19

LIAM ARCHER DIDN'T mind walking in the dark. It wasn't that far to the throne room and he walked quickly even in the dark. In his youth, he had trained his other senses to compensate for hampered vision in moonless forest nights. Through the years, he found himself drawing on this skill often during his hunts.

He had decided to leave all of his weapons in Dylan's room. He didn't want to show up at the throne room with his swords, and the guards would take them away before they let him enter anyway. He had always been uneasy with the idea of anyone else handling his weapons. Yet freed from the weight of his weapons, he felt his stride lighten as he walked past houses alive with the sound of families. He heard children laugh and play. His heart filled with joy to see people happy and families whole. But he also felt empty. He had a longing in his chest that would never go away.

He wondered if Dylan sometimes felt it too. He was so young when his mother died and he probably didn't remember her. But growing up without her surely left a hole in his life.

Liam tried not to think about Mary. There was no point in lingering on the past. It couldn't be changed, and he needed to stay focused and think about the future.

This was hard to do with Lillian around. She brought back many memories. He loved her and she was a good mom for Dylan when Mary died. But she also drove Liam a bit crazy. All she ever wanted to do was hunt and kill. She couldn't sit still for a moment.

Still, she was a good influence on Dylan. She inspired and motivated him, and Liam liked that. He liked her honesty. She and Dylan were the only people he fully trusted to always tell him the truth. They were family; they shared the same blood. There were no secrets, no locked doors, among the three of them.

Liam walked through the halls to the throne room. The doors were open. The guards moved aside for him and nodded their heads. He gave them a half smile as he walked past them.

The king was sitting on his throne. He looked fierce and strong as always and he smiled when he saw Liam. The jeweled chair to the king's right was empty and that made Liam wonder where Lady Katherine was. She was almost always at the king's side.

Liam bowed low and only stood up when the king told him to.

"Liam Archer," King Leonard said. "It's good to see you again. I didn't expect you to be back so soon."

"Neither did I," Liam said.

"I trust you have some good news," the king smiled.

"I do," Liam said. "We had a very successful hunt. By setting traps, we quickly wiped out several shifter families."

"That is good to hear," the king said. "Thank you for bringing the news to me personally."

"It's the right thing to do after you gave me the honor of serving you, Your Majesty," Liam said humbly.

"Yes," the king said. "You should teach that to your son."

"Your Majesty?" Liam asked.

"He is a good hunter. And even faster at doing his work than you are," King Leonard said. "But some lessons in courtly graces would serve him well.... He sent a guard to me to tell me that his work is done."

"I apologize on his behalf. I will speak with him."

"Good. He is a good fighter. I might use his services again soon—especially after there was a shifter on the loose."

"There was a shifter on the loose?" Liam gaped.

"Yes," the king said. "A shifter-wolf tore through the castle. Didn't Dylan tell you this?"

Liam paused and chose his words carefully. "I only just got back. We didn't have a lot of time together. He hasn't had a chance to brief me yet."

The king looked like he believed him. He paid Liam well and thanked him. Then he dismissed him.

Liam left the throne room feeling confused about his son. Dylan had more than enough time to share what had happened here. So why hadn't he?

Caitlin held Rafe's hand. Lady Katherine had left the room again and Caitlin assumed she would be back shortly. She had not asked where Katherine had gone. The king's right hand was a very busy woman and she was constantly on the move. Healer Dan hadn't come back after he had taken Caitlin's blood. Caitlin was glad that he had stayed away. Now she had some alone time with Rafe. She could tell he was lost in thought. She knew him by now. She could read him and sometimes she could tell what he was thinking.

"You're worried," she said breaking the silence.

He snapped out of his gaze and looked at her. "Not really."

"I can see you are," she said. "What is it that you are thinking about?"

"The look on Gerald's face when he realized what I am," Rafe said. "I don't think he will ever forgive me."

"It doesn't matter," Caitlin said.

"It does," Rafe argued. "You see him as a father and he thinks you are his daughter. Family is important."

"I agree. And if I am important to them, they will let me love the man who is good for me."

"I'm good for you?" Rafe smiled.

"You make me happy," she said with butterflies dancing in her stomach. It was the truth. He made her happier than anything or anyone. "So when do you want to leave?" Caitlin asked enthusiastically.

"It will have to be soon," Rafe said. "I can't stay hidden in the tunnels."

"Then how about tonight?" she asked. "I really don't have anything to pack. We can just go. I still have some money that I took from River Town. That should keep us alive for a few months."

"And then what?" Rafe asked.

"We can find somewhere else to live.... Maybe in Southpaw?"

Rafe shook his head. "I don't ever want to go back there."

"Then you choose," she said. "Surprise me."

"Caitlin, are you sure about this? I don't think you've thought it through...."

"Why do you say that?"

"I'm a shifter—my whole life is dangerous. There is always going to be someone who wants to kill me."

"So it would be safer if you have a pack, even if it's just a pack of two."

"People would judge us and look down on our relationship. They'll think you are a non-Magic. Shifters won't accept it either."

"We don't need any of them," Caitlin said. "And I'm not non-Magic. I'm kind of in between."

"I know that," he said.

She asked the next question cautiously. "Rafe, do you *want* me to come with you?"

"Of course I do!" he said and his tone convinced her. "It's just... you already have a great life and a family who loves you. I don't want you to come with me and then be unhappy or want more than I can give."

"All I want is you," she said. "I've never wanted anyone or anything more."

He put his hand on her cheek and she leaned against him. "And you don't mind being on the move a lot?"

"No," she smiled. "Not even a little bit."

"And you do realize that you might never see your family again?"

This made her heart ache and she held on to the little bit of hope she had left inside of her. "I can always visit them."

"We won't be staying close to the castle. It's too dangerous for me. I have no idea how Lady Katherine has been keeping her secret so well."

"She's a smart woman," Caitlin said.

"I don't want to stay here with her knowing what I

am. She has a lot more power than me and could easily use it to her advantage."

"Why would she do that? Don't shifters all stick together?"

"Don't humans?" Rafe asked with a quirk of his brow.

Their eyes met and there was a moment of silence. Caitlin craved a kiss. She couldn't get enough of Rafe. And all this talk of running away had her mind spinning.

But Rafe wasn't thinking about kisses. He changed the subject. "Before we go, I would like to check this place out. I would like to see the MOP. I want to know what she is planning to do with the people that they keep down here."

"Me too," Caitlin said. "Let's get all of this done tonight and then we leave tomorrow morning at first light."

"Alright," Rafe said. "Make sure you say goodbye to your family. You will regret it if you don't."

"You should too," she said.

"I will," Rafe said courageously. "I have to say good-bye to Maggie. And I'll at least try to explain to your parents that I'm not that bad...."

"You don't have to explain anything," she told him. "But if you really want to, I think you should do it sooner than later."

"I'll head over now. I'll take the back roads so not many people will see me. I doubt anyone would connect me to the shifter."

"Alright, I'll come with you."

They both jumped at a knock on the door. It swung

open and Lady Katherine entered. She could be frighteningly silent, like a cat. "Caitlin, I would like to show you some things about your past."

"Does it have to be now?" Caitlin asked, casting all courtly formalities aside. She wasn't sure if she wanted to see.

Katherine nodded. "If you're leaving the castle, then yes."

Caitlin wondered how much of the conversation she had overheard. It didn't really matter, did it? Yet, the idea of someone eavesdropping put Caitlin on edge. She turned to Rafe for an answer to her unspoken question.

"Should I come or wait for you?" he asked.

"It doesn't matter," she said.

"Maybe I should go to your family."

"Wouldn't you feel more confident with me by your side?"

"I don't lack confidence," Rafe smiled at her, playfully brushing the tip of her nose. "I think your father might handle it better if I spoke to him alone."

"Alright," she said. "I'll meet you there."

"Okay, and if something happens and we get split up, let's meet by our tower at first light?"

Our tower was a beautiful idea when Rafe said it. Caitlin knew he was referring to the tower where he had kissed her for the first time. "Okay."

He kissed her in front of Lady Katherine, whose expression didn't change as she watched them kiss. Caitlin gave him one last smile full of hope and meaning.

"I need to give the guards instructions. I'll be back in five minutes," Katherine said curtly and left.

Caitlin laughed. Her cheeks were red. "Do you think we made her uncomfortable?"

"No," Rafe said. "Maybe just jealous."

He kissed Caitlin again, and she wondered if he was really as confident as he looked. If he was not, he was very good at faking it.

Caitlin was a bit scared, but she also felt exhilarated. She couldn't wait to run away with Rafe, to live happily ever after.

Lady Evelyn returned, this time without knocking. "Caitlin, I'd like to show you something."

Caitlin looked worriedly at Rafe.

"Don't worry," he said. "I'll be fine."

"He's gotten himself this far," Lady Evelyn said. "He'll be safer outside of the tunnel walls."

"Go on," Rafe encouraged Caitlin.

And they parted ways.

CHAPTER 20

"ARE YOU READY?" Katherine asked.

"As ready as I'll ever be," Caitlin replied. She wasn't sure what Katherine wanted to show her or why. "May I ask why you want to show me this?"

"It's important to know who you are and what you fight for," Lady Katherine said. She didn't look like she had any ulterior motives. She was calm as always and Caitlin wondered if the king was missing her at his side.

"Yes, it is. And as you told me before, it's something I get to decide."

Katherine nodded. "I take it you have decided then." Her voice wasn't curious. It was emotionless and Caitlin did not like that because she had trouble figuring out what Katherine was thinking. She was a difficult woman to read and that impenetrability made Caitlin cautious.

"I think so," Caitlin said. "I'm trying to make peace with the past."

"So you're not angry? You're not seeking revenge then?"

"No... Who would I get vengeance on? Campbell is already dead."

"But the king is not," Katherine said. "He is the one that ordered Campbell to create you...."

Caitlin knew that Katherine was checking to see if she was a threat to the kingdom. Katherine had to know if she would try to hurt anyone. Caitlin thought she would pass the test easily. There wasn't a lot of anger in her heart. "No," Caitlin repeated. "I'd never be stupid enough to go after the king...."

"Are you scared?" Katherine asked.

"Not scared... but if I harmed him, I would always have people hunting me. I'm sure the queen will pay a lot of money to have my head cut off. I don't want to be labeled as a kingslayer."

"But you're going to be hunted when you and Rafe run away..."

"That's different..."

"How?"

"I'm doing it for love," Caitlin said, and felt her cheeks flush. Together, Rafe and she could rule the world—at least, their own little world, which was all that mattered. She didn't expect Katherine to understand.

Katherine smiled. "Love is a powerful thing. It's almost as powerful as anger."

"I try not to get angry." Caitlin confessed.

"You're deadly when you are angry," Katherine told her. "You're ruled by your emotions."

Caitlin knew this was true. She would have to work on not losing her temper. She should never get as angry as she had when she ripped those patronizers apart.

"I'm sorry about Divan," Katherine said. "If only I took over this whole operation sooner, I could have saved him."

"I wish you had," Caitlin said. "I'll kill anyone who touches the people I love."

"You should be careful with your family then. Although they don't know it, they are Magic folk."

"But they are safe here where very few people the truth."

"You really want to leave with him," Katherine said bemusedly.

"Why are you so surprised?"

"Because you are the *weapon*. You are the most dangerous thing in the kingdom. I expected you to be more violent."

"Well... I don't remember much about being made into a weapon. I don't feel that rage. I don't think I ever will."

"That's surprising. I do think traumatic experiences would bring that back."

"Maybe," Caitlin said. "But I'm planning to *not* have any more traumatic experiences."

"Aren't we all?" Katherine replied.

"Lady Katherine, I was wondering something.... You know about Evelyn's School.... Are you two friends?"

"No. I can't help but always be a bit sharp with her. She undermines my intelligence."

"I think you intimidate her."

"I intimidate most people."

Katherine walked with her through multiple rooms. Caitlin didn't recognize most of them. The hole in her memories was still there. Some of the rooms were classrooms and some were exercise rooms. "I hardly remember any of this," she told Katherine.

"I thought you might remember more by being here. You're very brave to come here and face the past."

"I'm not brave. I can't remember all the things that I once feared," Caitlin said.

"I think you'll master any fears you might have."

"I think so too." Caitlin walked around. "There are little details that I remember from dreams. Like that fighting ring." She pointed at it. "I knocked out a teacher over there."

"I sure wouldn't want to fight you," Katherine said.

"I'm not that good anymore. I don't remember all of my training. Some of it does come back at times —like when my life is threatened."

"Then maybe the MOP doesn't work as flawlessly as I'd thought."

"It seems to be working on my family. Maybe it just doesn't work on me because I'm different."

"That could be," Katherine said. "I want to use the

obliteration device confident that it's fully functional."

"Do you really want to use it?" Caitlin asked.

"If it's for the greater good, then yes."

Caitlin didn't like her response. It made her sick to think about what they were doing to the Magic folk down here. She could imagine little Maggie locked up down here in the dark. That thought made her blood boil.

"I would like to see it," Caitlin said.

"What?" Katherine asked.

"The whole program." Caitlin met her eyes. She refused to back down. For a moment she thought Lady Katherine would deny her request.

Then Katherine smiled, but her smile didn't reach her eyes. "Follow me."

Caitlin didn't hesitate. She also didn't walk behind Katherine like a follower. She walked at her side like an equal. She didn't think Katherine was scared of her or intimidated. She wondered if she annoyed her by not trembling like everyone else did.

They walked to the big metal doors. No patronizers stood guard. "Where are the patronizers?" Caitlin asked.

"You've killed most of them. There hasn't been time to create new ones."

"Why would you want to create new ones?" Caitlin asked. "They're a failed experiment."

"In some ways they are, but they are also extra protection."

"Protection from whom?"

"From anyone who seeks to harm the ones they serve," Katherine replied cryptically.

They walked through the doors and down the halls. The torches made the air almost suffocatingly warm. "I don't think I've been down this way," Caitlin observed.

"It's where the MOP test subjects are kept. It's dinner time for them."

Caitlin walked with her to a door. It was made of glass and Caitlin could see through it into a big room that served as a dining hall. There were a lot of children. They laughed and ate and talked.

"You look surprised," Katherine pointed out.

"They look so... normal," Caitlin said. "And healthy."

"Of course. I see them as guests, not prisoners. They are taken care of."

"And the adults?"

"Their dining room is farther down this hall. They don't eat with the kids and there aren't as many of them."

Caitlin thought about this. The adults were capable of thinking for themselves and they would be more difficult to control than the kids. Caitlin looked through the glass door. She wondered if they couldn't see her —none of them looked her way. She saw the little red-haired girl, Roxy. She was laughing with a friend. Caitlin remembered how Maggie was almost taken with Roxy that night in Waterfall Haven. Her anger flared up. No one had the right to lock her little sister away.

"You're upset," Katherine said.

"I don't like this," Caitlin said.

"What part?"

"The part where children are being taken from their families and turned into people that they aren't."

"But it gives them a better life and ensures their survival," Lady Katherine said.

"How would you feel if someone did this to you?" Caitlin asked. "How would you feel if someone stole your memories and made you forget who you are?"

"That's different," Katherine said. "I am completely safe."

"So you just want to pick up where Campbell left off?"

"Only with the necessary experiments," Katherine said. "Someone has to make sure that our kind survives."

"But what you are doing is horrible!"

"Is it?" Katherine asked. "You chose to do it to yourself and you seem to be just fine."

"That's different," Caitlin said. "I was emotionally traumatized."

"And these kids aren't? They have been born into a word where hunters want to kill them for what they are. Take Maggie as an example. If her memories hadn't been obliterated, she would have been hunted and killed. But look at her now. She is happy and has a family who loves her."

"There has to be another way," Caitlin said.

"If you find one, let me know." Katherine said. "Are

you sure you want to continue our little tour?"

"Yes," Caitlin said. "I'm fine."

"Alright then. Let's move on." Katherine started to walk again.

After the vastness of the dining hall, the narrow tunnels felt like a prison to Caitlin. She felt claustrophobic and wanted to be outside in the fresh air. She reminded herself that soon she would be away from all this, away with Rafe. Then she could have all the fresh air and freedom she wanted.

They walked past the dining hall where the adults gathered to eat. They were much quieter than the kids and they didn't look happy.

"We have been doing our best to make their stay comfortable," Lady Katherine told Caitlin.

"Was my real mother like one of these people?" Caitlin asked.

"Your birthmother was a street woman," Katherine said. "The moment she heard she could make money out of a child, she took it. After she gave birth to you, she left and she was never seen again. She didn't want you."

"Then she's not my mother," Caitlin said.

Katherine studied her. "Daisy is your mother now, isn't she?"

"That's right," Caitlin said.

"You came to love those people very quickly. I think it's because of your hell horse instincts to be part of a herd."

169

"Maybe," Caitlin said. "You really are very interested in me...."

"I am fascinated by you," Katherine said. "You are one of a kind and you would make an excellent ally."

"I don't want any part of this."

"You are a part of this whether you want to be or not."

"But I'm leaving."

"You're running," Lady Katherine said. "You might be able to run away from this place, but you will never be able to run away from your past. Your memories will stay with you."

"Then I think it is best I don't remember much more than I already do," Caitlin said.

They reached a circular room. In the middle was a square cage. It looked as if a bunch of dungeon doors were slammed together to form a box.

"Is this it?" Caitlin asked but she already knew the answer.

"We call it the Obliterator," Lady Katherine said.

"How do you operate it?"

"You'll have to ask one of the people who work here," Katherine said.

"Are they also Magic folk?"

"Some are but not many," Katherine said. "The Magic folk were employed initially to cast spells and use their powers to make the Obliterator functional. It would never have come into being if only the alchemists, healers, and blacksmiths had worked on it alone."

170

"Are the non-Magic folk Magic sympathizers?"

"No."

"Then why would they help you?"

"You're a clever young lady," Katherine said. "Because the king commanded them to. Everyone believes that the MOP is being done for the king. They think we created this machine for him to use and they'd rather use Magic kids than non-Magic kids."

"Don't you ever get confused with all these lies you tell them?" Caitlin surprised herself by her unexpected outburst.

Katherine chuckled. "I just keep the story as close to the truth as possible."

"So you're not a very honest person..." was another unguarded observation.

"It depends," Katherine said, her eyes narrowing for a fraction of a second. "I will be honest with you right here and right now."

"Yes?"

"I don't want you to leave," Katherine said.

"Why? I am of no use to you." Caitlin said.

"I want you by my side. I want you to help me save all of our Magic folk, and that includes Rafe. We can work on you remembering your training. The two of us can accomplish anything together. We can make the world the way we want it. We can overthrow the king and bring peace to the kingdom."

"I'm not a hero," Caitlin said. "I'm not very good at saving people either."

"Are you sure you're not just saying this out of selfishness?"

"I'm not selfish."

"Yet you are running away with the wolf and leaving the people who love and need you here behind."

"They don't need me." Caitlin objected. "And they will understand."

"Will they?" Katherine asked.

CHAPTER 21

RAFE LEFT THE tunnels and didn't look back. He felt uneasy because there was so much going on. He tried to stay level-headed and allow himself time to think through the series of events and their impact on the future. He could handle everything. He could.

He felt a little nervous to walk out in public. He shouldn't have because the witnesses had only seen him as a wolf and would not associate that wolf with his current human form. No one had witnessed him actually shifting into his wolf form and so no one could possibly identify him.

So Rafe casually walked home. No one glanced in his direction. No one stopped him. He even strolled past a few guards, avoiding eye contact, and was rewarded when they didn't chase after him.

He was safe.

But he was still in a hurry to leave the castle. He'd learned about everything he wanted to know. He knew enough about the disease that was plaguing his kind. He was also confident that a cure would soon be found for Craybies. As a shifter herself, this would be Katherine's top priority. He knew that she didn't want to get sick herself so she was compelled to put a stop to it.

He still felt uneasy about the MOP and he debated whether there was something he could do about it. Well, what would he do? What *could* he do against Lady Katherine? She was the most powerful woman in the Silver Kingdom. He had listened to her steady heartbeat as she had spoken to them. Everything she told them was either the truth, or she was an outstanding liar—even better than Caitlin.

So Rafe decided that he was ready to leave. He wanted no part of the MOP. He was ready to get out before he got caught up in something he didn't want to be caught up in. And Caitlin wanted to come with...

Just thinking her name sent jolts of electricity through his body. She was so beautiful and smart. He'd never met another woman like her, and he never would meet anyone like her again. But there was something dark about her. There was an evil hidden deep inside. This was something Rafe hadn't seen before but the thought of it made him uncomfortable. He thought about how she ripped apart the patronizers.

A part of him was glad that he hadn't watched her do it; the evidence alone was gruesome enough.

He wondered if that part of her would vanish once they ran away. He hoped so. He hadn't had a lot of time to think their plans through, but he did look forward to a life with Caitlin.

And that's why he had to be brave and speak directly to her family. He had to at least try and get them to forgive him for taking her away. He wanted to be in Caitlin's life. He knew that she loved them. They were important to her so they were important to him.

He approached the house. He took a deep breath and released it. Then he walked to the front door. He stood there for a moment before he had the courage to knock.

It was Daisy who opened the door. She wore an apron, and the delicious smell of food was coming from the kitchen. Rafe glanced in that direction. It was weird not to see the black cat perched on the counter. Rafe also noticed that the wooden table was missing. It made the living room look too big and too empty.

"Rafe!" Daisy exclaimed. For a moment it looked like she would hug him, but then she remembered what he was and she stopped herself.

"The table is gone," Rafe said awkwardly, unable to bring himself to explain why he was really there.

"Caitlin got into a fight," Daisy began. Before she could say anything else, Maggie, who had heard her mother say his name, appeared. She rushed out of her room, pushed past her mother, and flung her arms around Rafe's waist. "You're back! You're alright!"

Rafe couldn't help himself. He picked the child up and hugged her back. He knew that she truly loved him. Kids loved so easily. "I'm alright."

"I thought they killed you! Did Lady Evelyn help you? And where is Caitlin?"

"Caitlin is fine," Rafe said. "She'll be home soon."

Daisy stood blocking the doorway. She looked very unsure about what she should do. "You should come in," she said at last. "I don't want anyone seeing you."

Rafe saw how Daisy looked at Maggie in his arms. He noticed that she showed no fear but that there was coldness to her that wasn't there before. Rafe nodded and walked into the living room. Daisy closed the door behind him.

"Where is Gerald?" Rafe asked. He didn't try to disentangle himself from Maggie who was still clinging to him.

"He is in the back," Daisy answered. "I will get him."

Rafe watched Daisy leave. He tried to put Maggie down but she hung on to him. He had a feeling that she could cling forever.

"Don't let me go!" she told him.

She didn't weigh much and was easy to hold. "Alright," he said.

"Where were you?" Maggie asked.

There was no way Rafe would tell a six-year-old

what he had been through. There was no way he would be responsible for giving her nightmares. "Somewhere safe."

"Didn't the guards take you to the king?"

"I'm fine now," Rafe reassured her while evading her direct question.

He heard Daisy's voice. "There's someone here to see you."

"Who?" Rafe heard Gerald ask.

"You best come inside and look," was Daisy's cryptic reply.

Rafe waited patiently. Daisy entered ahead of her husband. Gerald was dirty and sweaty. Rafe guessed that he was busy chopping wood. He looked up and froze when he saw Rafe.

"What are you doing here?" he growled.

"I thought we should talk," Rafe said.

"About what?" Gerald's eyes went to Maggie who was still clinging to Rafe. "Maggie! I grounded you for running away! Why aren't you in your room?"

"Because Rafe is back!" Maggie said. "Please don't be mad at him, Daddy. He is a good wolf. I promise."

Gerald walked up to Rafe and his daughter. Rafe could hear his heart hammering. Gerald was angry but he was more scared as he reached for Maggie.

"NO!" Maggie cried and clung to Rafe.

"Go with your dad," Rafe said gently. "Please."

"Fine," she huffed out. "But only because it's you asking."

When Gerald took her from his arms, Rafe suddenly felt very empty. Her father put her down on the ground behind him and shielded her with his body. Rafe could not help but feel hurt. He had risked his life to save Maggie. He would never ever hurt her.

"The grown-ups need to talk," Gerald told his younger daughter. "Go to your room."

"Okay, but don't be mean to Rafe," she said. Then she gave Rafe a happy smile and walked away obediently.

Rafe was glad she had listened. He didn't want a child to be in the middle of this particular conversation. Daisy was hiding behind Gerald and her heart was hammering. Rafe wondered whether she was scared of him or for him. He kept his distance and calmly sat down on the couch.

"What are you doing?" Gerald asked.

"I'm sitting down so we can talk. Calmly," Rafe said.

"There's nothing to talk about!" Gerald retorted. "Get out of my house!"

"Please hear me out," Rafe said.

"Hear you out? After all the lies you've fed us?"

"I've never lied to you," Rafe said. "I just didn't give you the entire story."

"And you will now?"

"I'll tell you everything you want to know," Rafe said truthfully.

"I can't trust you!" Gerald said. "How could you come back here? You're putting my family's lives at stake!"

"No one knows that I am the shifter," Rafe said.

"You are all safe."

"How did you escape the king? Why aren't you dead?"

Rafe didn't know how to answer Gerald. He wanted to be honest but he couldn't tell this man about the tunnels and the MOP and how he ended up down there. "You wish he had killed me," Rafe realized.

Daisy had her hands in front of her mouth. She was shaking behind Gerald. She was too scared to speak up.

"Yes," he said coldly. "You and all Magic folk deserve to die!"

"I'm sorry you feel that way," Rafe said calmly. "I didn't mean to deceive you, but I couldn't tell you what I am."

"You should never have joined us on the way to the castle!"

"With all due respect, had I not joined you on your journey, your family would be dead."

Gerald knew this was true. "We might get killed anyway because of you."

"No, you won't," Rafe said to him. "I'm leaving."

"Leaving? Where will you go?"

"As far away from here as possible, and I won't come back."

"Good! So leave now," Gerald said. Then he realized something. "You told Maggie and Caitlin what you are...."

"Yes."

"When did you tell them?"

"Caitlin knew the day she saved me in River Town and Maggie did too."

"Both of them knew all along?! And no one told me!" Gerald threw his hands up in the air in frustration. He thought he had a better relationship with his daughters than this.

"Because they knew you would react like this. They didn't want to upset you."

"They didn't want to upset me?! Why didn't you just kill us?"

"I'm not a killer," Rafe said.

"And what are your intentions with Caitlin? Does she know you are leaving?"

"I think you should talk to Caitlin once she gets here."

"Where is she?"

"She's safe."

"That's not an answer."

"You asked a question that's for her to answer and not for me."

"I'll ask her when she gets back then,"

"Don't be mad at her," Rafe said gently. "She does what she thinks is right."

"That doesn't make it right," Gerald said. "You've betrayed us."

"How did I do that? By being who I am?"

"By lying to me."

"I am sorry for keeping secrets. Please try and see if from my side. I'm not a killer and I mean you and your family no harm. I've only ever been good to you."

"And I've only ever been good to you," Gerald said.

"I know that," Rafe said. "I don't see why our relationship should change. I am still the same man who you've been living with for weeks."

"Rafe, I know you care. I can see it in your eyes. I can see it by the way you treat my daughters. I know you love them both."

"I do," Rafe said while he looked into Gerald's eyes.

"But whatever it is you want, we can't give it to you. Your kind and my kind just can't live together in harmony."

"So you're going to tell the king about me then?"

Gerald had started to calm down. "No, I would never hurt Caitlin and Maggie by having you killed."

"That's nice to hear."

"And I know you wouldn't hurt them intentionally, but if you stay here, we will all be caught and killed."

"I will leave," Rafe said. "Please forgive me for hiding my true identity from you."

"I'm sorry but I can't," Gerald said. "I can't ever forgive you or look at you the same way."

Daisy was crying now and she couldn't speak. Rafe got up as he did not want to upset them even more. He knew it was time for him to leave and never come back. He saw them as his family, and he had thought that they'd felt the same.

"Thank you for everything you've done for me, Daisy," he said.

She sniffed and nodded. She didn't hug him the way she used to, and she couldn't look into his eyes either.

Rafe left with his heart feeling colder than ever.

CHAPTER 22

LILLIAN STOOD STILL for a moment and stared into the darkness. She didn't have to think about what she would do. She climbed down fearlessly into the tunnel where it was very cold.

There were torches on the walls. She could barely make them out in the dark, but they were there. She lit one easily and didn't bother closing the trapdoor behind her. Then she started walking.

She didn't think Dylan would come back straight away. He would go back to Liam, and once they realized she was taking too long to arrive, they would search for her.

Why didn't that boy tell her about this place?

The tunnel was dirty and the ground was uneven. The torches were spaced every twenty feet or so against the stone walls. There were no windows, and the tunnels housed rats and mice that skittered away from her torchlight. Other than the vermin, it looked abandoned. In some places, the ceiling didn't look very sturdy. She wondered if the tunnels ever caved in. She didn't mind if they did—as long as they didn't cave in on top of her.

She was good at escaping and prided herself on being a survivor. If the tunnels decided to rain down on her, she would find her way out. She wasn't scared and if she was, then she would run toward what she feared.

She walked for a long time before considering turning back. She was just about to turn around when she saw stairs. They led up to the ceiling. She aimed her torchlight at the top of the stairs and saw a handle in the ceiling. Was it a trapdoor?

She climbed the stairs, took hold of the handle, and pushed up. The trapdoor moved easily. She pushed it aside and heard dogs barking. Then she climbed out of the tunnel and found herself inside a luxurious room.

The room was bright because it had candles on every counter and corner. She dropped the torch into the darkness of the tunnel and looked up. A woman with long blond hair was staring at her.

"Where on earth did you come from?" the woman asked in astonishment.

Three dogs were barking from a large canopy bed. They were noisy and annoying little things, too small to be guard dogs, and Lillian instantly disliked them.

The woman wore a pink silky nightgown that made Lillian realize she had a lot of money. The woman looked clean and pretty. Her long golden hair shimmered in the candlelight.

"I don't mean to intrude," Lillian said. "I wasn't even sure where I was going."

"You're a huntress..." Evelyn realized.

"Yes," Lillian said. She enjoyed seeing the woman scared, as it made Lillian Archer feel all-powerful. She was a brave and strong huntress. Her status made her worthy of fear and respect.

"How did you find the tunnel?" Evelyn asked.

"I don't think I said anything about a tunnel," Lillian said.

The woman was scared. She was panicking. She spoke too fast and made a stupid mistake by mentioning the tunnels.

"It's obvious isn't it?" she tried to cover up her error.

"Not really," Lillian said. "How do you know about it? What's happening down there?"

"I don't know," Evelyn said. She shifted her weight to the side of the bed as if she was about to jump off and run.

Lillian looked into her eyes with a smile. "I don't want to hurt you."

"My husband is a powerful man," Evelyn threatened. "Harming me will be the last thing you ever do."

"I can tell you're a rich little brat," Lillian laughed.

"Just look at those silk sheets. So tell me, who are you?"

"I would like you to leave my room." Evelyn said. "Now."

"I don't really feel like it."

"Then I will have to call the guards."

"I don't think you will do that with this tunnel open," Lillian said confidently.

"I know nothing about the tunnels. I didn't even know about them until you popped out from there."

Lillian looked at her and wondered if she was telling the truth. Maybe it was just a coincidence that the tunnel led here. Then Lillian looked to her left, where a door opened to a bathing chamber. On the floor lay a dirty gown soiled with the same dirt found in the tunnels. "And how do you explain that?" Lillian asked.

"Please leave," Evelyn asked.

"Who are you?"

"Get out," Evelyn said again. She was on her feet.

Lillian had to admit the woman was brave. Not many people would stand their ground like that. "Tell me who you are."

There was a knock at the door. It was a servant girl. "Lady Evelyn, may I come in?"

"Not now. Please come back later," Evelyn said, and the servant girl left.

"Evelyn... Lady Evelyn Patterson," Lillian realized. "There was a door to this tunnel in your school. It wasn't closed properly, so I decided to go exploring. It led me here. To you."

Then Evelyn shot a Magic ball at Lillian. It happened so fast Lillian didn't have time to process what had happened. She fell backward, back into the tunnel. She landed with a thump on the ground and on her back. She opened her eyes but the world was spinning. She had never been hit by a Magic ball before. She felt all her senses to numb and her vision go blurry.

Lillian stumbled around, unable to think straight. She fell again and went still.

Lady Evelyn was panicking. She didn't know what to do. That woman now knew she was a witch and would kill her and then burn the school down. Evelyn couldn't let that happen.

She searched through her closet. She didn't have any ropes, but she needed something to bind Lillian with so that she wouldn't have to kill her. She grabbed belts and scarves and dropped them down into the tunnel.

The torch was burning on the floor. It illuminated the tunnel and Lillian's figure. Evelyn closed the trap-door and climbed down the stairs.

"What did you do to me?" Lillian mumbled slowly. She was standing up again and she took a few shaky steps.

Evelyn picked up a belt.

"No," Lillian said. "Get away from me."

Evelyn knew the effects of the Magic ball wouldn't last long. She had to act now if she wanted to tie Lillian up.

Lillian swung a very weak punch into the air. She missed wide. Evelyn grabbed her wrist and Lillian resisted by pulling against her. She was stronger than the witch and she managed to pull free but lost her balance and fell.

Evelyn jumped on top of her and tried to pin her down with her weight. She used a silk belt to bind Lillian's wrists together. Then she did the same with her legs. She wasn't very good at tying knots and she prayed Lillian wouldn't break free.

Evelyn removed all of Lillian's weapons. She decided to leave them right there in the tunnel where no one would ever find them. She hoped no one came looking for Lillian. *What should I do with you?* she wondered.

This huntress had surely killed many of her kind. She would have killed her too had she gotten the chance. She didn't deserve to live, but was Evelyn strong enough to kill her? Evelyn wasn't a murderer. She had never taken a life before. She didn't want to do it now either, but she couldn't risk letting this woman kill her and others like her.

She wondered if she could just leave the huntress here to slowly die. Then she realized that if other hunters came searching for their friend and found this tunnel which was directly under her room, they would suspect her and kill her.

So Evelyn decided to dispose of the huntress's body −somewhere far from this tunnel. She would throw the huntress off the side of the mountain. So if someone found the body, then it would look like an accident.

Evelyn dragged the body onto a sheet. Then she grabbed the edges of the sheet and pulled. The huntress was heavy but she could drag her around like this.

She would kill the dangerous woman before she herself was killed.

CHAPTER 23

"MAYBE YOU SHOULD think about my offer," Lady Katherine suggested. "You're welcome to stay longer. As long as Rafe stays away from the king and the guards who saw him, I can keep him safe. And you can be with your family."

"It's a tempting offer," Caitlin confessed. "But I have to go. I don't want to be used as a weapon and I don't want to fight." Although Caitlin said these words confidently, she wasn't sure if she truly felt that way. She did enjoy fighting. She was good at it.

"You can't avoid the fight. Life is filled with battles—" Katherine told her.

"And I'm choosing mine carefully," Caitlin told *her*.

"What battles do you have in mind if you're not going to fight by my side then?" Katherine asked.

"The greatest battle I'll ever fight is a mental battle

within myself." Caitlin had already fought with herself over choices and actions, and her past. She lacked inner peace and doubted she would ever achieve it.

"Don't we all," Katherine mumbled.

They were silent for a moment. Caitlin was the first to speak. "You've been watching me as a cat."

"Yes," Katherine said. "I knew what you were the moment you set foot in the throne room. When your dad mentioned River Town, I just knew you all were important. And then you got sick because of that bite. I thought it would kill you, but you proved to be stronger than I imagined."

"And so you kept an eye on me?"

"I knew Campbell was after you and I knew about his assassin. I didn't want to see you, or your family, die."

"Thank you," Caitlin said. "I won't forget that you saved my life."

"Good," Katherine said. "Where will you go?"

"I don't know yet. But it will be far away."

"And you don't intend to return?"

"That's the idea."

Caitlin took one last look at the room. She hoped that Lady Katherine would use it for good. She didn't agree with the woman, but she was too selfish to fight for what she thought was right. The kids who were kidnapped and brainwashed weren't hers. She didn't care about saving them. She wasn't a hero.

If it was her family, it would be a different situation. But then again, they had already been brainwashed and there was nothing she could do about that. It was better that they had new memories and believed that they truly were a family. This way, they would enjoy a long and happy life together.

"Lady Katherine?"

"Yes?"

"I was wondering, can the Obliterator be used to restore memories?"

"I thought you didn't want to remember your past."

"I don't. I'm just curious."

"It can't, unfortunately."

Caitlin didn't know if she should feel disappointed. If Daisy and Gerald remembered their past, the whole family would fall apart. And what would happen to Maggie? She would become an orphan.

"You told me to leave the castle when I was in danger..." Caitlin said.

"I thought the Obliterator had done its job on you. I thought you couldn't even remember how to defend yourself. I thought you would die if you stayed here."

It was strange to think how she refused to leave her family then, and now leaving was all she wanted to do. She felt grounded with Rafe and free at the same time. She would miss her family, but he was worth the loss. She would give up anything and anyone for him.

Dylan reached the inn the same time his dad did. They both stopped in front of the inn and greeted each other.

"Where's Lillian?" Liam asked as he seated himself on one of the two chairs just outside the inn

"She's still looking around the school. She should be home soon. There's nothing there." Dylan took the other seat, looking quite comfortable with his weapons still slung across his shoulder and strapped to his waist. "Something is on your mind," he noticed. "Did the king say something?"

"He said you completed the task he gave you to do brilliantly," Liam said. His voice was tense and he stopped short of congratulating his son.

Dylan frowned. "That's good to hear...."

"He is very pleased with your work. But why didn't you go to him personally when you finished the task?"

"I got busy."

"That's a weak excuse," Liam said in his firm fatherly voice. "And it's unacceptable. It's an honor for the king to ask you personally for your services. If this ever happens again, I expect you to go thank him and tell him in person that you did what he wanted you to do."

"Yes, Father." Dylan wasn't used to getting scolded. He felt like he was fifteen years old and his father had to keep him in check. He shifted in his seat, feeling not quite as comfortable now as he had earlier.

"What is it he asked you to do anyway?"

"He asked me not to tell," Dylan said truthfully.

"Since when do we keep secrets?"

"Since the king asked me to."

Liam stared at his son and did not try to hide his surprise. Dylan thought about why the king had asked him to tell no one. Of course, he didn't want people finding out. But he'd specifically asked Dylan not to tell his own father. Maybe he thought Liam wouldn't approve of the task. But what would that matter? He couldn't go against the king.

Maybe he was testing Dylan's loyalty. Or maybe he thought Dylan was easier to control than his father.

Dylan didn't want to go back into those tunnels. After Divan's death, there was nothing there for him. He didn't want to go back and think about the children being kept there. He didn't want to have nightmares about the patronizers either.

"Did the king ask you to keep the wolf a secret too?" Liam asked coldly.

Dylan paused. "He did not."

"So why didn't you tell me?"

"Because I don't tell you everything that happens every second of every day that you aren't here."

"I don't expect that. I only expect to hear the important stuff." Liam met his son's eyes so that Dylan would know how serious he was.

"I'm sorry. I didn't mean to be disrespectful," Dylan said. "I'll tell you next time."

"Alright then." Liam was still annoyed and he didn't sound convinced. He got up, almost knocking his chair over, and went inside.

Dylan was alone with his thoughts. So much had happened in such a short time. He thought about the monster that Divan was. Surely, he hadn't always been like that.

He wondered if Caitlin could ever be the same. She seemed to be different from him. She wasn't a monster; she was a lady.

Then Dylan thought about the little girl, the young Caitlin who he had seen on that gruesome day on the battlefield among all the bloody corpses–the little girl who her uncle wanted dead. He wondered what would have happened if he had just been brave enough to kill Caitlin then and there. He would have spared her all the pain and suffering she'd experienced at the hands of the king's alchemists and healers. Furthermore, he wouldn't have had to wonder whether she should die. He also wouldn't have to figure out how he could save her.

Caitlin was different from other women. She was different from everyone. She was strong and smart, and there was some good in her. Dylan sensed it.

He thought about how he had another chance to kill her in the tunnels. She was not scared at all. She didn't fight back, but she didn't welcome death either.

Maybe he should kill her.... She's a lot like the monsters he had been killing his whole life. At the same time, the idea of slicing her neck with a blade made him sick.

He was different around her than when he was

around most women. Although she was beautiful, he didn't flirt with her the way he did with most girls. He also felt much more comfortable with her than he did with most people. She made him feel like she accepted him completely. She didn't want or need him to change and she held no expectations and made no demands of him.

He wondered if she was angry at him for holding the dagger at her throat. She didn't look angry. She knew he wasn't going to hurt her.

He wondered for a long time why he liked being around her. Then he realized that it was because she didn't make him feel excluded like other people did. With her he wasn't just a scary hunter, he was a possible friend.

Dylan hadn't realized how much time had passed when he saw his father come back out the door. Liam was carrying his weapons. "Where are we going?" Dylan asked, startled.

"To find Lillian," Liam replied.

CHAPTER 24

DYLAN'S THOUGHTS WENT straight to the tunnel. Was it possible that she had found it? What would he do if she had?

"She's probably just walking around somewhere," Dylan said. "She'll come home."

"She was supposed to be home shortly after you," Liam pointed out. "We have to look for her. She could be in trouble."

"She might come home and find no one here and then decide to go out again," Dylan said.

"Do you want to stay here and wait then?" Liam asked.

"Nah." Dylan got to his feet. There was no way that he would stay home. "Would you like to start at the school?"

"That's where she was last seen, wasn't it?" It wasn't a question. Liam was still irritated with his son.

Dylan acted like he didn't notice the irritation. He wasn't in the mood for an argument. "Yeah," he mumbled. He got up and together they left the house.

Things were tense between them. It was weird. Things were never like this with his dad. He didn't like it and he felt a pang of guilt as they walked.

It was a dark night because there wasn't a moon. The house lights illuminating the streets that they walked on were scant and meager. There weren't many people outside.

Then Dylan saw him.

Rafe was walking down the street. He was coming from the direction of the Wilde's house. Dylan almost stopped and stared. He had watched the king's guards drag the shifter to the throne room where the king would have sentenced him to die. Dylan thought about it. He hadn't heard anything about an execution taking place and he hadn't seen a crowd gather at the execution block.

If Rafe had managed to escape, the king would have had the guards on the lookout and people would be sleeping behind locked doors and shuttered windows. The streets would have been pitch-black. Dylan thought the king might not know that he was free.

Did Caitlin know? She most likely did. Maybe she was the one who got him out. She was certainly capable enough.

Since the shifter was lucky to get out, why was he still in the castle? He didn't look like an idiot to Dylan, so why hadn't he fled the moment he was able to? Staying here was dangerous and would get him killed.

Dylan knew he should kill him. They were natural enemies. Were the tables turned, Rafe would have killed him without thinking twice about it if he'd had a chance. Yet he had never hurt Caitlin nor would he ever do so. Was it because Caitlin wasn't a normal non-Magic? Or was it because Rafe was in love with her?

Dylan had never heard of a shifter falling in love with a non-Magic. He didn't think it was possible. But from the way Caitlin acted when Rafe was hurt, Dylan could tell that she loved him too. Love was a dangerous game. He hoped she knew that.

Rafe walked with his head down, eyes on the ground, and his arms limp at his side. He didn't look up. He looked like a kid who had dropped his ice cream.

Dylan noticed something else that was weird. He was clean and showed no signs of injury. Dylan had shot an arrow through his shoulder. How could he not be hurt when Dylan had thought he would have bled to death?

Liam was walking a few steps ahead of Dylan. Unlike his son, he was oblivious to the threat walking straight toward them.

Dylan wondered if it was possible that his aunt Lillian had encountered Rafe? If they'd run into each other, she wouldn't have known that Rafe was a dangerous shifter and so she would not have attacked him. But Rafe would have recognized her as a huntress and would have avoided her. Or would he have hurt her to get revenge on Dylan?

Dylan put his hand on his sword. He could do it. He could kill Rafe with one blow. The man was walking straight toward his death. Then he remembered asking Ears, "*Why ask me to go after the girl?*"

"*Because,*" Ears had said, "*I sense something good in you. And I think that good part might be what saves her.*" She had sensed something good in him. Of course, a witch's opinion meant nothing to him.

But she was right about him saving people. It's what he did. It's what he lived for. He wanted to save Caitlin Wilde, although he wasn't sure how. He was sure that killing the man she loved wasn't the way to do it.

Rafe was very close to Liam when he looked up. He jumped back in fright and looked paler than Dylan had ever seen.

"Whoa, easy there," Liam said and walked by.

Dylan was glad Rafe hadn't shifted. If he had, they would have had to fight and Rafe wouldn't have stood a chance against him and his father. They would have easily killed him.

Dylan's blue eyes locked with Rafe's gray ones. Dylan didn't turn it into a power struggle. He held himself back and walked past Rafe, breaking the eye contact. All the while he kept his hand on his sword.

He left Rafe right there in the dark to stare after him. The shifter would never understand why Dylan chose not to kill him. The shifter didn't understand that it wasn't about him at all.

Dylan let go of his sword after a while. Then he fell in step beside his dad. They reached the school and climbed over the fence easily.

The school door was unlocked like Dylan had left it. The halls were dark, quiet, and empty.

"Lillian!" Liam called but there was no answer. "Where could she be?"

"I don't know. Don't worry, she can look after herself."

"I know that," Liam said. "But I'm always worried about the two of you."

"You shouldn't be," Dylan said.

"It's how being a dad works. You'll understand one day."

Dylan snorted.

"Is something funny?" Liam asked.

"I'm never having kids."

"Many people your age feel that way and change their minds once they get older," Liam told him. "I also felt that way."

"And what changed?"

"I met the woman of my dreams and I wanted nothing more than to have children with her."

Dylan didn't know what to say. His father had never mentioned his mother. He wanted to have children with her. Not just one child. Dylan wondered if he would have had a little brother if she was still alive. He would have liked that.

"I don't want to bring kids into this life and worry myself sick about them," Dylan confessed.

Liam didn't say anything to that. They walked through the school for a long time in silence before he asked: "Do you wish you had a different lifestyle?"

"Sometimes," Dylan confessed.

They left the conversation there and Dylan headed to the headmistress's office. He looked behind the desk and found the entrance to the tunnel wide open. He had no doubt: Lillian had gone inside to explore.

"Great work, Dylan," Liam said when he saw the hole.

Dylan knew there was no hiding it and he couldn't talk his father out of going down there. Liam went in first. Dylan sighed before he did the same. He lit a torch. He hoped that they didn't run into any patronizers or monsters down there.

Lillian's senses were returning. Slowly, her blurred vision cleared and she noticed the light flickering. She turned her head to see what Lady Evelyn was doing with the torch. She was having a hard time holding it and dragging the sheet. Lillian wondered if she would accidently set the sheet on fire.

She dragged her attention away from the panting woman and focused on herself. Her hands were tied with a belt. She wasn't strong enough to break free. Her legs were bound with scarves so she couldn't run away. But it didn't look like the woman knew how to tie a proper knot.

Lillian's mouth was dry and her back hurt from the fall. Being dragged across the tunnel floor was very uncomfortable too. Where was she being taken?

Lillian wasn't sure how long they had been moving, but she didn't think it was very long. Slowly the numbness in her body went away and she could move normally again. Her sense of smell and hearing came back as well.

"And I thought you would have gagged me," Lillian said.

Evelyn jumped and let go of the sheet and torch at the same time. She was nervous. She wasn't used to doing these kinds of things.

"Careful," Lillian said. "You wouldn't want to catch fire, would you?"

"Shut up," Evelyn said.

She reached down and picked up the corners of the sheet and the stem of the torch. Then she started pulling.

"You don't strike me as someone who belongs in filthy tunnels," Lillian told her.

"But you do," Evelyn spat back. Sweat broke out on her skin and her arms were shaking.

"That's not very nice," Lillian said.

"I'm not trying to be nice!" Evelyn was tired and frustrated and scared.

Lillian never expected anyone to come and save her. She could handle any situation alone. She was *never* a damsel in distress. She was the hero of her own story. She looked around. How was she going to save herself? She wiggled her legs and realized that they weren't bound too tightly. Maybe she could wiggle free. Evelyn wouldn't even notice.

"Would you please tell me where you are taking me?" Lillian asked.

"I don't want to talk right now," Evelyn said as she pulled.

"That's a shame. I'm a very talkative person." Lillian worked her feet to try to loosen the binding around her ankles. Evelyn didn't see what she was doing, nor could she feel Lillian's struggles.

"Aren't you scared that I'll scream and help comes?" Lillian asked.

"No one can hear you down here," Evelyn told her.

Lillian believed her. But even if someone could hear, she wouldn't scream. Screaming would destroy her pride.

"Isn't there a spell to make me float? Then you don't have to drag me around like a horse pulling a wheelless cart."

Evelyn remained silent except for her ragged breathing. She regretted not gagging the huntress. She considered gagging her now but decided that the huntress would most likely bite her if she tried to. Would she ever shut up?

"Or aren't you a good enough witch to do such a spell?"

"Shut up," Evelyn said.

Lillian heard the irritation in her voice and continued taunting her. "I've not killed many witches, to be honest with you. But I look forward to adding one more to my list."

"I'll see to it that you never harm anyone again," Evelyn spat back.

"How nice of you," Lillian replied with sarcasm.

The knots in the binding around her feet weren't tight at all anymore. Soon she would be able to pull free. But she didn't have any weapons and she didn't want to get hit with another one of those balls again. She brought the belt binding her wrists to her mouth and bit into it. She tried to pull it loose. It wasn't working. "I didn't expect to find a witch, or any Magical being in the castle," Lillian kept talking.

"Well, surprise," Evelyn said.

"This is the last place I actually expected to find a witch," Lillian said. "But it got me thinking... If you, a duchess, are a witch right here under the king's nose, then how many others are there? And where do I start looking for them?"

Evelyn didn't look at her.

Lillian got one foot free and continued her chatter. "So, I figured why not start at the school? That's where

I found an entrance to the tunnels after all."

Evelyn was tense and Lillian knew she was onto something. Both her feet were now free.

They moved into a different tunnel. Lillian knew it was different because the lighting was better than before. Sunshine came in from a scatter of holes in the walls. Lillian realized that they were inside a wall now and not underground anymore.

"You're going to regret doing this to me," she told Evelyn. "My family and I are going to burn your school down and hang you for this."

"Stop it," Evelyn said.

"Or I could just kill you now."

Lillian was very fast. She swung her legs up and used the momentum to lift her body off the sheet. She landed gracefully on her feet. Evelyn didn't even have time to process what had happened. Lillian spun around and kicked her. The huntress's kick was powerful, sending the witch flying backward and landing with a thud against the wall.

"No!" Evelyn's scream echoed through the tunnels.

"Did you hear that?" Caitlin looked to Katherine.

"It sounded like someone screaming in the tunnels," Katherine said.

"I'm going to check it out," Caitlin said.

"It's probably nothing," Katherine said, although she did look curious.

"Probably not. Still..." Caitlin went in the direction of the scream while Katherine remained behind.

The scream had been far away, but it had been a scream nonetheless. Not many people knew about the tunnels.... Caitlin's thoughts went to Evelyn, because she knew the tunnels so well that she had drawn Caitlin a map in the sand.

Evelyn made another Magic ball and threw it, but this time Lillian was prepared. She dodged and it fizzled into a wall.

"Don't look so happy," Evelyn told her. "I can easily beat you in a fair fight."

"Maybe," Lillian said. "But it's not just me you'll be fighting."

They heard footsteps running toward them. Lillian knew that they would come looking for her. They had heard her screams and ran straight toward her.

"Lady Evelyn, I think it's time I introduce you to my family."

CHAPTER 25

EVELYN'S FACE WAS filled with horror. She thought about running but she knew the huntress was much faster. This was a fight she couldn't win.

The footsteps were getting closer. She would most certainly not win a fight if more hunters showed up. She was scared because she had never been in a physical fight before.

"Lillian!" Liam called.

"This way!" Lillian called back.

Evelyn saw the huntress's smile spread across her cheeks and reach her eyes. It made Evelyn want to punch her in the face. But she wasn't even sure how to throw a punch; she'd never had to do it before. She was pretty sure that she would break her nails if she tried.

She had to stand and fight. Her school and the lives of all those children depended on her. She told herself that her death wouldn't be all that bad because then their secret would die with her. Without her confession, the hunters had no way of proving that the kids in her school had Magic.

But if she died who would teach them? Who would help them? Who would protect them? How could she see herself as their protector if she didn't make a stand here? She told herself to focus and then looked down at the torch that was still in her hands.

Now she was the one smiling.

The flame was biting at the air. She held a hand over it. Although her hand was very close to the flame she didn't burn. She started mumbling.

"What are you doing?" Lillian asked. For once she was the one who said, "Stop that." She wanted to attack but then something in the fire caught her eyes. There, in the flames! Were those two eyes staring at her?

Lillian gaped as the flames climbed out of the torch. Its fiery claws came first, then its head, followed by its body. Its body looked like it was made of coal. It was burning hot. Although it didn't have teeth, it looked like a wingless dragon. "A big lizard?" Lillian said aloud, trying to sound fearless.

The coal lizard dropped to the ground and the fire left the torch. Evelyn held it as a weapon anyway and Lillian wondered fleetingly if the witch would swing it at her. She was more worried about the lizard than the witch. The lizard illuminated the tunnel as if it was a tiny sun. It looked at Lillian with fiery eyes before it charged her like a lion. She found herself walking backward. Her hands were still bound and she had no weapons—a thought that made her smile. "Is this the part where I beg for my life?" Lillian mocked.

"It's the part where you die," Evelyn said.

"Then you better start running because I might just drag you with me," Lillian sneered. She hadn't expected the witch to run so the next move came as a shock. Evelyn took off and left her with the lizard. Lillian reminded herself to prioritize and do one thing at a time. She had to focus on the lizard now and then she would catch the witch later.

The lizard sneezed and flames shot from its nose. Lillian wondered if it had a conscience. As it moved toward her, she realized it was only the size of a spaniel dog.

The lizard lashed out with one of its claws. Little pieces of coal flew around when it moved. Lillian bent down and picked up a rock. It was difficult to throw with her hands tied. She managed to throw it and hit the lizard square on the nose.

The lizard charged her. She held her ground until the very last minute and then she hurdled over it.

Confused, the lizard spun around and charged at her again. She jumped again but mistimed her leap. She landed with her legs straddling over its tail. The lizard swung its fiery tail, and she lifted her left leg. It missed and hit the wall. Lillian retreated a few steps to avoid getting burned.

"What is that!?" Lillian heard Dylan cry.

"It's an earthworm with legs and a little bit of a spark," she responded. "I'm glad you found me."

The lizard jumped toward them. Dylan moved to the left side of the wall and Lillian to the right. The lizard missed them and then charged Liam, who didn't dodge. He pulled out his sword and slashed at the creature. The lizard hissed in return. It opened its mouth and inhaled and then exhaled fire, like a little a dragon.

"Whoa!" Liam cried. His shirt caught fire and he smothered it with his hand. "You're a nasty one, aren't you?"

"My hands, Dylan!" Lillian cried. "Untie them!"

Dylan cut them free with his sword and Lillian shook her wrists to get the blood flowing. It felt good to be free. Dylan saw that she didn't have any weapons so he gave her his sword. Then he retreated a few steps and nocked an arrow into his bow.

"I wonder if you can feel pain...." Lillian mumbled to the lizard.

The lizard was facing Liam who was slashing at it with his sword. He kept missing and dodging fire. Lillian crept up behind it and lifted her sword above her head. Standing this close to the creature made her feel like she was being roasted alive. She was already sweating. She dropped the sword, like an executioner swinging an ax, onto the lizard's tail. She expected the tail to fall. Instead the sword melted.

The lizard noticed her now. It lashed out with its tail. Lillian moved back, but not fast enough. The tail tip grazed her knee and her skin sizzled. She cried out in pain and then cursed.

"If our weapons are no use, we can't win!" Liam pointed out.

"Move aside, Lillian!" Dylan cried.

She ignored the pain in her knee and moved to the side to give Dylan a clear shot. He drew back his bow, aimed, and released the arrow. It flew and sank into the lizard's coal-like back where it burned up.

"That's unfortunate," Lillian said.

Dylan watched the lizard turn toward him and charge. He knew his weapons were useless but maybe he could outrun it until they figured out how to kill it.

He turned and started to run, but his eyes had been looking into the fire for too long. He was running blind in the dark tunnel. He knew he'd made a critical mistake. He felt a rock under his left foot and tripped. He tried to stop himself from falling, stumbling a few steps in the dark before finally falling onto his hands.

"Dylan!" Lillian cried. She ignored the burn on her knee and crouched to pick up rocks, hurling them at the lizard. She hoped this would get its attention. Instead, it only made the lizard angry.

The lizard ran toward Dylan with its mouth open, hissing and spitting flames. Dylan hoped that he wouldn't get incinerated. He crawled back frantically and managed to get to his feet. "I don't think throwing rocks is helping!" he told his family.

"Do you have any other suggestions?" Liam yelled back.

Dylan looked at its burning body. Water was fire's natural enemy. Maybe water could kill it. But there was no water in the tunnel.

The lizard charged at Dylan again. He wished he could kick it. "Where in the castle do you think we are?" Dylan called out.

"What?" Liam asked.

"I want to know where we are! If we can find water, I think we can kill it."

"Very smart," Lillian said. "But I have no idea where we are."

Dylan looked at the walls where the light was shining through. He visualized the map the king had drawn for him showing all the secret entrances.

"I think we are close to the pool," he said.

"So how do we get out of here?" Liam asked.

"Not so fast. We have to kill it before we leave this place. We can't set it loose on the people!" Lillian said.

Dylan pressed himself against the wall. He could see his bow and arrow. The wall behind him was weak and had a lot of holes. He could easily break through. It was not an ideal plan, but they were desperate.

The lizard ran toward him. As it charged, Dylan readied himself. He moved aside and it ran head-first into the wall. Its head broke through the stones.

"Let's not break the wall down!" Lillian said.

Caitlin listened closely to the noises: it sounded like fighting. It was far away, deep in the tunnels. She didn't think she wanted to be part of a fight, but curiosity urged her forward.

The lizard pulled its head back into the tunnel. The wall didn't collapse. It shook its head from side to side and then opened its mouth so it could hiss at them in anger.

"Evelyn ran that way." Lillian pointed.

"So?" Liam asked.

"So," Lillian repeated, a bit annoyed. "She obviously knows the tunnels. There should be an exit over there."

"I think you are right," Dylan said. "I'm going to let

it chase me." He didn't wait for a response. He bent down and in one smooth motion he scooped up his bow and arrows.

The lizard charged as Dylan sprinted in the direction Lillian had indicated. He still couldn't see well in the dark and hoped he wouldn't trip again. The lizard was very fast. It was actually on his heels and Dylan could feel its heat on his back.

Lillian and Liam followed closely behind it, keeping their distance so that it wouldn't turn around.

Dylan stumbled again in the dark. He heard the lizard hissing behind him and silently cursed. *Keep this up and I'll be burned to a crisp. What an unpleasant way to die.* He told himself to remain calm and focused on his breathing. He had good endurance and he was fast. He was also very agile and had run away from a lot of creatures in his life. *If I'm really careful and stay really focused, there's no way I'll fall.*

And then he tripped.

CHAPTER 26

THERE WAS NOTHING Dylan could do to stop his fall. So he did the only thing he could: he tried not to fall right in front of the lizard. He shifted his weight to the side and ended up falling against the wall.

The moment his body weight slammed against the wall, Dylan felt its mass give way and felt his body crashing through. Half his body rested outside the tunnel while the other half remained inside the tunnel. He had fallen through a secret door.

He looked up and immediately knew where he was. Then he felt a burning pain in his leg. Luckily it was only the lizard's claw that had grazed him. If its mouth had clamped down, he'd have lost his leg below the knee.

He scrambled forward, carefully avoiding the burning lizard, and was back on his feet. He saw Lady Evelyn who had exited the tunnel not long before him. Her eyes widened in shock as she realized the hunters were still alive.

But Dylan didn't have time for her right now. Lillian could handle the witch. He started running again and the angry lizard followed. It hissed and stopped once to blow out a plume of fire.

Evelyn watched in horror as the monster that she had created escaped free from the tunnels. She had never intended for that to happen. She'd only wanted it to get rid of the hunters.

Dylan was relieved to know where he was in the castle. He would lead the lizard straight to the pool. Adrenaline pumped through him and helped him to ignore the pain in his leg. He ran without limping and without looking back.

"Get out of the way!" he yelled to some peasants. They looked confused until they saw the lizard. Then they retreated into their homes.

Dylan didn't know what had happened to Liam and Lillian. He didn't look back to find out either. They would be fine.

The lizard ran with its tail dragging. He swished it every now and then. Most of the time he only hit air, but when it swished again, it hit a pile of garbage, throwing stinking refuse everywhere.

Dylan stayed on the stone path. But the lizard was getting awfully close. He decided to make an unexpected sharp turn left, onto a patch of grass.

The lizard ran forward and then stopped. It took a moment to realize what had happened. Then it veered left too. The grass was green and lush from all the water it received. It didn't burn easily but it caught fire nonetheless.

Dylan realized that he had made an error in taking this path. He needed to get back to the stone path, the one that led to the pool....

Then Dylan saw a middle-aged man. He was without a doubt the gardener. He was watering a nearby flower bed with a watering ladle in his right hand. His left hand was dragging the handle of a wheeled barrel filled with water. The man looked up at Dylan and the coal lizard with a confused frown. He had never seen a creature like that in his garden before. Green lizards, yes, but never a fiery lizard.

"Water! Douse it with water!" Dylan cried.

The man's jaw dropped open as he stood there staring.

"Throw water on the lizard! NOW!" he cried.

But the man still didn't listen to him. Dylan wondered if he was deaf or frozen with fear.

Meanwhile, the lizard got tired from chasing Dylan who was now running around the flower bed. It stopped and glared at Dylan before it charged through the flowers, burning some, wilting others, and leaving little black clawed footprints wherever it went.

Dylan cursed in frustration at the still immobile gardener and charged toward him and the barrel of water. He grabbed the barrel's handle and swung it so that the barrel stood in direct line with the lizard's flight path.

Wait for it, wait for it, wait... NOW! Dylan upended the barrel full of water onto the running lizard.

The lizard screamed. People opened their doors to see what all the commotion was. Smoke erupted from the lizard's body as it tried to run out of the garden and as far from Dylan and the water barrel as possible, while swinging its head from side to side. Smoldering pieces of coal flaked off its body with each shake of its head. By the time the lizard made it to the edge of the garden, its body had so fallen apart that nothing was left but a trail of smoking embers and ash.

"That was close!" Dylan said. He looked back at the gardener who was still staring open-mouthed at him. "You have a lovely garden, sir," he said before disappearing back into the tunnel.

Lillian knew that Dylan could handle the lizard. He was a strong, experienced, and smart fighter. Lillian didn't know where he was leading the lizard but she trusted that Dylan knew what he was doing.

The moment she got out of the tunnel, she spotted Evelyn. The witch was still staring in the direction that Dylan and the lizard had gone, so it took Evelyn a moment to notice the approach of the hunters.

Evelyn slowly turned to face Lillian and Liam, raising her arms as if in surrender—but Lillian was smarter than to fall for that ruse. This witch wasn't going to give up without a fight. Lillian had a sword in her hands and Liam had his. The witch and huntress made eye contact.

"Is that her?" Liam asked.

"Yes, it is."

Liam looked at the witch who held her hands up and said, "I accept your surrender."

The words had just left his lips and when a Magic ball was thrown at him. Lillian pushed him out of the way in the nick of time. The Magic ball hit the ground, turned into mist, and disappeared.

"And here I thought you were going to make this easy," Liam said.

Evelyn didn't want to fight in public. She didn't want people to see her doing Magic. She didn't want her powers exposed. She desperately wanted her husband by her side—he would know what to do. He would be able to help her. But her husband was not here and he was not coming to rescue her. She was alone. She had to fight for her own life.

The huntress approached, a lion stalking her prey. She studied the witch in her torn and dirty night-gown, a stark contrast to Lillian's own sleek armored leather. But by now Lillian was ready for any surprises.

The huntress swung her sword and the witch ducked to the side. Then Evelyn ducked to the other side as Liam swung his sword. The witch held her hand out and tried to push him back with a gust of wind.

Lillian swung again and Evelyn used the wind to redirect her sword. But Lillian was still coming forward and crashed her shoulder into Evelyn. Evelyn fell to the ground and knew the fight was over. She cried out as Liam held his sword against her throat and said, "I think we should burn her at the stake."

CHAPTER 27

RAFE WAS WALKING back toward the tunnels where he had left Caitlin behind. Despite the fact that his wolf-shifter constitution sped his physical healing, he felt shaken emotionally and couldn't wait to embrace Caitlin. He felt like he had failed with her family. He would never forget the way Gerald had looked at him or the things he had said.

"You and all Magic folk deserve to die!"

How terrible that Gerald wished his own kind dead and didn't even know it. What the king did to the Wilde family was unforgivable. It was wrong and sick.

Rafe wondered what kind of Magic folk Gerald and Daisy were. He didn't think they were shifters like him. It probably didn't matter....

Rafe's thoughts drifted back to his close brush with Dylan and the older man who could have been his father, and his hands started shaking. Why hadn't they just killed him then and there?

The last thing Rafe expected was to see him again. Rafe was almost at the tunnel entrance when he saw Dylan being chased by—what? A lizard that was on fire? Rafe had never seen a creature like that before. He suspected that it was a form of witchcraft.

He wondered what kind of trouble Dylan had gotten himself into. Rafe watched the hunter turn into the garden in a desperate attempt to escape the red-hot jaws of the lizard.

Rafe's thoughts then jumped to Evelyn, the only witch he knew in the kingdom. She was aware of the tunnels and Dylan had just come from the tunnels. *Was that a coincidence?*

Rafe left Dylan to fight the lizard, headed for the tunnel entrance, and then froze. Evelyn was on the ground and the man who resembled Dylan was holding a sword to her throat. "Hey!" he cried. "What are you doing to that woman? Let her go!"

There were two hunters—a man and a woman—and Dylan would probably return before long. Rafe knew a fight was unavoidable. But could he beat all three of them? He would have turned away to run, but Evelyn lay shaking on the ground. He was also angry and had a lot of pent up frustration which he really needed to release.

"Get out of here," Liam told him. "This is hunter trade."

The woman was staring at him. She tilted her head to the side in recognition, but Rafe had never seen her before.

"You have no trade here," Liam said.

"Actually," Lillian said, "he does."

"What?" Liam asked.

"He is a wolf," Lillian said.

Rafe was caught off guard. He had no idea how she knew that. He had done nothing to betray his secret in front of her.

Liam looked at him, "My least favorite shifter." Liam pulled his sword back and slammed its hilt into Evelyn's head, immediately knocking her out. Then he stood up and pointed his sword at Rafe.

"How did you know I am a wolf?" Rafe asked Lillian.

She smiled secretively, and Rafe was ready to rip the smile off her face. He hated these hunters. He didn't care that Dylan hadn't attacked earlier—he should have taken the chance when he'd had it. Now it was too late.

Rafe remembered the pain in his shoulder from the arrow wound. He remembered how he had done nothing wrong and Dylan still tried to kill him. He thought about all of the innocent shifters that these monsters had killed and the families they had destroyed. *They deserved to die.*

Rafe jumped up into the air toward Liam and shifted in midair. When he touched down, he knocked Liam over and away from Evelyn's limp body.

Then he opened his jaw and went for Lillian. She

was very fast. She dodged to the left and his jaws snapped shut, biting only air. She lifted her sword so that she could bring it down on his neck and behead him. Quickly he threw himself to the side and into her. She stumbled back before she could hurt him. Her sword's tip dropped to the ground and she nearly lost her grip on it.

Liam scrambled to his feet again. He had his sword ready. Adrenalin coursed through his veins the way it always did before he killed a dangerous monster.

Rafe growled. He showed Lillian his white fangs. She didn't look scared at all, to his disappointment. It looked like this was just a game to her. Rafe realized that she must have been playing this game her whole life and that she was used to winning.

She kicked him and her foot collided with his teeth. Her boots were hard and chipped one of his front fangs. He retreated a few steps and licked his lips while Liam ran toward him with his sword outstretched. Rafe dodged the sword and bit down, his teeth closing on Liam's sleeve.

Unfortunately, all he got was a mouthful of fabric instead of flesh. But Rafe hung on, spinning Liam in a circle violently. The fabric tore, sending Liam flying into Lillian, knocking her backward and causing her to drop her sword.

Rafe pounced and Lillian ducked down, his breath warm on her back. She heard the snapping of jaws and was relieved that he missed her. She picked up a rock and flung it at his head. It distracted him long enough for her to retrieve her dropped sword.

"Stupid dog," she sneered.

Liam was on his feet and advancing toward Rafe as Lillian swung at the wolf's head twice and missed both times. The third time she swung, he sank his teeth into her forearm. She cried out in pain and let the sword drop to the ground. Her other arm clawed frantically at his face but her human fingernails did no damage.

Rafe tasted her blood and, for the first time, he rather liked it. Then like a dog, he shook his head. Lillian shook with him and he heard her flesh tear like paper. He could rip her arm off so easily.

Liam watched in helpless panic. He didn't know how to save his sister.

Dylan was on his way back to the tunnel when he heard Lillian screaming. He ran toward her and was horrified by what he saw. Rafe had his jaw clasped around her arm. Her blood was dripping from his mouth.

The witch was lying on the ground. She was not moving and looked dead.

Liam was swinging his sword at Rafe but Rafe kept Lillian in front of him as a shield.

One of the things every hunter knew was that, although shifters looked like stupid animals, they were not. They were intelligent creatures that could think for themselves and shouldn't be underestimated.

Dylan knew jumping in would only make things worse. He didn't want to provoke the wolf. He was so scared that Rafe would rip off his aunt's arm, and he regretted not killing Rafe when he'd had the chance. Didn't his father always say that wolves were the worst? What had he been thinking!?

It was too late to dwell on the past now. Dylan looked around, desperately hoping that an idea would come to him. Rafe was standing very close to the roof of a building. He hadn't seen Dylan yet. Dylan could attack him by surprise....

Dylan quietly made his way to the side of the building and then climbed onto the roof. Once on top he had a good view.

Below, Rafe didn't look up.

Dylan aimed his sword toward the ground—toward Rafe—as he stood at the edge of the building, ready to leap. He planned to land on the wolf and kill him. Dylan jumped down, crying out as he did—and that was his mistake.

Rafe heard him, looked up, and skittered off to the side so fast that he didn't even look where he was going. He smacked into a wall that already had a lot of holes punched in it. The wall gave way. Rafe opened his mouth to cry out, letting go of Lillian, while dust smothered the air as stones rained on his wolf body.

Dylan was on his feet. His sword had dug into the ground. He was very lucky to not have hurt himself. All three hunters waited for the dust to settle in tense silence.

Then they heard coughing. The pain had forced Rafe into his human form. He lay there covered in rocks. He was bleeding and Dylan hoped he was hurt badly. He struggled to rise but the rocks pinned him down. He wasn't going anywhere.

Lillian was bleeding and she was angrier than Dylan had ever seen her. She was shaking as she got to her feet.

"This monster's family ripped your mother to shreds," she told Dylan.

"What are you talking about?" Rafe coughed.

"You want to know how I know that you are a wolf?" Lillian said, turning to the shifter. "Well you look just like your pack with your dark hair, gray eyes, and pale skin."

"But I don't have a pack," Rafe argued.

"Not anymore," she smiled. "Because, all those years ago back in Southpaw, I slaughtered them."

CHAPTER 28

THE WORDS TOOK a moment to sink in. Rafe stared at her in shock. Lillian had her hand clasped around her wounded arm. The bite was bad. Her blood dripped to the ground and Rafe wondered if she would bleed to death. He hoped so.

"Why?" Rafe asked hoarsely. His body hurt but his rage was taking over. After all these years he had finally found the huntress responsible for his family's deaths.

"Because they killed my wife!" Liam cried. "You monsters killed her for no reason!"

"It's a shame you weren't there to see me rip them apart," Lillian told Rafe.

Dylan froze. Not even in his wildest dreams had he imagined meeting a wolf whose pack had killed his mother.

"We are going to make you suffer like my wife Mary suffered," Liam swore.

"You should have been there to see what I did to your pack," Lillian said through clenched teeth. "Your father was the brave one. The fighter. He died first trying to defend everyone else. Your mother screamed the most. And your little sister begged me not to kill her—right before I painted your walls with her blood."

"She was a kid!" Rafe cried.

He lost all control. His rage took over. Everyone thought he was trapped under the pile of rocks. Then he shifted into a wolf and leaped into the air, scattering the rocks in all directions as Lillian cried out. Rafe ran over Liam as if he was a tiny mouse, his sword clattering to the ground as he was knocked over.

Dylan knew there was no time to stop Rafe. He watched helplessly as the wolf locked his jaw around the same arm he had bitten earlier. He watched as Rafe threw his aunt to the ground. He watched in horror as the wolf climbed on top of her, a paw on either side of her face. He watched his aunt tremble as the wolf's saliva dripped onto her.

What could he do? A part of his heart broke as he saw his aunt there, weak and helpless on the ground. He loved her and he didn't want her to die.

Lillian had never begged and never cried in a battle before. Then again, she had never been defeated. Tears sprang to her eyes. Pain shot through her now broken arm. Her body was trembling against her will. "Please," she begged.

Caitlin was walking through the tunnels when she heard the wall collapse. She ran up and froze at the scene before her.

Rafe was lying under a pile of stones, pinned, his body bruised and bleeding.

Her first reaction was to run to him. But she stopped herself to scan for possible danger. She saw Evelyn sitting up, touching her head with one hand, her eyes closed. She saw Liam standing there looking smug, Dylan looking uncertain in the background, and Lillian looking furious, with blood dripping down her arm.

Then Caitlin focused on Rafe. They had hurt him. Again. She was ready to rip them apart.

But then Lillian spoke drawing all their attention; no one noticed Caitlin who was also listening.

Caitlin's heart went out to Rafe. She thought he would break down, but instead he got angrier than she had ever seen him get before. She didn't think it was possible for him to break free. It all happened so fast. Rafe was suddenly on top of Lillian. As a wolf.

Caitlin thought he would rip Lillian's head off. She didn't blame him.

Caitlin watched Dylan. She had never seen him look that helpless, hopeless, and broken. She didn't know what to do.

Dylan noticed her. He pressed his palms together and mouthed the word "HELP."

She didn't owe Dylan anything, but at the same time she felt sorry for him. She emerged from the tunnel. "Rafe!" she cried. "Think about what you are doing!"

Rafe didn't look up at Caitlin but he recognized her voice. He glared at Lillian and then he did something very unexpected. He shifted into human form. He wanted to be able to speak, but he kept his right hand clawed, pressing that claw into Lillian's neck. "If anyone moves, I'll kill her," he growled.

"Please..." Dylan begged but was ignored.

"If you tell them the truth, I will spare you," Rafe said to Lillian.

"How can I trust you?" she whimpered.

His claw pressed deeper into her neck. "You can't."

Lillian was too scared to even swallow.

"I *know* my family didn't kill this Mary-woman. We have never hurt anyone, and we never would have. So tell me, how did she die?"

Lillian didn't want to tell the truth: Dylan and Liam would hate her. Tears rolled down her cheeks.

"Tell me!" Rafe cried.

She closed her eyes in fear. "Okay! She was friends

with your family. The moment she told me about them, I knew what they were. I wanted to show her that all shifters are bad. So the day she went to visit them, I beat her to their house."

"Then what?"

"Your father was out, maybe he was hunting—I don't know. I tied the rest of your family up and put them next to each other. When Mary walked into the house, she saw them and we got into an argument. She didn't understand and she didn't want to listen. Your youngest sister saw us distracted and thought it would be a good chance to flee. She managed to shift but I immediately noticed. I shot and arrow at her, but Mary... Mary... jumped in the way. The arrow went through her heart."

"YOU killed her," Rafe sneered. "Not us."

Lillian was crying. "I'm sorry..." she said to Liam and Dylan, although she could not muster the courage to look at them.

"And then you slaughtered my family," Rafe said. "You killed good, peaceful people."

"I was scared and outraged at the same time. Your father came home and tried to defend them. So I fought back."

"You mutilated them," Rafe told her. "I came home and found them in pieces."

"I was angry—I couldn't stop myself!"

"What did you do with Mary? I smelled her blood, but there was no body."

"I buried her in a nearby ditch," Lillian confessed. "There was no way that I could bring her body home with an arrow through the heart. So I just told everyone she was ripped to shreds by shifters."

Dylan held back tears. Never, not in a million lifetimes, did he see this coming. The truth made his world fall apart. It shattered his trust in the people he loved. His family had taught him that shifters were monsters, that they killed his mother. But it was all a lie. Maybe his family, maybe he, were the real monsters.

Dylan looked at Rafe and waited for the claws to slice through his aunt's neck. It was no less than she deserved. But still, he didn't want to see her dead.

"Are you going to kill me now?" she asked Rafe, her voice low and hollow.

"I want to," Rafe told her. "You have no idea how much I want to." His claws dug a little deeper. She was shaking from her sobs but that did not make him pity her. His face was twisted in anger and, for a moment, Caitlin thought the Rafe she knew was gone. Then he leaned forward so Lillian could feel his breath on her face. "But I am better than you."

Rafe stood up and moved away from her.

CHAPTER 29

CAITLIN RAN TO Rafe and threw her arms around him.
She pressed her head against his chest. She wanted to
comfort him.

Rafe had been alone for so long that he never
learned how to express his own feelings. He gently
pushed her away, and she gave him a puzzled look.

Evelyn got to her feet. "Caitlin, the guards saw us...."

"What?" Caitlin asked.

"Yes, they walked past the whole thing."

"When?" Rafe asked.

"About fifteen minutes ago? Right about when I
woke up. When Rafe was buried under the stones."

"And they didn't stop to see what was going on?"
Dylan said, puzzled.

"Why would they just walk past?" Caitlin echoed his
thought.

"They would only do that if they had strict orders," Liam explained, his voice husky, his mind replaying everything that was said and done. The shifter had shown a compassion he had never believed possible in a creature of Magic. He slowly walked to Lillian and took his shirt off, wrapping it around her bleeding arm. *Compassion and forgiveness?* He shook his head, still deep in thought, deaf to his sister's whimpering and blind to the fact that she couldn't look him in the eyes.

"What orders?" Caitlin wondered.

"Caitlin," Liam said, coming back to the present. "Was your family ever seen with Rafe? Do people know they associated with Magic?"

"I went to the house earlier," Rafe said to Caitlin, but she already knew this. "I didn't think anyone would recognize me."

"Which direction did the guards go?" Rafe asked Evelyn.

She pointed in the direction of Caitlin's house. There was a thin stream of smoke rising up into the air in the distance.

"No..." Caitlin breathed.

Rafe shifted again and took off. He didn't care how many people had seen him. He didn't care if all of the castle's guards attacked him. He just had to reach the Wilde family in time.

He ran as fast as he could. He jumped over objects and around people. He didn't listen to people scream and cry out. He didn't care about any of them. He only cared about the Wilde family. He loved the Wilde family. If anything ever happened to them, he could never forgive himself.

He had to focus and he had to reach them. He could make it there in time. He *will* make it there in time! He won't be too late like he was with his family. He won't find them harmed....

He was probably overreacting. The guards surely had some other orders. They weren't really going to the Wilde family.... But if they were, Rafe would get there in time to save all of them.

The houses blurred by. The trees blurred by. The wind flattened Rafe's fur and ears. The ground felt solid beneath him. He could see the house.

It was burning.

Rafe didn't lose speed as he jumped through the door. The wood broke and splinters flew. There was a loud crack as the door tore off its hinges.

Rafe breathed in smoke which made his eyes water and his throat burn. He stopped right there as he eyes rested on the body in the living room.

Gerald.

Rafe walked toward him and the first thing he saw was the sword in his heart. There was a pool of blood around him. His head was turned to the right. His arms were stretched out in that direction as if he was reaching for something or someone. His lifeless eyes stared that way too.

I'm too late, Rafe thought. *I'm so sorry.*

His frozen heart started cracking as he left Gerald's corpse there. He went in the direction Gerald was looking—to the back of the house. There he found Daisy lying by the back door. She was coughing violently. Rafe shifted into human form so that he would look less intimidating. He didn't want to pick her broken body up because that could hurt her even more, but he had to get her out of the house.

"Rafe!" she croaked as she saw him. He bent down at her side and she let him take her hand.

"You came back for us," she said gratefully.

"Of course I did," he said. "I am going to get you out of here."

"No." She shook her head. It looked like the soldiers had beaten her. Her face was purple and her lip was broken. Her right thigh bone was poking out of the skin. There was blood all over her core. They had stabbed her. Repeatedly. "I'm already dead."

"Daisy," he said softly, wanting to lift her up and carry her to safety. He wiped away her tears.

"They got Maggie out back—save her!" Daisy begged. "Please, please save your little sister."

"I have to save you first."

"I can't be saved." Her hands were shaking. "Rafe, you need to know that Gerald didn't mean the things he said. He was just scared. He loves you. We all love you."

Rafe refused to cry.

"Now go..." she said.

Her body shook as Rafe held her hand. He tried his best to comfort her as he watched her die. He bit back his tears and shifted back into wolf form, leaving her body there, and charged outside to the backyard.

The guards had Maggie. One had his hand clamped around her wrist. The six-year-old was hysterical. She was screaming and kicking and fighting. The other guards were laughing at her and their laughter made Rafe's anger boil. The man holding her lifted his sword, ready to strike. She looked up at him with pleading eyes.

Rafe growled and immediately got the attention of all the guards. Rafe was only focused on the one who held Maggie.

"Rafe! Help me!" Maggie cried and struggled against the man.

The guard let go of her hand the moment the wolf started running toward him. Rafe sank his teeth into the man's torso, penetrating his armor. Rafe crushed his bones and pulled his guts inside out before flinging him to the side.

Then he tore through the other guards like the monster they made him out to be. He ripped their limbs off and licked their blood off his lips. They tried to put up a fight but didn't stand a chance.

Rafe killed them all.

CHAPTER 30

CAITLIN REACHED THE house. She couldn't enter through the front door because there were flames everywhere. So she ran around back where she found Maggie and Rafe.

Rafe was in human form. He was shirtless and wore an ill-fitting pair of pants that he must have taken off one of the guards. They lay dead all around him.

Caitlin didn't want to believe what she was seeing. Rafe had his arms wrapped around the hysterical six-year-old who was crying too much to speak.

Where were Daisy and Gerald?

Caitlin looked to the back door the same time Rafe noticed her. He got to his feet while holding little Maggie. He shook his head at Caitlin and she realized what he was telling her. Gerald and Daisy were dead.

But she didn't want to believe it.

"NO!" she cried as she ran toward the burning house.

Rafe put Maggie down and rushed to block Caitlin. "Caitlin, don't go in there…"

"Move!" she cried.

"You're only going to get hurt if you do."

"Get out of my way!"

Rafe didn't move. Of course he didn't move—he never jumped when Caitlin told him to. "Caitlin," he kept his voice soft. "No one in there can be saved."

"That's a lie!" she cried out.

Then Caitlin tried to run around him. Rafe grabbed her arm and pulled her back into a hug, but she pushed him away.

"This is your fault!" she cried.

Those words hurt Rafe more than any dagger or arrow ever could. He let go of her and watched as she stumbled backward a few steps.

"I got here as fast as I could," Rafe told her. His stormy eyes looked more cloudy than usual.

"The guards must have seen you here earlier and recognized you!"

She blames me, Rafe thought to himself. He had never seen her look at anyone the way she was looking at him. Like she hated him more than anyone and anything. Like she would never forgive him.

"No one could have recognized me…." Rafe said, although he wasn't sure. It was the only logical explanation, wasn't it? If he hadn't come earlier, they would still be alive. Their blood was on his hands. He might as well have killed them himself.

"How could you come back here? You're putting my family's lives at stake!"

Gerald had been right. He should never have traveled with them. He should never have gotten involved in their lives. He should never have loved them.

What had he been thinking?

The burning house reflected in Caitlin's eyes. Her parents were being cremated. Their belongings cracked and burned and part of the roof caved in. Her dream catcher was in the house, burning as well.

Caitlin was shaking but she wasn't crying. She looked toward her little sister. She couldn't break down in front of the child. She had to be the strong one.

She walked to Maggie who was kneeling on the grass crying and gently picked her up, bundling the child into her arms. Her little sister couldn't get a single word out and Caitlin knew she had sustained a trauma that would last a lifetime.

Caitlin squeezed her eyes shut and then opened them to look at the king's guards lying dead in their backyard. The king had ordered this. He had wanted them dead. He was to blame.

Something inside her twisted. The king wanted her to be a weapon, a merciless killing machine. That was exactly what she would be.

Rafe wished he knew what Caitlin was thinking. He didn't like the cold, determined look in her eyes. "What do you want to do?" he asked her. He wasn't sure if she would talk to him. He hoped she wouldn't start screaming again.

"I need to take Maggie to safety," she said at last. "Maggie is my first priority." She gently stroked Maggie's back. The six-year-old was clinging to her neck, still sobbing, her tears wetting Caitlin's shirt.

Rafe picked up one of the guards' capes and threw it over his head in case someone recognized him. He followed Caitlin. "Where are we going?"

"I'm going to find help," she said. Her voice was too calm. "You can't come with me...."

"Why?"

"Someone could recognize you," she said.

"I'll meet you there?" Rafe offered.

"I want you to stay here," her voice was cold.

Rafe wasn't sure what it was she was planning to do, but he knew it wasn't good. She never excluded him. She always shared her thoughts and plans. But he knew now wasn't the time to argue as he looked into her eyes and agreed, "Alright."

"Don't go away," she said more gently. "I'm going to need you."

He was surprised. A part of him thought that she'd already discarded him from her life. If she blamed him for her family's deaths, what could she possibly want or need from him?

243

She started walking away and he didn't try to stop her. To whom would she go? They didn't have any friends, and he was pretty sure no one would help them—no one except Evelyn.

Rafe waited until they were out of sight and then he trailed behind them, making sure to keep his distance. He kept his guard up but no one paid him any attention.

He watched as Caitlin made her way to Evelyn's quarters. She knocked on the door. Evelyn opened it and let her in. The door closed and he heard the lock click.

Rafe sat down by the door and listened.

What was Caitlin going to do that was so bad that she couldn't tell him?

CHAPTER 31

"WHAT HAPPENED?" EVELYN asked.

Maggie was in shock. She clung to Caitlin and her little body shook. The lady motioned for Caitlin to put her down on the bed. She didn't care that the child was filthy. Maggie look terrified but luckily not hurt.

"Someone must have spotted Rafe and recognized him as the wolf when he went to my house," Caitlin started. "I'm guessing that they went to the king and told him my family associated with Magic. He sent his guards and they killed my mom and dad. Rafe arrived just in time to save Maggie."

"She looks terrible," Evelyn said. "I will make her something to calm her down."

Maggie sat cross-legged on the bed. Her arms were wrapped around herself and she was looking down.

Her messy and dirty hair covered her face. Caitlin hoped that Evelyn could make a potion that would let the child relax.

"You're very good with herbs," Caitlin remarked as she watched the witch mix leaves and spices together.

"Every witch has their own special talent," Evelyn told her. "Mine is healing."

"The damage that has been done to her is permanent, isn't it?" Caitlin asked.

If Maggie heard them, she didn't show it. She just looked at her knees and let the tears roll freely down her cheeks.

Evelyn looked at her and shook her head slightly. "I can heal someone's body but not their soul."

Caitlin refused to cry. She refused to show any emotion. She had to keep herself together. She had to stay strong. That's what older sisters do.

"Have you ever thought about having kids?" she asked Evelyn who was mixing the potion.

"I have always wanted them, but I can't get pregnant," Evelyn confessed. It was weird how easily she told Caitlin the truth. She had kept her secret for so long, but after she'd told her husband, she felt at peace with it.

"How does your husband feel about it?" Caitlin asked and then caught herself.

It was an intrusive question but Evelyn answered anyway. Speaking about something so mundane lessened the tension and distracted them from the murders of Gerald and Daisy. "He suggested adoption."

"That could work..." Caitlin said absentmindedly. She folded her arms around herself and looked down at the ground. Evelyn wondered what she was thinking about. She looked so intense, and conflicted—as if she was fighting herself.

"Absolutely. It's a brilliant idea," Evelyn said. "And there are so many children that need a good home."

Caitlin paused and looked closely at Lady Evelyn. The duchess was wealthy, kind, smart, and good. She was confident, protective, and loving. She was also one of the Magic folk, like her and Maggie. "You would make a great parent," Caitlin told her softly.

"Thank you, I would love having my own little girl. I would raise her to be a lady and I would teach her everything I know about healing," Evelyn said. The idea of having a child always excited her. She would raise her child as best as she could, and Riley would be the greatest dad in the world.

"That's perfect," Caitlin said. She was pacing now and she avoided looking at Evelyn. Her eyes lingered on Maggie for a while before she managed to tear them away.

"Why do you ask?"

Caitlin swallowed. It was not easy for her to talk. She refused to choke up. "I can't be a mother.... My life isn't safe enough for a kid...." The idea of being a parent terrified Caitlin. She wasn't responsible enough to take care of someone else. She wasn't stable enough either. She didn't have work, a house, or money. She could never give a kid a good life.

"What are you saying?" Evelyn asked.

It took all of Caitlin's courage to speak her mind. "Would you adopt Maggie and do all the things with her that you would have done with your own daughter?"

Evelyn looked at Caitlin. "Of course... but she's your sister...."

Caitlin nodded. Maggie was her sister and she would always love her. She loved her so much and that was why she had to do what would be best for her. Caitlin was a weapon—definitely not what her sister needed.

"I need a moment to think," Caitlin said. "Please finish making that drink." She left the room with Evelyn's eyes following her. Once outside she closed the door, leaning against it.

Rafe looked up at her from the floor where he was sitting.

"I should have known you would follow us," she said to him. She didn't sound happy to see him, but she didn't sound unhappy either. Her voice was neutral. Rafe knew she was fighting to keep her emotions under control.

"Do you want me to go?" he asked as he got to his feet. He wanted to touch her but he was scared that she would push him away again. So instead he kept his distance.

"No," Caitlin said as she flung her arms around his neck. She couldn't stop herself.

Rafe was so surprised that it took him a moment to hug her back, but when he did, he held her for a long time.

Caitlin had snapped at him earlier because she was hurting. She didn't mean to say everything that she had said. At this moment she was still too emotional to apologize but she knew that Rafe was her emotional pillar. He was what kept her sane and held her together. She needed him now more than ever.

"Are you planning on leaving Maggie with Evelyn?" he asked. He didn't like the idea of leaving Maggie with the witch. Yes, the witch was a good woman who would take good care of her, but she wasn't Maggie's family. Maggie didn't love her the way she loved Caitlin and Rafe.

"I think it would be best for her," Caitlin whispered.

"I disagree," Rafe said. "She's your sister and your responsibility. You can't give family away to another woman. She'll never be able to forget her real family and she will need her big sister. She's got so much damage done to her after... everything. You can't just abandon her."

Caitlin looked up at him but didn't say anything.

"She'll never be able to let you go," Rafe told her. He knew all too well how hard it was to let go of the people you loved. For a kid, this would be almost impossible.

"So what are you saying? We should take her with us when we go? That's no life for a kid," Caitlin argued. She couldn't imagine little Maggie traveling with them everywhere. That wasn't a stable life. Few things would be constant for her. Maggie needed a school and friends and stability: she needed to feel secure.

"But it's not right to leave her behind either," Rafe persisted. "Your family has been broken and you should work on fixing it. Don't break it even more."

Caitlin thought about this. She understood what Rafe was saying. He meant well. He probably wanted nothing more than to fix his own family—but that would never be possible. She took a deep breath and then she kissed Rafe on the cheek. "I will fix Maggie," she reassured him. "I will."

Then she stepped away from him and went back inside. She closed the door between them, locking it behind her.

CHAPTER 32

"IS THE DRINK ready?" Caitlin asked Evelyn.

"Yes," Evelyn said as she walked toward Maggie, holding a cup of greenish liquid in her hands. "I was just about to give it to her."

Caitlin took the cup from Evelyn who was confused by her action but let her take it. Caitlin put it down on the bedside cupboard and took a deep breath.

"What are you doing?" Evelyn asked.

"Just adding the final ingredient," Caitlin said. Her back was turned to Evelyn.

"I have already added everything..." Evelyn said.

She didn't understand what Caitlin was doing. Caitlin stuck her hand into her pocket and pulled out a small black vial. She opened it and poured its contents into the drink. It mixed with the liquid inside the cup and its color didn't change.

"What is that?" Evelyn asked.

Caitlin didn't answer her. She didn't tell her that it was Blankness, the potion for forgetting. She just could not get the words out. With a heavy heart she made her way to the bed and sat down next to her sister.

Maggie jumped when Caitlin put her arm around her. It was as if Maggie had forgotten she wasn't alone. She looked at her older sister. She was still shaking and crying.

"I need you to drink this," Caitlin said and handed Maggie the cup.

Maggie looked at the cup and slowly took it. She didn't speak. She didn't ask what it was or what it would do to her.

"It will help," Caitlin said.

Maggie brought the cup to her lips and started drinking. She drank two sips and then she stopped.

"Drink all of it," Caitlin prompted when she stopped.

Maggie obediently drank it all. When she was done, she went into a state of calmness. Her body stopped shaking and her tears stopped flowing. She dropped the cup onto the bed and looked in front of her without showing any emotion.

"Maggie..." Caitlin said.

The little girl looked at her. There was no recognition in her eyes. Caitlin readied herself. She didn't have much time. She started talking. "Your name is Maggie Patterson. Your mother is Evelyn Patterson and your father is Riley Patterson. They love you dearly.

You live with them here in Sky Castle. You're a beautiful young lady and training to become a healer."

Caitlin swallowed and drew a breath before she continued.

"You will remember nothing of your previous life. You will remember no hardship and no suffering. You will not remember your parents, Daisy and Gerald, or everything you've been through. You will not remember having a bad or a hard life. Your soul is whole and your wounds are healed." Caitlin took a deep, shaky breath. "You will forget all about Rafe, the wolf. He no longer lives in your mind or heart. And..." She fought the tears. She would not cry. "You are an only-child. You do not have an older sister. The name Caitlin means nothing to you."

Caitlin moved away from the bed. She had said everything that needed to be said. She had fixed Maggie as best she could. Blankness would work effectively on Maggie because she was so young. It would probably work as well as the obliteration device had.

For a few seconds, she and Evelyn just stared at the little girl as if they were waiting for something to happen. Then Maggie snapped out of her gaze. She looked at Caitlin and then she turned to Evelyn.

"Mommy, who is that?" she asked.

Evelyn silently looked at Caitlin.

"Nobody. I'm nobody," Caitlin said softly and smiled sadly before leaving the room. Never again would she return.

Rafe sat outside the door, listening to every word. At first, he wasn't sure what was going on. Nothing Caitlin was saying made sense. Then he remembered giving her the Blankness potion. He had given her the power to make this tremendous mistake.

He couldn't believe what he was hearing. He wanted to stop it with all his heart. He considered breaking the door down, but he knew it was too late. There was no stopping it. If he interfered now, things could only go wrong and Maggie's mind could be damaged.

He pictured sweet little Maggie who always laughed and always wanted to help everyone. He thought about little Maggie who used to cling to him and fall asleep on his chest. He remembered little Maggie as one of the few people he loved and who loved him in return.

But that was in the past now. The Maggie he knew was gone.

He listened as Caitlin stole her memories and replaced them with new ones. A piece of his heart broke. It physically hurt. His hand went to his chest and pressed down where his heart was. He refused to cry.

How could Caitlin do that? How could she do that

after something similar had been done to her? She knew how bad it was. She suffered through it herself! And she promised him that she would never ever do this to someone. She broke that promise. She lied.

"You will forget all about Rafe, the wolf. He no longer lives in your mind or heart."

Rafe clenched his hands when Caitlin made Maggie forget him. How could she do that? He had known Maggie almost as long as Caitlin had! He'd put in so much effort and time with her. Maggie was as much his sister as she was Caitlin's.

Rafe was pacing now. His heart ached like it hadn't in a long time. He had lost a second family. Once again, he was too late to save them. Once again, he had to find their lifeless bodies....

But he had saved Maggie. She would have been fine. They would have helped her recover. Once again, Rafe felt completely alone.

Rafe blamed Caitlin. He couldn't forgive this. He couldn't let this go. How was he supposed to look into Caitlin's eyes again? Things would never be the same between them.

She had made this decision without him. The consequences of this decision rested on her shoulders and her shoulders alone. She would have to figure out how to live with herself.

He watched the sunlight creeping through the window. It was morning. It was first light. It was the time that he and Caitlin had agreed to run away together.

He got to his feet and he started running. He was leaving the castle at first light as they had planned. But he was leaving alone.

CHAPTER 33

CAITLIN SHUT THE door behind her. That was the hardest thing she'd ever had to do. She didn't want to do it, but now Maggie would be happy. She deserved to be happy.

Maggie now had everything she'd ever wanted. She would be taught how to sit and talk and walk like a lady. She would wear all the elaborate gowns she loved so much. She'd have servants to wait on her and pamper her. She would always look gorgeous. And she would be training to become a healer and she would be brilliant at it.

It was the most selfless decision Caitlin had ever made. She was glad that she did it. She felt she did what was right.

But it was still hard and her heart still hurt. She had rushed out of the room. She longed for Rafe's arms.

She needed to hear him tell her that she'd done the right thing. She needed him to tell her that everything would be fine. He always made everything better. He could fix the worst situation.

Once she was out of the room she looked around. Rafe wasn't there. She knew he reacted very differently than she did when he was hurt. He usually needed some space. Maybe that was it. He'd just walked away to be alone for a while.

She wondered how upset he would be that she didn't tell him about her plans. She couldn't tell him. He would have talked her out of it. She had to do what was best for Maggie, not what was best for herself. This was the only way she could ensure Maggie's happiness.

Caitlin sat down next to Evelyn's door and pressed her back against the wall. She wrapped her arms around herself although it wasn't cold. She closed her eyes and breathed in deeply. She would not cry. This wasn't the place to cry. She had to stay strong.

A servant girl walked by and stared at her. Caitlin faked a smile. She was surprised at just how good she was with it. The servant girl passed and left her alone.

She was glad Evelyn didn't open the door. She didn't want to see them right now. She didn't know if she could handle it.

Just sitting on the other side of the door made her happy and sad at the same time. She heard Maggie laughing. It was a real laugh that started in her stomach and worked its way up. It was the most beautiful sound in the world.

Caitlin sat there for an hour before the door opened and shielded her. Maggie and Evelyn left the room without noticing her. She pushed the door shut and watched them leave.

It was midday by the time she got up. She wondered what could be keeping Rafe. Where could he be?

"*Okay. If something happens and we split up, we meet each other by our tower at first light.*" How had she forgotten that? Rafe was probably sitting at the foot of the tower waiting for her. She would show up late and he would laugh at her.

She started jogging toward it. She passed the throne room and tried not to glare. She meant what she had said about being a weapon. She wanted to kill them all.

But she was thinking with a clearer mind now. If she did that, she would have a lot of enemies. And that would also endanger Rafe's life. So she couldn't do that.

She just had to get away from here as fast as possible. She could outrun the pain. She didn't have to face it ever again.

She didn't look in the direction of her old house and tried to block those memories out. No good would come from thinking about it.

She picked up her pace. She couldn't wait to get there! She couldn't wait to look into Rafe's gray eyes. She craved his strong arms around her, making the world fade away. She wanted to lean her head against his chest and hear his heart beating just for her.

She reached the tower and slowed her pace. There was no one there. The silence gathered all around her in a solid wall and pushed against her so hard that her breathing stopped. She stood there, looking lost and out of place.

"Rafe!" she called. Her voice bounced off the stone walls and was carried through the corridors. She looked around, expecting him to jump out at any moment. "Rafe," she whispered.

She wrapped her arms around herself and felt truly alone. She held onto herself like she used to hold onto Rafe. She bit back tears. This couldn't be happening. Rafe would show up like he always did. He would not have left without her—he could not have left without her.

"*You'll never lose me.*" He had told her that. She still believed him.

Slowly Caitlin walked toward the staircase and started climbing. She tried to keep her mind as blank as possible. She started running, taking two steps at a time. Although she felt her world spinning out of control, she didn't get dizzy from the spiral.

When she reached the top of the staircase, the wind blew into her hair and cooled her down. She took her first step onto their tower. Her eyes lingered on the spot where they sat and ate that day. It was one of her favorite memories.

She could see the castle grounds. The people looked so small and unrecognizable from up here. She could see the mountainside and the cliffs. She could see the dark gray clouds around her.

But she couldn't see Rafe. He wasn't here. He hadn't met her like he said he would. A little part of her knew then and there what had happened. He'd left when she needed him most.

But she loved him. She trusted him. She believed in him and she was fiercely loyal. So she sat with her back against one of the tower's four pillars and waited. She sat there by herself and looked down. The clouds were rolling in. They hid the sunlight. Then lightning split the sky open and thunder roared, answering her silent screams.

I love you. He had said those words. Why didn't she say them back? She did love him. She loved him with all her heart. Truthfully, he was the only person she really needed in her life.

The rain cried its pity. Despite the roof covering the tower, the wind blew the rain onto Caitlin. It soaked her clothes and ran down her cheeks like tears.

She waited for what seemed like an eternity and yet also seemed like a single heartbeat that then stopped. Her brave heart shattered once midnight came.

She began to rouse herself and listened carefully as she continued to sit alone in her tower. She heard people talk, walk, heard the crying of the rain. Then once the moon reached its highest, she heard the crying of a wolf. Another wolf answered the first cry as if to say, "It's alright. You're not alone."

She lay down on the cold stone floor of the tower and a part of her wished she was dead. She didn't move except for her breathing. She closed her eyes and remembered how Rafe used to sing her to sleep. She knew it was him out there–crying for her, crying over his decision.

If he came back, she would forgive him.

But he didn't come back.

So as the night deepened, she closed her eyes to a mournful lullaby, the faraway cries of the wolves.

CHAPTER 34

CAITLIN WOKE UP. She groaned as she didn't want to wake up. She was cold and wet where she had lain on the stone floor of the tower. Her body was almost as sore as her head. She was very cold.

She sat up. It was a new day, a new beginning, and a time for change. She managed to get to her feet although her knees were shaking. She looked over the castle and at the Whispering Mountains. Rafe would be far away from the castle by now.

She was hungry and dehydrated. She started making her way down the staircase, amazed that she wasn't slipping or that her shaky knees weren't buckling. If she fell down these spiral stairs she would get hurt badly.

The necklace that Maggie gave her dangled from her neck. It was a constant reminder of her sister's love—a love that no longer existed.

She remembered getting the necklace and thinking it was ugly and sloppy. Back then she was very ungrateful. Now she swore she would never take it off.

There would be no funeral for Daisy and Gerald. They were cremated as their house burned down. So there were no bodies to bury and no one besides Caitlin to go to their funeral.

She wondered how she could honor them.

She walked for a long time with an empty belly. She knew what she had to do. But she couldn't do it while she felt like this.

She saw a beautiful flower bed and sat down next to it. Some of the flowers were burned and black paw prints charred the grass. She wondered what had made them.

She sat there and breathed in the flowers. This was what Maggie used to do in her free time.... There were plenty of flowers in the castle. She was probably happy.

"Excuse me miss," someone asked. "Are you okay?"

She turned her head to see a middle-aged man staring at her. Judging from his clothes and the dirt under his fingernails, he looked like the public gardener. A frown creased his forehead.

Caitlin was tired of pretending. She was tired of fake smiles. She was tired of being someone she wasn't. "No," she told the old man. What could he do? She watched him walk away and let her head hang. Her stomach rumbled and the grass tickled her legs.

Ten minutes later the man came back with some bread and water. He knelt down beside her and handed it to her.

She didn't know what to say. She was so hungry her instincts took over and she started shoving everything down her throat. It took her a moment to realize the gardener was watching her eat. She expected him to be staring at her, looking disgusted. Instead, he was smiling. She wanted to thank him for the food but her mouth was too full to speak. She tried to gulp the bread down.

"It's a shame our king doesn't take better care of his people," the gardener said. "No one should be homeless or go to bed hungry."

She was about to tell him that she had a home. Then she remembered how she had watched it burn. She was homeless. She was a street person. She had gone to bed hungry and it was a horrible feeling. But she had been so sad yesterday that she wouldn't have been able to eat anyway.

Without another word, the man sat down next to her. He was keeping her company. He knew she needed both food and comfort. The way he cared for her reminded her of Daisy. She missed her mother. She missed having someone watching out for her, making sure that she was always alright.

She shoved the last piece of bread down her throat

and then started gulping down the water. Her cheeks flushed red. She wanted to thank him but said instead, "Your garden is beautiful."

He smiled. "Well, thank you. I work very hard on it. Believe it or not, a lizard from hell ran through it and burned some of it down."

She raised her eyebrows. Maybe he was batty.

He laughed. "If someone said that to me, I would also not believe them."

She shrugged and touched the closest flower. It was red and white and had tiny little thorns on its stem. "My family loved flowers."

The old man hesitated before he said, "You should take them some. These flowers are going to die soon anyway and then I will plant new ones."

"Thank you, sir. You are very kind."

"I try to be. It's all one can do in a world as cruel as this one."

"Or you could just be crueler than the rest of the world," Caitlin found herself saying.

"Those are some strong words...." the old man said. "What happened to you, child?"

She paused. "Someone hurt me."

"If they hurt you, they are hurting themselves. You should forgive them. That's what they need."

"Forgiveness isn't what I need," she responded.

"So what is it you want to do then?"

"I want to hurt them so bad that they will never be able to touch me again."

"Take it from someone who's seen his share of living —the only things in life you'll regret doing more than the things you didn't do are the things you did to intentionally hurt someone."

She didn't say anything to that. She got to her feet. "I'll take you up on your offer of the flowers," she said and started picking them.

"Alright." The gardener also got up. "Let me help you get all the pretty ones and arrange them in a nice bundle."

They did it in silence. The flowers were gorgeous. They were in all shapes, sizes, and colors. The gardener tied their stems together and handed them to Caitlin. There were so many that they hardly fit in her arm, yet they still didn't feel like enough.

She thanked him and left the garden behind. She didn't look back but knew he was staring after her.

Caitlin walked to what was left of their house. The walls were black. The roof had fallen in. The flowers and garden were burned to a crisp. Their furniture was eaten by the fire.

Daisy and Gerald were turned to ash.

And no one cared.

The world carried on like it always did. All around her people were laughing and living their lives. No one cared about the deaths of two amazing people who they didn't know.

Caitlin walked to the porch. She placed the flowers in front of the broken door. She couldn't bring herself to walk into the house. She turned away and decided to leave the past behind her.

Then she went looking for the armory. She would need weapons before barging into the throne room.

CHAPTER 35

LILLIAN WOKE UP in the healer's house. She ran her right hand over the rough cast of clay and twine that had hardened around her left arm, effectively immobilizing it. Her body felt bruised and sore. She looked down at her body. She had purple marks and scratch marks everywhere.

Her eyes squinted at the sunlight streaming through the open window. Although the brightness hurt her eyes, the wind that blew revived and refreshed her.

She expected to be alone, thinking that her family would want nothing to do with her. But when she looked to her right, she saw Dylan. He was clean, face scrubbed, hair washed and combed neatly, and no weapons in sight. He sat in the chair by her bed and slept. His head was propped up against the wall and her bedpost, and his eyelids fluttered as he dreamed.

He looked so peaceful. Lillian didn't want to wake him up. She just wanted to touch him. She reached for him and put her hand on his arm. Slowly his eyes opened and he yawned.

"I didn't mean to wake you," she said hoarsely.

"It's alright," he said. "I feel well rested." He took her hand in his, in a comforting and caring way, and she knew he wasn't mad at her. He looked at her with blue eyes that matched her own.

"How long was I out?" she asked.

"It's almost been two days," Dylan said. "They have you on some very strong medication."

"What did the healer say about my arm?"

"Amazingly you aren't going to lose it," Dylan said. "But it won't work the way it used to."

She looked at the cast. "You broke your arm as a kid and it works just fine."

"Yes, but that's different," he laughed. "I fell off a swing. Mine wasn't almost ripped off by a shifter."

"My story is so much cooler than yours," she teased.

"Absolutely," he agreed.

She moved her arm to study the cast. She let go of Dylan's hand and touched it. "I remember writing on yours...."

"I will look for a quill and an inkwell," Dylan said and sounded excited. "It's an honor to be the first person to write on your cast."

He left the room and Lillian stared out the window. She had so much to think about. Her heart was hurting.

Dylan came back brandishing the writing implements. The ink was red. "Found them." He sat down again and looked at her arm.

"You better write something nice," she said.

"You didn't write something nice on mine," Dylan said.

"That never happened."

"It did."

"Don't argue with me. I'm never wrong."

Dylan looked at her broken left arm. "You're all right."

She glared at him. "You're a bit young to be making lame dad jokes."

He smiled. Then the moment turned serious.

"Dylan... about what happened..."

He looked at her. Her eyes were shiny.

"I understand if you are angry with me."

"I'm not angry," Dylan said.

"Then what are you?"

"I'm sad and a bit disappointed. I understand why you didn't tell me."

The truth had broken the trust between them. Their relationship would never be the same. It was like Lillian's arm. It was broken and would be healed but it would also leave a nasty scar.

"I wanted to..." she said. "There were so many times that I wanted to."

"I believe that," he said.

"I loved your mother," Lillian said. "I couldn't read

her mind. I couldn't predict that she would jump in front of an arrow. If I could, I would never have gone to the shifter's house. If I could, I would change the past, but I can't."

"Regret comes too late," he said.

"I can't forgive myself," she confessed. "I've been trying to for years. It's a scar I will bear for the rest of my life."

"What are you going to do from now on?" Dylan asked.

"What I've always done—protect those who cannot protect themselves."

"So you will stay a hunter...."

"That is who I am. It's the life I was born into. I don't know how to be anything else."

"You don't want to be something else," Dylan mumbled.

"Excuse me?"

"Someone once told me that I'm only one decision away from a completely different life," he smiled. "I just need to want it bad enough."

"And you think it's that simple?"

He nodded. "It's that simple. I must just be brave enough to make that decision."

"What decision have you made?" she asked.

"To live a different life."

"And are you leaving me behind in this life?"

Dylan looked at her. She was still his aunt. She still helped raise him. He was raised to be a good man, and never abandon anyone. He forgave her.

He opened the small red pot. Its ink looked like blood. Lillian held out her arm so that he could write on her cast.

Dylan dipped his quill in the ink. *I never leave family behind,* he wrote on the hardened clay. Lillian read his words with tears in her eyes as he got up to leave the room.

"She's awake," Liam said by way of greeting. His large body blocked most of the doorway as he hesitated before entering the room. He kept his eyes on his son and avoided looking at his sister.

Dylan nodded. "You need to talk to her," he said to his father.

"We need to talk as well," Liam replied, briefly laying his hand on his son's shoulder.

Dylan held his father's eyes before answering, "Yes... afterwards." Then he nodded and smiled at his aunt as he said to his father before leaving, "I'll meet you at the inn, Dad."

CHAPTER 36

LIAM DIDN'T WANT to see his sister. He didn't ever want to talk to her again. If it was up to him, she would have bled out where the wolf had nearly killed her. A part of him wished the wolf had killed her. But Dylan was a much better man than his father ever was or could be. He had picked her up and rushed her to the healer's house. He was able to forgive and release his anger. Liam envied that. He was bitter with pain. He knew it would shoot through him like a thousand arrows when he looked at Lillian. He thought about everything that had happened in the past....

Their parents were both hunters so they grew up in the trade. Lillian was very competitive. She took great pleasure in beating him at everything they did. They couldn't even play a game without it turning into a competition. She took great pride in winning at every-thing. But she also loved her brother. Ever since they were children, they were best friends.

As the years went by, it was nice to have someone who understood him and knew him better than any-one. Brother and sister shared secrets and fought side by side for a long time. Lillian saved his life much more than he ever saved hers.

He watched her go through her first heartbreak and sat with her when she swore off boys. He told her he didn't see himself getting married either.

But then he met Mary, and everything changed. She was not the ideal person to bring into a family of hunters. She was too soft and too kind. She had so much compassion and love in her. Liam remembered her saving his life like it was yesterday.

He couldn't stop himself from falling in love. He never thought a woman like that would love him back. He never thought a woman like that would want a hunter as a husband. But she did. She supported him in his career as best she could.

The closer that Liam and Mary became, the less space there was for Lillian. Lillian advised him to not get married. She warned him that Mary wasn't made to live the life that they lived.

He didn't listen. Liam never listened. He didn't think about what was best for Mary. He only thought about what was best for him and what he wanted.

Mary struggled to deal with the things Liam did

and the creatures he killed. She felt a guilt that he had never known or understood. Although she tried to support him, it was hard. The only time they ever fought was because of his work. She never asked him to quit until Dylan was born.

Dylan was their world. Mary didn't want her son to be raised into such a violent lifestyle. She wanted him to go to school, like she did. She wanted him to be educated, like she was. She knew he was smart, much smarter than she could ever be.

Lillian and Mary fought as well. Lillian said that Dylan had a hunter's blood and heart and that he had the right to be raised as a hunter. Liam agreed with his sister. But Mary held her ground and tried to keep Dylan as far away from that life as she possibly could.

Despite their differences, Lillian did love Mary. They were friends and spent a great amount of time together. But three was a crowd. Dylan coming into the word was a blessing, drawing husband and wife closer together.

Liam knew Mary didn't hate Magic the way he did. She wasn't raised like him at all. She was raised as a healer. She saved lives instead of taking them.

Lillian always tried to change Mary's mind. She always tried to get Mary to see things differently and to switch to their side. Liam didn't know how far she was willing to go to accomplish this.

He remembered seeing Lillian cry for the first time. It was when she came home covered in blood and dirt. She told him that Mary had been brutally ripped apart.

She also said she got her revenge, and Liam believed her. He never doubted what happened that day because he trusted his sister to tell him the truth, no matter what.

Now, their bond was broken.

Liam thought about his intense hatred for wolves. All these years, he had misdirected his hatred. The real murderer was right under his nose.

Liam stood in the middle of Lillian's room looking at his sister. She was staring at the window and he wondered if she was imagining herself running away. He reached into his pocket, took out a little pouch, and placed it on her bedside table.

"What is this?" Lillian asked.

"Your half of the payment from the king for our work out west," Liam said.

"Thank you." She didn't touch the bag or count the coins inside. She knew Liam wouldn't cheat her. She couldn't look into his eyes—just as he'd expected.

I never leave family behind. Liam read his son's handwriting on her cast. He taught Dylan those three very important rules for hunters:

    1. *I run toward what I fear.*

    2. *I never leave family behind.*

    3. *I protect those who can't protect themselves*

Liam's world had fallen apart. Lillian had feared telling him the truth and instead she ran away from her fears and lied. She broke the second rule too when she left Mary behind. She didn't bring her body home, so Liam's wife was deprived of a proper burial. And the third rule: Mary couldn't protect herself and Lillian didn't protect her.

"Please say something," Lillian said.

Liam was deathly quiet. He stood in her room and looked down at her for what seemed like forever. "There's not much to say," he said at long last.

She knew that was true. "I'm sorry..." she said.

"Sorry doesn't fix anything," he spat. "After Mary died, I wanted to quit hunting. YOU talked me out of it. I knew it was a dangerous life to raise a kid in. Mary was right about that."

"I know I talked you out of it," she said. "I just didn't want to be alone."

"You *are* alone," he said as he turned away from her and left the room.

CHAPTER 37

DYLAN SAT OUTSIDE the house waiting for Liam. He had taken his shirt off, letting the sun kiss his already tanned skin. He leaned his head back and closed his eyes.

He needed some time to relax. His body hurt from fighting. He needed a break. He felt his muscles unwind, but his brow remained furrowed as his emotions continued their internal war.

"Are you falling asleep in the middle of the day?" Liam asked.

Dylan opened his eyes. "I'm just resting." He sat up. "You are back early."

Liam just nodded and Dylan sensed he didn't want to talk about his visit with Lillian. Dylan knew his dad well enough: he was done with his sister.

Liam took a seat next to his son and for a while

they enjoyed the sun's warmth. It felt so good. Then Liam turned to look at Dylan before announcing, "We should start packing soon."

Dylan swallowed.

"There's no point in staying here," Liam continued.

"I know that, Dad."

"There's no work for us here."

"Are you serious?" Dylan asked, sitting upright.

Liam looked confused. "Yes? We won't find any more shifters here..."

"You're kidding me!" Dylan said and got to his feet. "You want to continue hunting?"

Liam looked baffled. "Of course I do. Why do you look so upset? Hunting is what we do!"

Dylan shook his head. "I never wanted this life."

His father looked at him with guilt. "I didn't mean to force you into it."

"But you *did* force me into it," Dylan said. "You never asked me what I want. You never cared about what was important to me."

"I do care," Liam said.

"Well you sure don't show it!" Dylan snapped, his anger flaring. Liam expected Dylan to forgive him when Liam couldn't even forgive Lillian!

"Dylan..."

"Don't say whatever it is you want to say to change my mind," Dylan said. "When I was growing up, you never let me think for myself. I always had to do every-thing your way. My opinion didn't matter then."

"It matters now," Liam said.

"Does it really?"

"Yes, son!"

"Then listen to what I'm saying! How could you want to continue hunting the shifters? You saw how that wolf spared Lillian. He's a more forgiving man—yes, I meant 'man'!—than either of us will ever be."

"Maybe... maybe he was just too weak to kill her. Maybe—"

"Rubbish!" Dylan threw his hands up in the air. "That wolf could have killed her and both of us! If you were in his position, you wouldn't have thought twice about ripping our heads off. What that wolf did back there? That was more *human* than you are behaving now."

"Take. That. Back."

"But it's the truth! You can't even forgive Lillian for accidently killing Mother. Rafe forgave her for purposefully slaughtering his whole family." Dylan rose to his feet as their argument intensified.

"He's still a shifter."

"And a good man!" Dylan cried. "He is a better man than I will ever be. Just look at the killer I have become."

"You save innocent people."

"No, Father, I kill innocent people," he swallowed. "I am just as bad as Aunt Lillian! How many families have we murdered?"

"They have Magic..."

"SO WHAT?"

"So what?! Magic is evil!"

"You brainwashed me into believing that lie for a long time," Dylan said. "But I don't anymore. Non-Magics are scared of Magic because we don't understand it."

"Magic is a threat!"

"Is it?" Dylan asked. "The kingdom is ruled by a non-Magic man! The war with the Magic folk ended over twenty years ago."

"They could come back."

"But they aren't coming back. They are all hiding like animals because we are the true monsters."

"I didn't know you hated yourself this much," Liam said.

"I hate myself no more than you hate yourself," Dylan said. "Killing shifters won't bring Mom back. It won't justify her death and it won't get you revenge."

"So what would you have us do then?"

"I don't know about you, Father, but I'm going to go my own way. I'm going to become a healer, like mom was, and live a life where I truly help others."

"I can't talk you out of this, can I?" Liam said solemnly.

"No," Dylan said.

"Should I come with you then?"

"No," Dylan said. "I love you, Father, but after everything we've been through, I just need to be alone for a while."

"Is this because of that girl?"

"What girl?"

"The pretty one. I think her name is Caitlin."

"She's in love with someone else," Dylan confessed.

"Love between a boy and a girl is a temporary thing. It can change like the seasons."

"I don't think this will change."

"The love that a parent has for his child is eternal."

"I love you too, Dad." Dylan said. The anger had disappeared from his voice.

"Go find that girl anyway," Liam said. "Maybe she's changed her mind."

"I will do that," Dylan said as he gave his father a long hug in parting.

When Dylan got to the Wilde home, he was horrified. He thought Evelyn had made a mistake when she'd said she'd seen guards. He thought she'd just been dazed from the blow to her head. But once he reached the front door, he knew she had been right. The place was destroyed.

Dylan scanned the blackened timbers and saw the flowers on what remained of the porch. He realized that someone had died. He panicked. *No, not Caitlin*

—she must have brought the flowers here, he thought. This was enough to tip her over the edge. She would be dangerous and deadly. She would kill anyone who wronged her.

"*By the time you hear of her being a threat it will be too late,*" the witch had warned him.

Dylan started running. He only hoped he would get there in time to stop her from killing the man who was responsible for this. The king.

Dylan ran and ran, the witch's words echoing in his mind, driving him to run faster and faster.

"*The castle isn't a good place for her. You should take her away.*"

Liam packed his belongings. There wasn't much. Then he made his way toward the stables. He was about to saddle his horse when he saw the white mare.

He called the stable boy. "Why doesn't this horse have water?"

"The owner has not paid his stable fees."

"So you are letting this animal suffer."

"It's not me! My boss's orders," the boy defended himself.

Liam stroked the horse's neck. She whinnied softly and affectionately.

"He said we will have to put her down or let her go if her owner doesn't retrieve her. We can't sell her since she is not ours."

"I'll take her. Her owner won't be returning for her," Liam told the stable boy. He knew the mare to be Jasmine, Black Blade's valiant and trusty steed, and he also knew that the assassin was never coming back. "You can sell my horse," Liam offered. "I am leaving and I don't need her anymore. And keep the money."

"Thank you, sir!" The boy walked away to clean some more stables.

Liam fed and watered Jasmine. She was a stunning horse and she had the sweetest temperament. When she finished her meal, he saddled her. Then he walked her out of the stable and mounted. He patted her neck. They had each lost a partner and best friend here, he thought as they rode away from Sky Castle.

CHAPTER 38

THE KING SAT on his throne. To his right sat Lady
Katherine, as always. She wore a beautiful dark gray
dress streaked with silver. Her long black hair was in a
French braid to the side of her face. Her lips were
colored red. She sat with her back straight and looked
down through long lashes at the king's men.

A table had been placed in front of the throne.
Chairs ranged around it for the king's most trusted
allies. All of them were non-Magic and all had fought
beside King Leonard during the Age of Magic. All of
them were ruthless men who hated Magic and had
worked hard to vanquish it from the Silver Kingdom.
They were his second family.

None of them approved of a woman being the king's
right hand. They were all too scared to say something

about it, especially since she had been there forever. They knew the king would choose her side above theirs without a second thought.

None of them ever argued with her either. She was ruthless and cunning. She had a way of always getting what she wanted as she was frightfully smart. They knew she was more powerful than all of them combined.

"The shifters are out of control," one man said to the other men who sat at the table.

"They've been killing both Magic and non-Magic folk all around the kingdom," another man agreed with him.

"They're clearly becoming crazed," a third chimed in.

"The hunters you sent out west, My Lord, completed the task wonderfully but there are even more shifters. They keep popping up out of nowhere," the man that had spoken first said.

"It's happening because they want revenge," a man with a droopy moustache shared his opinion.

"It's happening because they hate us," another said.

Lady Katherine was used to these meetings. She attended all of them to advise the king on the problems in the Silver Kingdom. It was always the same. The men brought their complaints and she resolved them. One of the reasons the king valued her was because she was irreplaceable. She was brilliant at her trade and always got things done. The king never had to worry about anything he placed in her hands.

Lady Katherine spoke up and all the heads instantly turned in her direction. "It's happening because they are sick," she said. "But don't worry gentlemen. I have found a cure."

"A cure?" the man with the droopy moustache asked skeptically.

She knew all of them were just waiting for her to make a mistake. They had tried getting her away from the table more than once and more than once she had outsmarted them. "I will see to it that this disease disappears," she said confidently.

"And so the shifters will live?" one of the men asked.

No one dared to ask if the shifters would benefit from the cure—which they would. Everyone was too scared to say something to upset the lady.

"Yes, but they will no longer be killing us once they're cured," Lady Katherine said.

"I trust Lady Katherine to handle the situation," the king said as he waved and waggled his fingers in front of himself in dismissal. Gold and silver rings glinted on his fingers. "What else do you gentlemen want to talk about?"

"The floors in the castle have been caving in," one man said. "Luckily, no one has been hurt yet."

"Don't worry about that either," Lady Katherine said soothingly before the king even had to think about a solution. "I've already sent people to fill up the holes and rebuild the floors."

"We don't have to worry about anything with you running things," one lord mumbled.

Katherine met his eyes. "Indeed," she said. He looked

away first and she smiled. She could intimidate even the most powerful lords in the kingdom.

Katherine despised these men, and they knew it. She had worked long, hard, and smart to be in the position she was in. Many of them envied her. Some wanted to be her, some wanted her for themselves, and others wanted her dead.

She was the first woman ever to be in the right-hand seat and she occupied it with pride. No one could take this position from her.

"My son tells me that we are having a drought to the north," the king said to one of the lords.

"Yes, the prince told me he would speak to you," this lord said. "Your esteemed son has a very kind heart."

"I will have our people send water that way," Lady Katherine offered. She knew the prince well. He was young and easy to manipulate. He had a good, soft heart but he wasn't a strong person, and he was nothing like his father.

Suddenly, someone screamed. All heads turned to the big doors. They were shut and two guards stood on the outside so that no one in the halls could hear what the king and his men were talking about.

"What was that?" the king asked.

"Maybe the guards got into a brawl?" the lord with the moustache suggested.

"I'll find out," one man said valiantly and got up. "It's probably nothing." He walked to the big doors as everyone watched. When he reached for the handles, the doors swung open and slammed into him. He was knocked backward and fell to the ground. He looked up and touched his bloody nose.

In front of him stood a woman. She was tall and beautiful. She had daggers strapped to her thighs and a sword in each had. Slung over her shoulders were a bow and a quiver of arrows. Fresh blood stained her clothes.

No one was ever allowed to enter the throne room with weapons. The guards at the doors were supposed to have taken them away. But behind her, lay the guards in a puddle of their own blood.

"What is this? Explain yourself!" the king ordered.

"I'm here to deliver the weapon you'd commissioned," she said to the king. She watched the blood drain from his face. He wasn't nearly as scary as she had first thought. He looked like a little boy who was about to cry.

"What's the weapon?" the man asked angrily, still on the ground.

"I am," she said. Then she drove her sword through his neck.

The other men jumped up from the table instantly. Caitlin spun around, shutting and bolting the doors so no one could enter.

The only person who didn't move was Katherine. She watched Caitlin with her dark eyes. She didn't flinch and didn't interfere.

Caitlin went for the lords first. They were easy to kill because they didn't have any weapons. One threw a chair at her. It was big and heavy but easy to dodge. Another broke his chair and used its leg as a weapon. He held the sharp, splintered end out in front of him. It was no match for her sword. She slashed through the chair leg. The man gaped at her as she stuck her sword into his stomach.

Caitlin smiled as she pulled her blade free. All of her training kicked in. She remembered.

She flipped herself over the table and rammed the outer edge of her foot into a man's jaw. She ducked as another tried to hit her and drove her sword through his abdomen. He made a sickening sound as he fell to the ground. She spun around and swung both swords, beheading two lords at once. Then one man tried to tackle her but she moved to the side and kicked him over. All of them together were no match for her.

The king was up and out of his chair. He called for more guards. They came and hammered on the big, strong, locked doors—blocked from entry.

Caitlin wiped the blood from her cheek. She looked around her. All of the men were dead. She felt no pity.

The king tried to sprint toward the trapdoor behind Katherine's throne but Caitlin was much faster. She beat him to it and stood on top of it, triumphantly cutting off that exit too.

"You were created to protect me and fight for me. You are supposed to do what I say. You belong to me," said the king in a broken, high-pitched voice.

Caitlin was gratified to see the big man trembling. "I belong to myself before I belong to any land or liege," she said.

She walked toward him and he backed up. She wondered if he would run away. He looked into her eyes.

"I left you for last," she said. "I wanted you to watch your men die. They were like family, weren't they?"

He nodded.

"Good," she smiled. "Now you can feel my pain."

He was about to say something when her first sword raked across his stomach. He cried out and sank to his knees.

"Katherine!" he cried.

She still sat in her chair. She looked calm and relaxed, or maybe bored. She tilted her heard to the side and looked at the king maliciously.

"She's not going to help you," Caitlin said. "No one is going to help you."

"What d-do you want? M-money?"

"You can pay with your life," she said.

Her sword sliced through his head the way his executioner's ax had sliced through many Magic folks' necks.

Then she dropped her weapons and looked around the room at what she had done.

CHAPTER 39

THE KING'S GUARDS continued banging on the door.

Caitlin's eyes came to a rest on Lady Katherine. She was sitting in her jeweled chair. She didn't look horrified as she surveyed the bodies. She almost looked irritated because of the mess. Katherine's eyes met Caitlin's. For a moment they just looked at each other. Neither moved.

Then Katherine broke the silence. "Are you going to kill me too?"

Caitlin shook her head. "No, you're not the one who wronged me."

Lady Katherine got to her feet in one swift yet elegant motion. She walked regally over to Caitlin. Caitlin was surprised when she stood so close. She could easily strike her down with a sword.

"What happened?" Lady Katherine asked. "I thought you'd be long gone by now."

"I thought so too," Caitlin said.

The banging intensified. There were voices barking out orders now. Caitlin knew it was only a matter of time before they got in.

"Are you planning on escaping through there?" Katherine pointed to the trapdoor.

"The thought crossed my mind," Caitlin said. "But they'll find it suspicious if I left you alive."

Katherine tilted her head to the side. "They're going to find it suspicious that I'm not hurt."

Caitlin hesitated. "I didn't mean to get you into this mess. I was just so angry at the king. I couldn't wait."

"It doesn't matter when you decided to do it. The odds are that I would have been present to witness it anyway."

Caitlin sighed. "I know I owe you my life," she said, remembering how the cat had woken her up when Black Blade had tried to kill her and how she'd manipulated the king into executing Campbell so he could no longer harm her. "I'll hand myself over."

"That easily?" Katherine asked. "What happened to the fighter I just saw?"

"I have nothing left to fight for," Caitlin said.

Katherine looked confused. "What do you mean, child?"

"Rafe left me," Caitlin said, aware of how much her voice shook. "He's never going to come back." She looked up and blinked away tears and then dropped her swords to the floor. "My family is dead. The king had them murdered."

"So that's why you did this," Katherine realized. "Not because you are wronged by being turned into a weapon but because of your family."

Caitlin nodded and she couldn't stop the tears. She had been holding them back for too long. Her whole body shook.

"Oh, dear child," Katherine said. She took a step forward and embraced Caitlin. She held her tight and let her cry her heart out. Caitlin's knees gave way. She sank to the cold stone floor and Lady Katherine bent down with her. "I'm so sorry, child."

It sounded sincere. Caitlin hugged her back, and she cried and she cried and she cried.

"They're going to kill me, aren't they?" Caitlin asked moments later. As much as she wanted to, she knew she couldn't cry forever. So she wiped the tears off her pink cheeks and straightened her back.

"I won't let them," Lady Katherine said.

"Well then I am going to be locked up for life."

"We'll figure it out," Katherine said.

The doors bulged once. Caitlin wondered what they were hitting it with.

"I need you to pick up those swords again," Lady Katherine said.

Caitlin did as she was instructed and looked Katherine in the eyes before cutting her arm. She didn't cut it very deep but there was enough blood to make it look bad.

Then Katherine got down on the floor so that it looked like Caitlin was standing over her, ready to strike. Caitlin held her breath, expecting the big doors to give way any moment.

Then the trapdoor lifted. A blond head emerged.

"Dylan?" Caitlin asked.

"Caitlin!" He was out of the tunnel. He looked down at Katherine who lay on the ground with one hand up as if she could block the sword. Then he looked around the room. "What have you done!?" he asked.

She didn't answer. How could she answer? He had no idea how much pain she was in. He had no idea what she was going through.

He drew his sword. "Get away from the king's advisor."

Caitlin turned toward him. "I don't want to fight you."

"So you only fight unarmed men?"

"I like winning," she sneered. There was no honor in

what she did today. She didn't mind. All that mattered was that they were dead and that no one could ever hurt her again.

"This wasn't a victory," he told her, nodding his head toward the carnage around them. "This was butchery."

"Does this mean I am just like you?" she found herself saying.

Dylan flinched and she knew her words had cut deep. "I'm sorry for the things I've done," he confessed.

"I'm not," she said. "My only regret is that they didn't suffer more before they died."

"Who are you?" Dylan found himself asking.

"I'm the monster you let live ten years ago," she told him. "Now, please leave. I don't want to fight you."

He walked closer. He extended his sword. "I can't let you kill her."

"You don't know what you are talking about."

He swung his sword and she blocked. He then kicked away her other sword that was on the ground. She still had daggers strapped to her thighs. She wondered how she looked through his eyes, awash in other men's blood.

"Don't do this, Dylan," she warned. "You cannot beat me."

"I disagree," he said. He knew she was a good fighter. But he had been trained by the best and he had been fighting for years. All of his experience counted against her.

But he didn't want to kill her. He only wanted to get her under control. He knew that the guards would surely behead her once they broke the door down. He didn't want that to happen, but he wasn't sure how he could stop it either.

He swung again. She leaned back and the sword missed her. Then she moved away from Katherine. That came as a surprise to Dylan. He thought she would use her as leverage.

Caitlin didn't attack back. She blocked each of Dylan's blows with ease. She had both hands on her sword's hilt so that she could put all her strength into it when she blocked.

"I'm not the bad guy," she told him. "You don't understand what he's done to me."

Dylan swung again; she sidestepped. "He created you, I know."

"That's not what I meant." She twirled around and Dylan missed again.

"I was at your house," Dylan said. "I know about that too." He could see her pain. He could see how red her eyes were from crying. He knew her pain was unimaginable. "What he did to you wasn't right," he continued. "But slaughtering all these people wasn't right either."

She kicked and got his shin. He cried out. She didn't attack. She stood there and waited for him to recover. "It's too late to undo it," she said.

"Caitlin, you just threw your life away," Dylan said.

"Why?"

"I have nothing left to live for."

"It's a pity you feel that way," Dylan said. "I really don't want to kill you."

He wasn't even sure how it happened. She must have been holding back the whole time. Or maybe she was just toying with him. But suddenly she started fighting back. She swung her sword and he blocked several times. Then she kicked his feet out from under him and he fell onto his back. She could have killed him then and there.

"Get up," she said.

He got to his feet and the fighting resumed.

The doors cracked. The men were almost inside.

The next moment, Caitlin grabbed Dylan's wrist. She twisted the sword away, twirled her body inward, and jammed her elbow into his stomach. His breath left him. Then she threw her head back, straight into his nose. Blood spurted.

Without missing a beat, she bit his hand and he dropped his sword. Then she turned again and kicked him in the torso. He fell onto his back and found her sword aimed at his chest. Both of them were panting.

"I don't want to kill you either," she said as she stepped back.

Then the doors swung open and the guards rushed in.

Dylan watched from the ground as they circled Caitlin. He realized that she could kill all of them and walk out unharmed. But instead of fighting, she dropped her sword and raised her hands in surrender.

"Don't kill her," Lady Katherine ordered. "Throw her in the dungeons."

Katherine and Dylan watched as the guards dragged her out of the throne room and to the dungeons. Caitlin didn't resist.

CHAPTER 40

CAITLIN SAT IN her dungeon cell. All around her were thieves and murderers. She was glad she got a cell all to herself. The guards probably thought she would kill someone if she had to share.

She had one tiny window in her cell and stared out of it, counting the people passing by. She looked up to see the sun coming out behind the clouds. She decided to count all the clouds that formed animal shapes, and then those that formed non-animal shapes. She was bored.

Her hands were cuffed. The cuffs were too tight. They hurt her but she didn't mind. She was tired of fighting.

The guards hurt her when they dragged her in here. They didn't treat her any gentler because she was a woman. They pushed her and pulled her and threw her inside. She scraped her knee in the process. They also called her names but she found it easy to block out their voices.

They didn't feed her. She was probably not worthy of food. She also hadn't had a sip of water since before she barged into the throne room. The last water she drank was the water that the kind gardener had given her. She wondered when she would be executed. The whole castle was probably eager to watch.

As she sat in her cell, she thought about the people she loved and lost. She thought about how she'd fought—and almost always failed—to protect them. She marveled at the fighting skills that came flooding back to her when she needed them most. She realized that the recent traumatic events triggered her memories and awakened her fighting skills.

But she didn't want to relive her brutal past, so she tried to block it out by redirecting her thoughts. She focused on Divan. She had promised to go back and bury him. She couldn't keep that promise. *Well this line of thinking isn't really helping*, she smiled bitterly as she cast about for a more promising topic to keep herself occupied.

Caitlin wondered how much power Katherine lost when the king died. The prince would be crowned king—would he use her as his right hand as his father had done?

Caitlin jerked at her shackles in frustration. Lady

Katherine wouldn't be able to get her out of this mess. The royal family would see her hanged for what she had done.

But Caitlin didn't fear death. After three days in her cell, she actually welcomed it. Things would be easier if she died. It was far preferable to rotting alive in this stinking dungeon.

She heard footsteps approaching and thought it was the guards. She lay prone on a filthy straw pallet with her face toward the window and her back toward the cell door. She didn't want to see them. She didn't want to talk to them. They meant nothing to her.

"I know you're not sleeping," Dylan said.

She didn't expect to hear his voice. He wouldn't have come here just to patronize her, so she decided to hear what he had to say. She rolled over to look at him. "Why are you here?" She hadn't spoken in a while. Her voice was hoarse and she barely recognized it.

"I thought you might be hungry," Dylan said. In his arms were some fruit, meat, bread, and water. He sat down by the cell door. She crawled closer and he handed her the food and water through the bars.

"Why are you helping me?" she asked after downing several gulps of water.

"I guess I feel responsible for you," he confessed. "And I can see how much you are hurting."

"You have no idea how much I am hurting," she said. She took some bread and stuffed it into her mouth. She accepted that she was never going to be a neat eater, especially after being food deprived for days.

"I wish I could help you," Dylan said.

She believed him. His eyes were soft and kind as he looked at her. His hands were caring and giving as he passed her the food.

"I'm fine," she told him. "It will all be over soon."

He didn't look happy at the thought. She wondered if he would miss her when she died. No one else would miss her.

"I've not heard anything about the execution dates."

"Just wait. You will," Caitlin said and glanced at her window. It was getting dark outside. She had made it through another day.

"Actually, the royal family, what's left of it anyway, disappeared from court the day after the king died—and only just resurfaced early this morning."

"They were probably sitting somewhere and debating how to kill me."

"I don't know," Dylan said. "Something is wrong. Katherine has also been missing ever since you killed the king. No one has seen her."

"She's always up to something," Caitlin muttered while chewing a chunk from an apple. She didn't really care about any of them. But at the same time, it was nice having someone to talk to. So she listened to everything Dylan said.

"And I heard from the servants that the prince is acting strangely—has been since he resurfaced."

"How?"

"When he heard his father died, he was crying inconsolably, but today he's behaving as if everything is fine. He seems to be in unusually good spirits."

"Maybe he is just eager to sit on the throne, or excited."

"I don't know..." Dylan said, puzzled.

"Like I said, they were probably plotting something.... Do you... do you think I will have a trial?" she asked, switching to a more pressing topic.

"I don't know," Dylan said again. "I think it's pointless. I don't think anyone will fight for you."

She nodded. This was true. No one would stand up to defend a kingslayer. She finished her meal. "Thank you."

"I'm going to miss you," Dylan told her.

"Why?" she blurted out. He caught her by surprise. She thought he might miss her but didn't think he would actually say it aloud.

"You're my only friend," he confessed.

His words were sweet and sad at the same time. He said she was a friend. If so, they had a weird friendship. Friends don't try to kill each other.

"We're not friends," she told him. She wasn't sure why she pushed him away. Maybe because she felt everyone who came close to her either died or left. She shouldn't have friends.

"Then you're my only almost-friend."

She smiled sadly. "I will miss you too." It was the

truth. She wasn't sure how it happened, but she had grown to care about Dylan. They had a lot in common. His father had turned him into a hunter; the king had turned her into a killer. He had lost his mother; she had lost her family. Both of them knew pain and wanted different lives.

Dylan wished he could break her out of the cell and get her as far away from the castle as possible. He felt he had failed her. So he sat there and kept her company for hours. Every time he got her to smile, it felt like a victory for him. He only left once the guards told him he had to.

CHAPTER 41

THE NEXT MORNING Caitlin woke to the sound of her cell door being unlocked. She looked at the door. Only one guard stood there. She was surprised as it would take much more than one to restrain her.

"You're being let go," the guard said.

"What?" she blurted out.

"Get out," he said.

She couldn't believe her ears. She sprang to her feet and slowly walked out of the cell. She wondered if it was a trick as she cautiously walked out of the dungeon and found more guards waiting for her. Would they kill her in a staged escape attempt? She stopped and stared at them. But no one attacked and none of them had weapons.

"Please follow us to your room," one guard said.

She didn't object. She followed them and they left her standing in front of a door. It was slightly ajar and she pushed it open all the way and stepped inside.

It was luxurious. It had big windows that let the sunlight in. The bed was huge and the sheets looked soft. She had her own bathing chamber, and a walk-in closet was open, displaying a rich collection of clothes in her size.

An elderly lady came in and walked softly across the rug to greet Caitlin. She had wrinkles and freckles but a young smile. "Hello," she said. "I'm Wendy. Lady Katherine employed me as your servant."

"What?" Caitlin gaped.

"She would very much like to speak with you," Wendy added. "She's invited you for lunch."

"What?" Caitlin blurted out again.

"Let's get you all cleaned up and dressed nicely." The old lady went to the bathing chamber where servants had already filled the tub full of hot water.

Caitlin heard Wendy pour some salts into the bath and swish the water around. She eyed her servant's back. Did Wendy know who she was? If she did, why wasn't she scared to turn her back on the king's weapon?

Caitlin had so many questions. She'd fully expected her head to be separated from her shoulders by now. This didn't feel real.

"Your bath is ready," Wendy told her.

Hesitantly, Caitlin walked into the bathing chamber.

There were mirrors everywhere. She hardly recognized herself. The blood on her clothes had dried and left dark red patches that were easily visible. She was covered in dirt.

The tub was big and inviting. Fragrant bubbles burst and steam rose out of the water.

"You can get in, dear," Wendy said.

She hesitated.

"Lady Katherine told me that you've never had a servant before," Wendy said. "If you are more comfortable alone, I can wait in your room."

"That's alright," Caitlin said. She took off her clothes and ignored her sore muscles. She got into the hot water. It felt fantastic. She closed her eyes for a moment.

Wendy was there to help wash her hair for her. No one had ever done this for Caitlin. At first it felt awkward, and then she started to relax. It soothed her to have someone's fingers rub against her scalp.

Wendy rinsed her hair and then helped her wash her body. Caitlin wasn't sure what to do besides sit there.

Wendy held a towel out for her so that she could get out of the water. She did that and Wendy wrapped the towel around her.

"Thank you," Caitlin said as she dried herself. She felt warm and safe and clean. It was nice to look into the mirror.

They made their way to the closet where Wendy helped her choose a dress. It was gorgeous! It was the exact type of dress that Maggie would love. It had a tight purple corset and a wide skirt with bows on it. Caitlin's heart ached when she thought about her little sister.

"Your ears aren't pierced," Wendy observed, "so these will have to do." She gave her clip-on earrings and a necklace. "This one is much nicer than the one you have on now."

"I prefer the one I'm wearing," Caitlin said, clutching Maggie's gift to her collarbone.

Luckily Wendy didn't argue. The necklace Maggie had made for her didn't match the purple dress. It looked childlike and out of place, but Caitlin wasn't going to take it off and replace it with the diamond necklace.

The corset was tight. Caitlin had never worn anything like that before. Although it looked beautiful, she preferred a loose shirt in which she could breathe. She chose flat shoes because she was scared that she would fall over in heels.

"Now you look like a real lady," Wendy remarked.

Caitlin looked at herself in the mirror. Everything looked perfect: her hair, her hands, her skin, her dress.... All she needed was a smile.

Then Wendy ushered her to Lady Katherine's private chambers and opened the doors so Caitlin could walk inside. Then she closed them.

The room was magnificent. It was the size of five other bedrooms. It had a balcony and a huge bed. On the balcony was a long table. On either end of it was a chair. Katherine sat in one of them.

On the table were all sorts of food: pies, chicken, salad, vegetables. There were also all kinds of wine and beautiful goblets.

Caitlin walked out onto the balcony. The sun was shining brightly, warming her skin and drying her hair.

"I'm glad you could join me," Katherine said. "Please take a seat."

Caitlin sat down. "I don't understand what's going on."

"I can imagine you have a thousand questions," Katherine said while scooping some food into her plate. "Please eat."

Caitlin was hungry. She started plating her food but her mind was still racing. "Why am I not dead?"

"The royal family has ordered that you be released," Katherine told her.

Caitlin struggled to believe that. "Did you have something to do with this?"

"Of course," Katherine smiled. "Caitlin, I would like for us to have an honest relationship. I want to be able to trust you and I want you to be able to trust me."

"Alright," Caitlin said.

"So what I am about to tell you is confidential."

"I understand."

"When the king died, things fell apart and I had to fix them. The royal family was outraged. They were going to have you tortured and they would not have killed you for a very long time. Death would have been painfully slow. You would have been in unimaginable agony."

"You saved me once again," Caitlin realized. "How did you convince them to let me go?"

"I put them in the obliteration device," Katherine confessed. "I erased their memories."

"You did what?" Suddenly everything Dylan had told her made sense. She could see why this prince was acting "strange."

"A necessary expedient. There was no other way to save you."

"So what happens now?"

"The prince will become king. I will be his right hand and advisor."

"So your life will stay the same," Caitlin realized.

Katherine nodded. "But yours won't."

"I didn't think it would."

"I would love it if you stayed," Katherine said. "I'll obliterate the minds of the guards so that they don't recognize you. You will be safe and will have a place at my side. You're the perfect ally. No one would dare stand against us."

Caitlin had nothing left in her life. The offer was a good one. She knew Lady Katherine was smart. The prince would now be easier to control than the king ever was.

No wonder Katherine didn't care when Caitlin had killed the king. She had seen her opportunity. Now she would stay secure in her position of power and protect the Magic folk.

"I will stay," Caitlin decided.

CHAPTER 42

WHEN THEY FINISHED eating, Caitlin asked if she could have a week to herself before assuming her new role. She needed time to deal with everything that had happened to her. Lady Katherine told her to take as much time as she needed. She understood that Caitlin's wounds were deep and would take long to heal.

Caitlin made her way back to her room. She changed into a loose tunic, knit leggings, a chunky leather belt, and her own pair of worn moccasins, all in a stone-brown color. Infinitely more comfortable than the courtly attire she wore to her dinner meeting with Lady Katherine. She didn't think she would ever get used to the big fancy dresses.

She knew she would have a lot of time on her hands.

But before she could lie around and do nothing, she had a promise to keep.

Caitlin went back into the tunnels, carrying a shovel. Although it was dark, she knew her way and her eyes adjusted soon enough—so no torch needed.

As she approached the cave entrance, she let her shovel drag behind her and continued walking. She stopped when she saw the sunlight and looked in the direction of Divan's body—but spoke to the person behind her. "Why are you following me?" she asked without turning.

"I was curious to see where you were going," Dylan confessed.

"You know you could have just asked."

"This was more exciting…. When did you realize I was behind you?"

"The moment you followed me into the tunnel."

"I was careful. I didn't think you could hear me."

"How could I not? You tripped once, scraped against the tunnel wall twice, and banged your head into a support beam," she sighed. "I came to bury him."

Divan's body smelled terrible. Caitlin walked outside into the light. She chose a spot and started to dig.

"If you give me the shovel, I can do that," Dylan offered.

"This is something I have to do," she said.

He sat down on the rocks close by and watched her dig. He could see her pain as she slammed the shovel into the ground. "I'm sorry about his death."

She didn't say anything. Dylan did try to kill him and she wouldn't forget that. She dug a little more before she spoke. "Do you think the world is better off with him dead?"

"I think there is already too much death in this world," Dylan said. "But he couldn't have been saved."

"And I can?"

"You can. You are different."

"Not really. I'm just like him. He just spent more time down here and that drove him crazy."

"You wouldn't have gone crazy."

"You don't know that," she said. "I was born and raised just like he was. We're the same kind of monster."

"I understand why you feel that way," he said.

"Why aren't you scared of me?" Caitlin asked. "Everyone else is."

"If you were going to hurt me, you would have done it already."

"That's true," she said. She didn't want to hurt Dylan. He was the only man who was still kind to her. But why was he here? "I think you should leave the castle. Why are you still here anyway?"

"Because I want you to leave with me," he said.

"That's not going to happen," she told him.

The hole in the ground was very big now and it was getting deeper. She worked fast and hard to dig the grave.

"Why not?" he asked. "There's nothing for you here."

"Katherine offered me a position to help her."

"That doesn't sound good," Dylan said. "Katherine always gets what she wants. You should be the exception. She can get someone else to do her dirty work."

"I'm staying," Caitlin said stubbornly.

"It won't be good for you to stay here," Dylan said.

"I have nowhere else to go."

"We can go anywhere you want. We can run away together."

"Someone else already beat you to making me that promise."

"But I won't break it," Dylan said. He walked closer to her. She was standing in the hole so he had to look down at her. He wanted to look into her eyes to convince her that he was different. "Let's bury Divan and get out of here."

Caitlin grasped his outstretched hand and he pulled her out of the hole. They walked over to Divan. Then together they picked up his rotting body and lowered him gently into the grave. Then Caitlin picked up the shovel and silently filled Divan's grave.

"There's nothing out there for me," she said after tamping down the loose earth with her shovel. Sweat and dirt smeared her face, neck, and arms.

"You're so wrong," Dylan said. "You can have whatever you want."

"Do you realize what position I will be in if I stay?"

"A position of power...," Dylan said.

She nodded. "I will be fine here."

"You're choosing to turn into the weapon that the

king wanted you to be."

She shrugged. "It's everything I was meant to be."

"That's not true. You know love and have family. You know what it is like to care. Don't forget who you are when you're trying so hard to be what they want you to be."

"They?"

"The king and Katherine."

"Katherine has no part in this," Caitlin said a bit defensively.

"She is the king's right hand. She wants you because you are powerful. She's greedy that way."

"And that's understandable. You have to have power to do the things she does."

Caitlin turned away from Dylan and started laying down stones to mark the grave. She didn't want to argue with him so she focused all her attention on each stone.

"I can't leave with you, Dylan," she finally said when she finished.

"So you will stay here and help with *whatever* Lady Katherine asks?"

"I will do what I feel is right."

Dylan knew she was afraid. She was afraid of herself and she was afraid of change when change had only ever hurt her. "It's alright to be scared."

"I'm not scared, and I don't feel trapped. I'm *choosing* to stay."

"Then I am staying too," Dylan said.

"Until when?"

"Until you decide that you are ready to leave with me."

Caitlin had no response to that as she stared at Divan's grave. It was such a lonely, secluded spot on the side of a mountain. No one would bring him flowers or mourn his passing.

She sat down and looked at the cliffs and the far-away valleys. It was a beautiful view. Dylan sat quietly by her side and she found his presence comforting.

CHAPTER 43

THEY WALKED BACK through the tunnels, but instead of exiting and going to her newly assigned quarters, Caitlin decided to find Healer Dan. On the way, she told Dylan everything she knew about the tunnels and the things that were happening down there.

"I want to see if Healer Dan has developed a cure for Craybies," she told Dylan.

"Alright, where do we find him?"

"I'm not sure," she said. "I guess somewhere in the MOP area."

They walked to the big steel doors where only one patronizer stood guard. Caitlin thought it wasn't going to let them enter. Dylan thought the same. But when they reached the door, it didn't move. It didn't even look at them as they pushed the door open.

"Maybe Katherine told them that you can come and go as you please," Dylan suggested.

"Maybe," Caitlin said. She wondered if the patronizer knew she had slaughtered its brothers. It didn't look sad or vengeful. It just stood there.

"I think the medical rooms are this way," Caitlin said. She walked to the room where Rafe had been taken when he was hurt.

Dylan followed her. He hadn't been in this section before. He didn't like this place at all and he hated what they were doing here.

"Do you think Katherine will stop what they are doing down here now that the king is dead?" Caitlin asked him.

"No," Dylan said. "I think she likes the power this place gives her."

Caitlin agreed with Dylan. Katherine would only use this place. Who could stop her if she obliterated people's minds and replaced their memories with those of her choosing? If she could control what people were thinking, no one would stand against her.

She had already gone so far as to obliterate the minds of the royal family. They were now her puppets. Who could stop her?

Caitlin wasn't a non-Magic. But she wasn't Magic folk either. She was something in between. Did that mean neither side would want her, or that she could choose a side? If she could, she would definitely choose the winning side. Katherine's side.

She found Healer Dan in what appeared to be his office. He was sitting at a desk going through paperwork. She knocked on the open door and he looked up.

"Caitlin," he said, surprised. "I didn't expect to see you here ever again."

"I didn't think I'd come back." She remembered everything. She remembered the things this man did to her. She considered killing him.

"And you brought a friend," he observed.

"I'm Dylan Archer." Dylan realized she wasn't going to introduce him so he did so himself and shook the healer's hand.

"You're the hunter I've heard so much about," said the healer.

"Yes," Dylan said tightly.

Dylan used to feel pride when people recognized who he was and what he did. Caitlin wondered if he now felt shame. When the truth came out about his mother, he changed. He became much humbler and more cautious. Caitlin thought he was trying to save her in an attempt to redeem himself. She didn't feel she needed any saving.

"Can I help the two of you?" the healer asked. He looked at Dylan. "You are welcome to take a seat, if you want to."

"Thank you," Dylan said as he sat down across the desk from the healer.

Caitlin didn't sit. Not because she didn't want to

CRY OF THE SHIFTERS

get the chair dirty but because she didn't feel comfortable in this particular room. "I came to see if you were making progress with the cure," she said.

"It's all done," the healer said with a smile. He opened his desk drawer and pulled out a bottle with liquid inside. The orange liquid sloshed around. "This is one of many antidotes. The antidote has to come in contact with the infected shifters' bloodstream. It will take time to have an effect, but it will cure the shifter."

"That's some fast work," Dylan observed.

"Brilliant," Caitlin smiled.

"Thank you."

"Has Katherine given orders to start using it?" Caitlin asked.

"She has," the healer said. "She has distributed it to many people so they can start using it on those infected with Craybies."

"I'd like to help distribute the cure," Dylan said. "Even if I just use it in areas that are close to the castle for now."

"I can't just give this to you," the healer replied. "Go speak to Lady Katherine. With her permission, I will hand it over."

"We're not asking for permission," Caitlin growled. She met his eyes and could tell that he was frightened. "Hand it over."

The healer gulped nervously. He didn't want to fight because he knew he couldn't win. So he handed the bottle to Dylan.

"How many more bottles of cure are there?" Caitlin asked.

"Many," the healer said. "And many more are being made."

Dylan had learned the truth about everything from Caitlin as they were walking through the tunnels. He had listened in silence and sensed that she trusted him. "So tell me," Dylan said. "How is it that you created this disease?"

"It wasn't intentional," the healer said, startled into confirming their suspicions. "Before the obliteration device was built, we tried to develop a serum that would work like the device. We used it on a shifter, but instead of giving us control over his mind, it made him mad. He escaped and infected others."

"You've killed hundreds of shifters," Caitlin said.

"It wasn't intentional," the healer said again. "None of us knew the serum would make them crazy and violent."

"It doesn't fix what you did," Caitlin said.

"We are trying to right that wrong now," the healer defended himself.

Caitlin could be at his side in a flash and snap his neck. She wanted to do it. But Katherine would be displeased if she did....

"I'm leaving," she told Dylan.

He followed her out of the room.

CHAPTER 44

TWO DAYS PASSED. Caitlin spent her time going for long walks and sleeping. Dylan came to find her each day and they talked and laughed. He made her feel better.

"Since Lady Katherine gave me permission to distribute the cure, I've been riding all around the castle grounds," he said. "I've found more shifters than I thought I would. This disease not only makes them crazy but it also makes them forget that they are in danger here."

"And you cured them?" she asked.

He nodded. "Yes. I have laced my arrows with it–"

"So you shoot them?!" she asked in shock.

"It's the only way to get it into their blood without getting too close," he confessed. "I just shoot in the shoulder or somewhere it won't kill them."

"I'm glad your aim is so good!" she chuckled.

"You should join me sometime," he suggested.

"I don't feel like it." She didn't feel like doing anything. She'd been spending most of her time she lying around being unproductive and getting lost in her own mind.

"Come on!" he said. "It will be fun! Can you shoot a bow and arrow?"

"Of course I can shoot!" she snapped. "I'm a weapon, remember?"

"How could I forget?"

"I think I can teach you a thing or two at the shooting range."

"Challenge accepted."

Dylan fetched his bow and Caitlin decided to buy one for herself. Katherine had given her a lot of spending money. Caitlin had done nothing to deserve this money. Maybe she should have felt guilty for taking it, but she did not. So armed with her brand-new bow and a quiver full of arrows, Caitlin walked with Dylan to the target range.

"Do I need to go easy on you?" Dylan teased.

"It doesn't matter," she smiled. "You'll lose either way."

She was glad that he was here. He made her feel less alone and he distracted her from her thoughts and nightmares. She wasn't good at making friends and she didn't feel the need to make new ones. They couldn't replace the old ones. Dylan was enough.

He shot the first arrow at the closest target and hit the bullseye. Then he lowered his bow and grinned at her.

"I see you chose the easiest target," she pointed out as she aimed and shot for a target that was farther away. Her arrow hit the bullseye as well. Now it was her turn to grin.

"Show off," he said and pulled out another arrow and aimed. He let it go and hit the center of a target a little bit farther away from hers.

She aimed for that same target. Her arrow struck his, splintering his into two pieces as her arrow's tip sank into the bullseye. He glared at her. She shrugged and then smiled. "The one who hits the farthest target wins," she told him.

He aimed. The target was very far. His arrow came to a stop. It hit just outside the bullseye.

"My turn," she said. She drew her arrow and breathed in. But right before she released, Dylan shoved her. The arrow flew free and fell wide off the target.

"Ha-ha. You lose," Dylan said with a wink.

She turned to him and hit him playfully with the bow. "That's cheating!"

"Ow, don't hit me!"

Caitlin laughed. It felt like she hadn't laughed in forever. It felt good. "And here I thought you were a very serious person," she remarked.

"I am a serious person," he said and tried to keep his face blank.

She laughed again. They walked away from the targets. She thought they each would go their separate ways, but instead Dylan decided he wanted to spend more time with her. "What do you want to do now?" he asked.

"Do I have to do something?" she asked him.

"Well you can't sleep anymore. It's all you've been doing."

"That's not true," she objected.

"Oh yeah? What else have you been doing?"

"I've been going for walks."

"To get food from the kitchen?" He smiled teasingly.

She glared at him. "It's a far walk to the kitchen!"

"So why don't you just ask your servants to bring food to your room?"

"It feels weird to tell others what to do," she confessed.

"Speaking of that... Has your boss told you to do anything yet?"

"She's not my boss," Caitlin glared. "And no, I haven't seen much of her lately."

"She's probably busy planning the Freedom Ball."

"The what?" Caitlin asked.

"Do you know what Freedom Day is?" Dylan asked.

"It's the day the Witch King died." Caitlin remembered that Gerald had told her this. "It's celebrated as a holiday now."

"Correct," Dylan said. "The royal family hosts a ball to which only the most important people are invited. Even our neighboring kingdom's royal family will come."

"The Forevermore Kingdom's royals will come here?" she said. "That's far to travel."

"They are probably on their way already," Dylan said. "I thought you might be invited."

"ME?" she said. "But I killed our king..."

"Shh!" he warned. "Someone might hear you."

She gave him a look that suggested she didn't care.

"No one knows it was you," Dylan told her. "Katherine completely covered it up. Not even the guards who dragged you away know you as the kingslayer. I've asked around but no one knows the truth. No one knows who killed the king."

Caitlin gaped at him. How many people did Lady Katherine obliterate? How easy had this been for her? And why would she go through all that effort to save Caitlin?

"She either really cares about you or she wants you badly for something," Dylan said.

"There's nothing I can give her.... I can fight and I am the best... but still... Do you think she did all of this just to have me in her service?"

"I don't know what the king's right hand wants— you need to be careful," Dylan cautioned her.

CHAPTER 45

IT WAS GETTING dark outside when Caitlin returned to her room. Dylan suggested they stay out a little longer but she was still not feeling up for it. She flopped down on her bed and stared at the ceiling.

She frowned at the knocking on her door and was about to tell whoever it was to go away, but the door opened before she could say anything.

Lady Katherine entered, her long dress dragging on the floor behind her as she walked. "Hello Caitlin," she said, closing the door behind her.

"Hello," Caitlin said, sitting up.

"I came to see you earlier today," Lady Katherine said.

"I was practicing archery," she said. "I only just got back."

"Were you practicing with Dylan?" she asked.

Caitlin nodded.

"That's good. He's a nice young man and very loyal too."

Caitlin didn't say anything. It was weird that Katherine treated her like a friend when she spoke down to most people. With Caitlin she was much more laid back. Katherine sat down on the bed next to Caitlin and gave her a warm smile. Her long nails scratched the soft blankets on the bed.

"What is it you came to talk to me about?" Caitlin asked.

"I came to see how you are doing," Katherine said. "I know I haven't been around much."

"I understand," Caitlin said. "You are a very busy woman."

"Sometimes too busy," Katherine said. She was still smiling gently. "So, tell me, how are you doing?"

"As good as I can be," Caitlin confessed.

"Are you comfortable? Is there anything you would like me to change?" Katherine asked as she looked around the big luxurious room.

It was messy. Caitlin hadn't given her clothes to the washer woman—they covered the floor. Her bed was unmade and there were cookie crumbs on the counter. Caitlin liked her privacy and shooed away the servants who tried to clean in the mornings.

"I'm all good," Caitlin said. She now regretted not keeping the place cleaner.

"How's your heart feeling?' Katherine asked the sensitive personal question.

"Not that good," Caitlin confessed.

Katherine put a comforting hand on her arm. Caitlin looked at it, but she didn't pull away. "I can always help you with those memories."

Caitlin met her eyes. Her chest felt tight but she didn't cry. She had no tears left.

"It's a simple procedure," Katherine said. "The obliteration device has proven to be both safe and very effective."

"I don't know..." Caitlin said. Was it weird that she was actually considering it? She had done it to herself once before and it had helped with the emotional trauma. Sometimes it was just better to forget.

"You don't have to, of course. It's your choice. I'll only take away what you want me to."

"Part of me wants to take you up on that offer," Caitlin said. "I sometimes want nothing more than to forget my parents. I try to stay away from Maggie because seeing her only brings back the pain. And the more I try not to think about Rafe, the more I wind up thinking about him."

"It's normal to feel this way," Katherine told her.

"But the pain and the memories are all that I have left of them. I can't risk losing those."

Katherine nodded. "I'm here whenever you need to talk."

"Thank you," Caitlin said. "Katherine, are we friends?"

"I'd like us to be," Katherine said. "I'll need your help running the kingdom."

"What kind of help?"

"Well, there are a lot of people who want to bring us down. There are a lot of people who still defy my authority. We have enemies in our kingdom and in others. It's good to keep them in their place."

"What is it you expect me to do?"

"For now, I just want you to be loyal to me," Lady Katherine said. She made eye contact. "Can you do that? Loyalty is in your nature after all."

"You saved my life. You gave me a place to stay, and you cleared my name," Caitlin listed the things Katherine had done for her. "Of course I am loyal to you."

Katherine smiled. She was pleased. "There's one more thing I want now of you," she said.

"What's that?"

"Your support with the obliteration device."

Caitlin swallowed and looked down.

"I know it is a hard one for you. I know it is a sensitive subject. But that device gives me the power to keep peace throughout the kingdom."

"By erasing people's minds," Caitlin said.

"By filling their minds with the right thoughts," Katherine said.

"What about the experiments down there? The device works. You no longer have use for the subjects you still keep."

"What do you want me to do with them?" Lady Katherine asked.

Caitlin thought about this and answered, "Send them home."

"I can do that. I can make sure all of them get home safely. But I will have to wipe their memories of this place."

Caitlin didn't like that but she understood why it was necessary.

"It's no different than what you did to Maggie," Katherine said.

"I know."

"So if I do this, if I right the wrongs that Campbell did... Will you support me in my use of the obliteration device?"

"Yes, you'll have my support," Caitlin said.

"Good," Katherine smiled. "Feel free to visit the MOP area of the tunnels anytime. Then you will see with your own eyes that I keep my word."

"I'll do that," Caitlin smiled.

Katherine stood up from the bed. "There's one more thing."

"What is it?" Caitlin asked.

Katherine pulled an envelope from her purse. It displayed the royal family's seal and Caitlin's name.

"What is this?" she asked as she took the envelope.

"An invitation to the Freedom Ball," Katherine said.

"You're inviting me?" Caitlin gaped. "But—"

"But nothing," Katherine smiled. "It's important for

me that you come. You are welcome to bring an escort."

"I'll ask Dylan," she said quickly.

"Caitlin, this ball is going to be much more exciting than ever before," Katherine said, her eyes gleaming. "Come prepared."

Caitlin wasn't sure what she meant but nevertheless smiled as she watched Katherine leave.

CHAPTER 46

THE NEXT MORNING Caitlin woke up feeling excited. She was aware that it was a great honor to be invited to the Freedom Ball.

She decided to shop for a new ball gown. It took her forever to find the perfect dress. It was red with black twine that tied the corset together. It was strapless and had little diamonds sewn into its skirt so that it shimmered whenever she moved.

Caitlin found black heels to match the dress. They were really high and she would have to practice every day to walk in them. They hurt her feet, but she didn't mind.

Katherine had given her more than enough money to live comfortably. She hadn't earned it—yet. But she would. Her week of resting was almost up.

It was late evening when she completed her shopping

and went home. She was pacing in her room while wearing her new shoes. She observed herself in her full-length mirror.

Someone knocked and she turned her head in the direction of the door. "Come in."

The door opened and Dylan stepped in. He looked her up and down, his eyes lingering on her heels. He had never seen her wear shoes like those before. "Where have you been?" Dylan asked her. "I couldn't find you this morning."

"I went shopping," she told him.

Dylan gaped at her. "Are you feeling alright?" he asked, reaching for her forehead.

"I'm fine!" she said as she laughed and dodged his hand. She felt happy. She twirled around and forgot that she wasn't used to the new shoes. She stumbled and Dylan stepped forward. He was only just fast enough to catch her. She giggled.

He smiled and pulled her upright. "I never thought I would see you in shoes as ridiculous as those."

"I know," she said. "It's only this one time."

"What's happening?' Dylan asked.

"Katherine invited me to the Freedom Ball."

Dylan's jaw dropped. "No way!"

"Yes way!" she said. She considered twirling again but didn't want to embarrass herself again. So instead she just paced around.

"I thought that was only for royals, lords, and noblemen."

"And us."

"Us?" he asked.

"You are my date," she told him as she performed a mock curtsy.

"Usually you ask someone to be your date," he said, laughing in response.

"If I ask, it means you have the option to say no. So I decided to tell you instead."

"Gee, I'll have to think about it…. I'm awfully busy."

She punched him gently on the shoulder.

"Alright! I suppose I'll have to go with you!"

"Good," she smiled.

"I'll need to go buy clothes."

"My dress is red," she told him so that his clothes would match.

"Are you coming to shop with me?" he asked.

"No," she said. "I'm going down to the tunnels. Katherine told me she would send all of the experiments home."

"That's a surprise," Dylan said. "I didn't think she would put in the time or effort for them."

"She cares about everyone—Magic and non-Magic alike."

Dylan made a sound in the back of his throat. He wasn't sure if he believed that. But he didn't argue with Caitlin either. "I'll swing by tonight."

"Are you bringing dinner?" she asked.

"Of course! It's the least I can do in return for your spectacular invitation." He grinned and exited her quarters, whistling as he went.

Caitlin took off her shoes and placed them in the closet. She admired them briefly before putting on her boots and leaving her room.

She walked to the closest tunnel entrance and made sure that no one was watching before she entered. As always, the tunnels were dark. She stood still for a little while to allow her eyes to adjust before she started walking in the direction of the MOP.

The patronizer guarding the steel doors let her pass undeterred. She wondered what would happen to them. Should she have bargained for their lives as well? She eyed the emotionless, soulless creature as she walked past it and decided that there was no life inside of it to save.

She turned right and walked toward the dining hall. The children were having lunch. There were already fewer than usual. She walked to the adult's dining room. There were also not many of them left. Lady Katherine had kept her word.

Caitlin decided to cut her tour of the MOP area short. She didn't like being there. It stirred up painful memories that she was trying to forget. She skipped having a look at the obliteration device. She could still remember how she had flipped its switches when she wasn't sure how it worked. She could still remember throwing herself inside it. She hadn't been sure what it would do to her back then and had felt that death would have been better than being taken back to her cell by the patronizers.

Caitlin's thoughts wandered to Campbell. He had never approved of her. He'd always known she was too dangerous and too unpredictable. The strange thing was that after killing the king, she understood why Campbell had wanted her dead.

Caitlin wondered if it would have been better if she had died. She'd felt so alone and purposeless. Maybe that was one of the reasons she had chosen to stay with Lady Katherine—to have a purpose in life.

Caitlin returned to her quarters and patiently waited for Dylan to come and make her feel better.

CHAPTER 47

THE DAYS PASSED quickly with Dylan there to entertain her. Dylan even convinced her to go riding around the castle armed with arrows laced with the cure. They had a great time horseback riding but unfortunately didn't find any shifters.

On their way back to the castle, they saw plenty of guards that they had never seen before. They wore different armor and were standing around a carriage. The carriage was pulled by four massive shire horses, their coats a gleaming black and their legs thickly fringed with collars of white hair, clean and free of any traces of dust and mud. Caitlin wondered how it got up the steep mountain road. The carriage's door was opened by the driver and the royal family got out —the royal family from the Forevermore Kingdom.

First came the king, Arson Reid. He was reed-thin and walked with a limp from an old war injury to his right knee. He sported a bald spot on his head and cultivated a long beard to compensate for it. He stood upright and his clothes were beautifully tailored.

Next, Queen Helena Reid got out of the carriage. She took her husband's hand with jeweled fingers and stepped out cautiously with her high, high heels. Her dress was a radiant pink. Her long hair was piled up high in the latest fashion and powdered beneath a tall and elaborately feathered hat. Her entire ensemble made her look much taller than she actually was.

Last to emerge was their daughter, Princess Eugenie Reid. She was only a kid, but she was dressed like an adult. Her dress was a similar style as her mother's. She also wore heels higher than Caitlin could walk in. But unlike her mother, her long hair hung loose and unpowdered over her shoulders.

People bowed as the royal family made their way in stately fashion to the throne room. The guards stood at attention as the royal procession passed and then closed the gilded doors behind them.

"They always arrive a day before the ball," Dylan told Caitlin. "Then they are greeted and welcomed in the throne room before they are given the finest sleeping quarters in the castle."

"Who is that?" Caitlin asked, pointing to a man who stood beside the carriage. He wore a hood over his face and was as still as a statue. He was very tall—

taller than Dylan—and his arms were big and more muscular. Caitlin squinted to see what she could of the face under the hood: she thought she saw heavy scars around his mouth.

"He is the Reid's protector and assassin," Dylan said. "His name is Flynn Slayer. He has worked for the royal family ever since he was a boy after they'd freed him from slavery."

"He doesn't look like someone I'd want to tangle with."

"I agree," Dylan said. "No one has ever beaten him in combat. He goes everywhere the royal family goes. They only send him away on occasion."

"What occasions?"

"When he has to go kill somebody," Dylan replied.

Caitlin studied the man. He was staring at the throne room's doors as if they were about to be blown from their hinges. Everyone kept their distance around him. Everyone was cautious. His presence even made Dylan uneasy.

Caitlin wondered if she could beat him in a fair fight. Then she wondered if it was weird that she wanted to try. "Do you think I can challenge him to a duel?" she asked Dylan.

He stared at her. "Are you serious?"

She nodded. "I can't help but wonder who would win."

"Caitlin, he is twice your size!"

"Size isn't everything," Caitlin said. "So, can I challenge him to a duel?"

"You can," Dylan said. "But do it after the ball.... I don't want my date to be full of bruises."

She smiled. "After the ball it is then."

"I'm sure the whole kingdom would show up to see that," Dylan laughed.

"You don't think I'll do it?"

"Oh, I think you will do it." Dylan said.

The two of them went to unsaddle their horses. It was time for lunch and so they headed to a bakery reputed to have the most delicious chicken pie in the kingdom.

After lunch, their bellies full and their spirits high from joking and happy conversation, they raced each other around Sky Castle's battlement walls, hopping from merlon to merlon over crenelation after crenelation. Dylan bobbled to regain his balance every so often and his legs quivered a bit as he looked down the steep walls and sheer cliffside, nervous about the height and the thought of falling. But Caitlin relished the thrill as she confidently and gracefully hurdled over each four-foot gap in the stone walls without hesitation or pause, her laughter echoing down the sheer cliffside.

After an hour of risky fun, they finally slowed to a leisurely pace. Caitlin steered them away from her and Rafe's tower and they wandered in the other direction instead. They sat on the wall until dark, chatting away and gazing at the stars.

"There's a shooting star!" Dylan said, touching her arm.

She looked in time to see it arc across the sky. It was beautiful, bright, and fast. "Make a wish," she told Dylan.

"I'll give you my wish," Dylan said.

She thought about it. She knew what she wanted most, the one thing she would never have again. She wished for Rafe to come back.

"What did you wish for?" Dylan asked.

"I can't tell you that," she said.

"Why?"

"Because then it won't come true."

"Nonsense! It was my wish, so you can tell me."

"I just wished that I will beat Flynn Slayer when I challenge him to a duel," she lied.

It was getting late, so the two of them climbed off the battlements and headed back to their rooms. As always, Dylan walked with Caitlin to hers. On the way there, they passed the hallway that led to the Reid family's suite of rooms.

Caitlin stopped in her tracks. For a moment she thought that she saw a red cape—the cape of a patronizer. It disappeared down the hallway as she blinked.

"What is it?" Dylan asked.

"I thought I saw something," she said, and then she second-guessed herself. "It's probably nothing."

Caitlin said goodnight to Dylan and stayed awake in bed. She struggled to sleep. An uneasy feeling kept her awake as Katherine's words kept replaying in her mind....

"*Caitlin, this ball is going to be much more exciting than ever before,*" Katherine had said. "*Come prepared.*"

CHAPTER 48

CAITLIN DIDN'T SLEEP in the next morning. She had risen early wishing she had slept more because the hours preceding the Freedom Ball crawled at a snail's pace that tried her patience and drained some of her usually boundless energy.

On a positive note, she managed to spend time with Dylan who was happy to see her talking and laughing more. Caitlin couldn't believe how excited she was for the ball that night. She never thought she would go to such a grand event. She felt a little nervous too, partly because she didn't know anyone there.

By the time that Wendy arrived to help her prepare, Caitlin was in such a good mood that she talked to the servant much more than usual. Wendy curled her hair and tied it up on her head, letting strands fall on either side of her face.

Caitlin held onto the bedpost as Wendy tied her corset, pulling in her stomach when she felt the laces fasten snugly. She stepped into her shoes and Wendy bent down to tie their diamond straps. Once everything was tied, strapped, buttoned, and otherwise affixed into place, Wendy took a step back to observe Caitlin and then beckoned her to look at herself in the mirror. The red silk dress fit her perfectly, hugging every curve of her body yet giving her enough room to breathe and move. Its skirt came together in two rectangular panels: the front panel was separated from the back panel at mid-thigh by two long slits traveling up each leg. The ensemble was both glamorous and functional as it allowed her to stride as freely as she dared.

"You look magnificent!" Wendy said, clapping her hands. "Now, off you go, and enjoy the ball!"

"Thank you for all your help. And please go home so you can enjoy your evening too!"

"Yes, I will. Thank you!" Wendy said.

Caitlin smiled with her red lips. She exited the room, her heels clicking smartly on the stone floors. She was on her way to meet Dylan and was half-thinking about how he would react to her glammed-up look. Then she slowed to a stop.

"Caitlin, this ball is going to be much more exciting than ever before," Katherine had said. *"Come prepared."*

Caitlin thought about that. *Come prepared. What did she mean?*

She thought about seeing the patronizer walking down the hall outside the Reid's guest quarters. It had happened so fast. Had she really seen it? They never leave the tunnels.

Caitlin decided to go back to her room. She strapped daggers to each of her thighs, just in case. She secured their holsters high enough on her thighs to be hidden by her skirt but still be easily accessible through the two long slits between her skirt's front and back panels. She sent a silent thanks to the talents of the gown's designer before stepping outside.

Dylan was already waiting. He looked handsome as he absentmindedly stared up at the clouds. His arms were crossed and he was leaning against a tree. His suit was black and his neckerchief was red.

"Are you dozing off?" she asked to distract him from the fact that she was a little bit late.

He snapped back to reality and turned his head to her. Then his jaw dropped—actually dropped. Caitlin couldn't help it. She blushed.

"It does feel like I'm in a dream," he confessed. "You look..." he trailed off.

She smiled. "Yes?"

"I—I don't have the words." He laughed nervously.

She'd never heard him sound nervous before. She had also never seen him look at her like that—like she was the only girl in the world. He extended his arm and she took it with one hand.

"Do you have the... uh... uh..."

"Invitation?" she supplied, quirking an eyebrow up. "Yes, I do." She smiled, pleased with the impression she'd made.

The two of them walked to the ballroom. It wasn't far to walk. Everyone they passed stared at them. People stopped what they were doing to look.

"They're staring at us," Caitlin pointed out.

"They're staring at you!" Dylan corrected.

Caitlin realized that he was right. Even the women were looking at her enviously. She wondered who they thought she was. Maybe they thought she was a rich duchess. For once she didn't mind the attention. She was flattered. She walked beside Dylan and felt like the most beautiful woman in the world. She blushed as she realized that he couldn't keep his eyes off her. Every time she looked at him, he would look quickly away and mumble something about how pretty she was.

The ballroom was beautiful. It was very spacious with tables arranged around a dance floor. Each table was ladened with flowers and food and wine. The dance floor was big and people were already dancing, although the ball wasn't officially opened yet. Music, talking, and laughter filled her ears. A big glittering chandelier hung from the ceiling and trembled slightly in resonance with each percussive beat.

The royal family's table stood apart from the others and was raised on a dais. Caitlin wasn't surprised to see that Flynn Slayer had assumed his position and was already standing guard on one side of the dais. The royals weren't there yet. They would wait until everyone had shown up and taken their seats before they made their entrance.

Caitlin handed her invitation to a man who was directing people to their tables. He looked at it and ushered them to their table.

"I don't think I know anyone here," Caitlin whispered to Dylan.

She wondered if he was as nervous as she felt. If he was nervous, he didn't show it. He walked with confidence and nodded to some of the lords they passed.

"I know some by reputation," Dylan said, nodding and smiling to a lord sporting a perfectly trimmed and waxed imperial mustache. "The same way most of them know me."

"You've not spent a lot of time at the castle, have you?" she asked.

"No," Dylan confessed. "There aren't enough shifters here, so my father and I hunted far away in the countryside. I did always want to see the castle, but I never thought I would stay here as long as I am now."

"Are you happy here?" Caitlin realized just how

selfish she had been this past week. With everything that had happened, she only ever thought of herself and how much her heart was hurting. She relied on Dylan to make her smile but never wondered if he was happy.

"I am," Dylan said. "But I don't want to stay here forever."

She spun her head toward him and looked at him with wide eyes. She held on a little tighter to his arm—as if that could stop him from running away.

"Relax," he laughed. "When I leave, you are coming with."

"I don't think I will leave anytime soon," she said. "Besides, where would I go?"

"We can always travel the Silver Kingdom," Dylan said. "I've been everywhere so I can take you to all the most beautiful places. Pretty villages filled with cottage gardens... green woodland where thousand-year-old oaks grow... crystal clear lakes beneath waterfalls deep in hidden canyons... We'll visit every hill and valley, every mountain and farmland, every village both small and large, until you decide where you want to stay and what you want to do."

"It sounds like a fairy tale," she confessed.

"So what's holding you back then?"

"Fairy tales don't exist," she said.

He pulled her chair back from the table and she took her seat. There were six other chairs at their table. Four of them were already taken. Caitlin's first instinct was to be quiet and avoid eye contact with the others, but Dylan introduced himself and kissed the ladies' hands.

He also introduced Caitlin. She managed a smile. She was aware that both men were gaping and their women were glaring. Dylan sat down beside her. Caitlin stared at her place setting: a goblet, a plate, and on either side of that plate, more cutlery than she knew what to do with.

Dylan noticed her wide eyes and whispered, "Just start from the outside and work your way in."

She managed a small smile and then looked up. A line had formed at the door.

Dylan made small talk with the people sitting at their table. He was so comfortable and fit in so easily. Caitlin never knew what to say to strangers. She didn't have a need to talk to them either. So she simply sat back and observed.

Dylan noticed how quiet she had gotten. "Would you like to dance?" he asked her.

"The dance floor hasn't been opened by the royal family yet," she pointed out.

"Let's be adventurous and break the rules," Dylan smiled, elbowing her ribs.

He didn't have to ask twice. She got up and followed him to the dance floor. It was an upbeat tune that was familiar to most of the guests.

"Dylan, I just realized something," she said.

"What?" he asked.

"I don't know how to dance."

He smiled at her and chuckled. "It's really easy. First, I bow and you curtsy."

She looked at him and did what he said. She was glad that Wendy had taught her how to curtsy. Then he reached his hand out. She took it and he pulled her in. His arm wrapped around her waist and he pulled her closer. She could feel his breath on her cheek.

"Now, you just follow me," he said.

He took a step forward. She took one backward. Slowly she started feeling the rhythm. She became less tense and started smiling. It really was easy. He twirled her in a circle again and again. She got drunk on music and laughter.

They went back to their seats when the music ended. Everyone else did the same, and slowly the chattering died down as all heads turned toward the door.

Prince Reagan and Queen Isabella walked into the room. They were followed by Lady Katherine who wore an elegant black dress. They smiled at the people as they made their way to the royal table.

On the one side of the table, Flynn Slayer stood guard. On the other side, the Silver Kingdom's guard stood. He was half the size of Flynn and looked comical by comparison.

"Good evening, ladies and gentlemen," the prince said.

He was very young and he looked like his father. Caitlin saw how he nervously fidgeted with his hands and guessed that he hadn't given a speech like this before. He would be crowned king soon. She hoped he would be a better king than his father.

"Thank you very much for joining us on this fine evening. It is now my great honor to welcome the Reid family from the Forevermore Kingdom," Prince Reagan said in a stilted voice and then managed a tight smile.

The people clapped as Arson, Helena, and Eugenie walked into the room and made their way up the dais to take their places at the royal's table.

"Today we celebrate our freedom. It is a day set aside to remember that evil has been banished and replaced by good. It is a day we celebrate because of the best man I know: my father. He cannot be here to dine with us tonight, but he is always in our hearts." The prince paused dramatically. Caitlin wondered if he was speaking from the heart or if someone else had written his speech for him. "Let the feast begin!"

The people clapped and cheered and the music resumed. Caitlin sat back, ready for the party to begin, ready to enjoy the night, ready for the music, the dancing, the food and wine.

Caitlin did not expect Lady Katherine to get to her feet; no one did. Everyone else at her table was seated and they stared up at her as she rose.

Lady Katherine had a bandage wrapped around the arm that Caitlin had cut. She cleared her throat and the music died down. The chattering stopped and all attention turned to her. This was unexpected. The king's right hand was not supposed to give a speech.

"Ladies and gentlemen," she said. "I know there have been many questions about the king's death that haven't been answered." She had everyone's attention. "I know many of you have been wondering how I witnessed it and didn't give you someone to blame."

King Arson Reid chuckled as if he knew something no one else did. Caitlin couldn't tear her eyes away from Katherine.

"Many of you think that I am hiding someone and protecting them. Everyone knows that killing the king is an unforgivable crime. A most heinous act of treason. Many of you think I don't know who it was. Well the truth is... I do know."

The people started whispering. Dylan's spine stiffened next to Caitlin and she realized that she was gripping his hand because she was nervous. She loosened her grip slightly but she did not let go. There was no way that Lady Katherine had brought her here just to give her up. That didn't make sense.

Caitlin tried to make eye contact, but Katherine was avoiding it. Her stomach turned. She couldn't move. Her heart was hammering.

Lady Katherine Black waited for the whispering to die down before she continued speaking. "I cannot keep the unbearable truth to myself any longer. I have to tell all of you that the king's killer is in the room right here and right now."

CHAPTER 49

LADY KATHERINE POINTED. Caitlin's hand went to her chest as if asking, "Are you pointing to me?"

It sure looked like it.

Then she realized that Lady Katherine was not pointing at her but at Flynn Slayer who was standing in front of their table.

Some people got to their feet. Others gasped. Some cried out in shock. The Reid family went dreadfully pale.

"That is a lie!" Queen Helena cried.

"I was there," Lady Katherine said. "I saw him with my own eyes. He spared me because he thought that I would switch sides and aid them in the war they were going to start. They have been preparing their armies to attack."

"Lies!" Queen Helena cried again.

"Think about it, ladies and gentlemen." Katherine said. "Flynn shows up and kills our king and all of his men. The castle is weakened—"

"He traveled with us here!" Helena cried. "Everyone saw him!"

"Thank you for the prompt," Lady Katherine said. "So how did he do it? How did he manage to travel so fast, to appear to be two places at once?" She paused. "The answer is simple: Magic."

The crowd gasped.

Katherine continued. "We've all known for years now that the Reid family are Magic sympathizers. All those years ago they only showed up to 'aid' us after the war against Magic had been won! Ever since King Leonard took the throne, they have been trying to bring us down. They want the throne for themselves."

"This isn't true!" Helena cried. "Arson, say something!"

King Reid sat beside her in silence. His face was white.

"It is my duty to inform you all that the royal ring was stolen from the king's finger after he was murdered," Katherine said. "The person who him killed would have that ring." She turned to King Reid. "Prove me wrong," she said. "Turn out your pockets."

Everyone was staring at the Forevermore king now. His lips were pressed together in a tight line as he glared at Katherine. He stuck his hand into his pocket and pulled out the royal ring.

The crowd gasped.

Then he did something unexpected. He looked around like a crazy person. "It's a trick! She's messing with my mind!" Then his eyes found Flynn Slayer. "Kill her!"

The guards were too far away. They would never be able to reach Katherine in time. The one guard that stood by the table tried to defend Katherine but Flynn cut his head off before he could even draw his sword. Even if the other guards managed to get to the dais, Flynn would kill all of the Silver Kingdom's royalty, including its right hand.

But Caitlin was unnaturally fast. She knocked her chair over as she jumped up and moved toward Flynn like lightning. His eyes were fixed on Katherine and he was swinging his sword, so he didn't see Caitlin coming.

Katherine held her hands out in front of her as if she could block the sword. She knew she couldn't outrun or fight the big henchman.

Caitlin knew she didn't have the weight to knock such a big man over. So she slammed into his arm instead, spoiling his swing and giving Katherine the time to step back and out of reach and call for the guards to come.

Flynn grabbed Caitlin with his other hand, easily pulling her body weight forward. She wasn't used to wearing such heels so she tripped when he did this and fell to the floor. He brought his sword down, but she rolled off to the side as it slammed into the stone floor.

Caitlin kicked his shin with her stiletto heel, losing the shoe in the process. He cried out and stabbed at her again. She rolled once more.

Hobbling on just one heel, Caitlin felt really off-balance. Dodging the sword again, she managed to pull her remaining shoe off and then threw it at his face. It collided with his nose. He cried out and stepped back, giving her enough time to get back to her feet.

The guards were in the room now. Caitlin thought they were going to interfere until–"Don't!"–Katherine stopped them.

Caitlin nodded her thanks. She wanted this fight and she wanted to fight alone and fair. She was ready for it.

The crowed formed a wide ring around the two fighters. All of them wanted to watch; none of them wanted to join. Caitlin was glad that they stayed out of her way.

Flynn brandished his sword. She still had the two daggers strapped to her thighs. She reached into the slits in her dress and pulled both free of their holsters. The daggers were short so she would have to throw them or get really close to him.

He moved closer with his long sword. She wasn't intimated although he towered above her and had a long reach. He swung again and she moved to the left, where she spotted an opening to get in closer. She slashed out with her little daggers and only just missed. She got very close—too close. His elbow came up and smashed her in the cheek. She fell to the side and only just managed to twist away from his sword —that neatly cut the front panel of her skirt off just above the knee.

Well, thank you! You just made moving in this dress easier, she thought with a smirk as a square of red silk fluttered softly to the polished white stone floor.

She bent down and his next blow cut the air over her head. Her arms shot forward and both of her dagger tips sank into his thighs. Then she popped both daggers out of his huge muscles, wondering if he'd even felt the slightest ping.

Apparently not, she thought as her eyes widened when he lifted his knee and just missed her face. Then he grabbed her hair and tossed her back. But she remained on her feet. He sprinted toward her. She waited until the last moment to drop to her knees, right between his legs, and he flew right over her and past her.

She jumped to her feet and turned to face him just as he turned to her. She could throw a dagger, but what if he dodged and she hit an innocent person?

She decided not to throw it and fight the hard way. He came closer and she kicked upward, left leg aiming for his face. But he caught her leg midair. She had to be quick or he would pull her off balance. As he held her left leg up, Caitlin jumped into the air and kicked out with her right leg. This time she got him in the jaw and he let go of her left leg. She spun in the air and landed on the ground with both feet, her hands outstretched for balance.

She faced him and saw that he was already recovering. Losing no time, she moved forward, spinning with her hands and daggers outstretched. They raked across his chest. Although the cuts weren't very deep, he still cried out, and then he tried to grab her. Since she was now well inside his reach, he couldn't effectively use his sword.

She was too quick for him. She ducked as he grabbed and then she sank her first dagger into his arm, the one that held the sword. He cried out as his sword fell to the ground.

She pulled her dagger out of his arm and stepped back, but not fast enough this time. His enormous fist collided with her mouth. She staggered backward and realized she had let go of both her daggers.

She tasted the blood that dripped from her lips. Now she was angry.

His arm was bleeding, and she knew that he was hurting although he showed no pain. He advanced. She punched first this time and he blocked. Then his arm swung out and she dodged. She hit his face twice, but not nearly hard enough. He punched again and his fist collided with her stomach. She fell to the ground and gasped. Her arms wrapped around herself.

He kicked her in the chest before she could fully recover. She shot backward and landed on her side. He was coming for her. She dodged his foot and realized he was trying to step on her neck—like she was an insect.

Well, that's just not happening, big guy! She grunted as she kicked up and struck his knee. His leg bent and she kicked again. His knee gave way and when his face came down toward her, she punched it. Hard. Then she jumped to her feet.

He blocked her next punch and pushed her away. She stumbled backward and realized that the dinner tables were behind her.

He came for her and she ducked under a table. He was too big to follow. She moved to the right and then he did the same. She moved to the left and he mirrored her movement again. Then she gave him a taunting smile.

With a howl of frustration, he lifted the table and threw it at her. Caitlin managed to duck just in time. Goblets and plates crashed to the floor. Wine spilled. Dishes broke.

Caitlin was still barefoot so she moved to the side instead. She was not going to cut her feet on broken dinnerware. She backed up against a wall. When he came for her, she pushed off from the wall and flipped over his head. She landed on another table and kicked him in the back of the head before he had time to turn around. The momentum sent him face-first into the wall.

He spun around and kicked the table out from under her. She had anticipated his move and she fell forward. He reached for her but missed as she rolled under his legs. Then she got up and jumped. Her hands tangled in his hair.

He fell backward and she pulled herself up onto his shoulders. He reached for her with his meaty hands, but she was too fast. She grabbed his jaw and twisted his neck.

There was a sickening crack as his neck broke. Then his body fell to the ground. Caitlin landed gracefully on her feet.

She stood up and looked down at Flynn Slayer, whose body lay still, neck twisted in an unnatural angle.

Caitlin looked at the people gathered around her and then raised her arms in victory.

CHAPTER 50

ONE BY ONE, the people started clapping and stomping their feet until their applause became a deafening roar. Their energy lifted Caitlin up and made her feel as if she could fly. She found Dylan in the crowd. He wasn't clapping, but he did return her smile.

Then Caitlin looked at Katherine. She had a malicious smile on her face. She made eye contact with Caitlin and smiled even wider.

The Reid family was surrounded by guards. They all looked scared. At the far edge of the dais, Helena had distanced herself from her husband and had her arms wrapped around her daughter like a shield.

"Take them away," Katherine ordered the guards. "Lock them up. They will have a fair trial soon enough."

The crowd watched as the Reid family was led away

in shame. Everyone who traveled with them to the castle would be locked up too.

Nervous chatter filled the ballroom. Everyone had something to say about what they'd just witnessed. Many approached Caitlin. They wanted to know who she was and where she had learned to fight like that. She felt smothered by the tight knot of people who not only wanted to speak to her but also kept touching her—perhaps to assure themselves that she was real—so she picked up her shoes and left the ballroom.

"Wait for me!" Dylan called.

She turned around and gave him a bloody smile. He caught up easily and started walking alongside her.

"Where are you going?" he asked.

"I don't feel like staying there," she replied and licked some dried blood from her lips.

"Are you alright?" He asked.

"I feel spectacular!" she said. She turned to Dylan in excitement. "Dylan! I won!"

"I knew you would."

"It was epic! And Lady Katherine told the guards not to help! It was a fair fight. I did that all by myself!" She victory-punched the air but soon realized how unladylike it was. She self-consciously dropped her hand to her side and hazarded a look around her.

Then she realized nothing about her was ladylike. Her hair was falling out of its pins, she was barefoot, her dress was torn, and her mouth was bloody.

"Did you know this would happen?" Dylan asked.

"What? Of course not! Why do you ask?"

"You had daggers strapped to your legs.... You came prepared."

"Katherine kind of told me to."

"Kind of?"

"She didn't tell me what would happen, but she did tell me to come prepared. So I took extra precaution." She patted her holstered daggers.

Dylan looked down. They were now far from everyone and out of earshot.

"What's wrong?" she asked. "Aren't you glad I won?"

"Of course I am glad you won!" Dylan exclaimed. "I would have killed that man myself if you'd lost."

"Then what is it?"

"It's about the bigger picture."

"I don't understand."

"Katherine started a war. There has been a fragile peace between the two kingdoms for years now. They just needed a reason for a war. Now Katherine has framed the royal family for a murder that they didn't commit. Most kingdoms will join our side. She will conquer the Forevermore Kingdom and rule over it."

"We've always known Katherine was after power."

"But we didn't know to what extremes she would go to get it."

"I don't see what the big deal is," Caitlin said. "My name is cleared. She got what she wanted, and she will rule better than any of the Reids ever could."

"And what about the Reid family? They'll be sentenced

to death for killing our king."

"It's not my problem."

"Do you feel no guilt at all?"

"It's not in my nature to," she said.

Dylan gaped at her. "Caitlin, do you realize how serious this is?"

She rolled her eyes at him.

"The king pulled our royal ring from his pocket. We both know Katherine planted it there. I wouldn't be surprised if she had his mind obliterated so that he would cooperate."

"So she messed with his mind. So what?"

Dylan gasped. "So what?! Are you kidding me?! If she could do that to a royal, she won't hesitate to do it to commoners like us!"

"She won't ever do that to me."

"How do you know that?"

"I trust her."

"Then you are a fool," Dylan sneered. "This woman clearly has no limits."

"Neither do I." Caitlin was getting irritated with him. "What would you have me do then?"

"If you really feel like the two of you are so close, maybe you should go talk to her."

"And say what? I have no objections to what she is doing. She's only ever helped me."

"She's using you!" Dylan objected. "We both assumed she cleared your name for your sake, but she only did it for herself. She only does things if she sees the benefit to herself. You killing the king gave her exactly what she wanted–the opportunity to frame the royal family of the Forevermore Kingdom–the kingdom she wants for herself."

"Stop it."

"You need to hear the truth whether you like it or not," Dylan told her.

"And you know the truth?" She glared at him.

"You're just too infatuated with Katherine to see what she truly is."

"And what's that?"

"A snake."

Caitlin rolled her eyes. "She's not going to backstab me."

"Of course not. Not when she can use you. You were a great help to her tonight. She'll thank you later and make you feel special."

"And so what if I feel special?"

"Framing and killing people shouldn't make one feel special."

"You're a funny one to talk," she said. "You've killed more people than I have."

"Yes," he said. "And it took me this long to figure out that killing is wrong."

"I've got killer blood running in my veins, remember?" she reminded him.

"I know that."

"And I'm not going to change. This is who I am. This is how I feel. If you don't like it, you can do us both a favor and remove yourself from my life." She turned to walk away but he pulled her back.

"I'm sorry," he said. "I won't leave."

"And why won't you leave? Because you are trying to save me?"

"I *can* save you," he said. "You just need to let me."

She pulled free and met his gaze. Then she walked away.

CHAPTER 51

THE NEXT MORNING Caitlin rose early. She had left what remained of her dress on the floor and slept in her underwear. She wasn't planning on picking it up. She'd slowly gotten used to having servants do everything for her.

She opened her closet door and decided to dress in comfortable clothes. *Surely no one would mind me wearing something like this?* she thought as she slipped on a plain linen dress that draped shapelessly down to mid-calf. She grabbed a chunky leather belt and a pair of worn boots. The ensemble looked nothing like the form-fitting red gown that now lay in tatters on the floor near her bed.

But as she left her room and made her way to Lady Katherine's room, she realized people were staring and whispering as she walked by. Everyone she passed recognized her so she kept her eyes forward and tried to ignore them.

She knocked on Katherine's door. There was no answer. At first she thought that Katherine was out or was busy but then the door swung open.

"Good morning," Lady Katherine said. "It's nice to see you!" She moved aside so Caitlin could enter and then she closed the door. Morning sun poured into the room from the large mullioned windows, warming the stone floor while creating a crisscross pattern of shadows. It was nice.

"I was wondering when I'd see you," Katherine said. "I thought you would sleep in after the ball."

"I didn't stay that long," Caitlin confessed. "I went to bed much earlier than expected."

If Katherine didn't know this, then she hadn't stayed long either. Caitlin wondered if she had gone to see the royal family after leaving the ball.

"Did you get tired of all the attention?" Katherine asked. "You're the castle's new celebrity."

"I'm not used to the attention," Caitlin confessed.

"You'll get used to it soon enough," Katherine said. "Many of the knights want to challenge you to duels. If you say yes, you will be the first woman ever to fight them."

"Of course I'll say yes!" Caitlin exclaimed. "That sounds fun!"

Katherine smiled. "Let's sit outside. It's a beautiful day."

She took the teapot and teacups outside to the patio where a pretty little table and chairs perched over a garden view. Then she sat down and poured the tea.

"Don't you have a servant to do that?" Caitlin asked.

"I do," Katherine said. "But I also prefer doing things on my own.... It keeps me from getting lazy. Besides, with a servant around, I lose much of my privacy."

"I can understand that." Caitlin took her teacup. It was made of the most delicate porcelain she'd ever seen, almost translucent in the morning sun.

Lady Katherine took a sip of her own tea and then breathed in the morning air. "You looked stunning last night! Without a doubt, you'll have a lot of men lining up to marry you."

Caitlin laughed. "I doubt that. I think most of them are now too scared of me."

"Dylan Archer isn't scared," Katherine pointed out.

Caitlin sipped her tea and looked down. "He's not scared of anything."

"Everyone is scared of something," Katherine said and then paused to contemplate a nearby rose before turning back to Caitlin. "He's scared of heartbreak."

Caitlin met her eyes. "I don't think anyone has that power over him."

Katherine tilted her head to the side. "Sweet girl, are you really that blind? Don't you see the way he looks at you?"

Caitlin shot Katherine a look of bewilderment.

"He is in love with you, my dear."

Caitlin looked down and felt her stomach turn. Did she want Dylan to feel that way about her? That would ruin everything.

"So, I take it you don't feel the same?" Katherine said.

"I'm in love with Rafe," Caitlin confessed. "I don't know if I'll ever get over Rafe."

"You will. You're young, and a strong person."

"My dad once told me that nothing can break a girl's heart like a first love."

"But you can put it back together," Katherine said optimistically. "You just need time."

"I'll take my time," Caitlin nodded. She felt so comfortable here. She felt like she had known Katherine for years. It was nice to have her as a friend.

"I still haven't thanked you for saving me," Lady Katherine said.

"I was just returning the favor," Caitlin said. Then she changed the subject. "What you did last night was wicked—but brilliant."

Katherine smiled. "I've wanted to talk to you about that."

"So talk," Caitlin said.

"Placing the blame on someone else was the easiest way to clear your name. Everyone saw King Arson with the royal ring. That piece of evidence convinced them all."

"But this wasn't about me...." Caitlin said.

"No," Katherine admitted. "We've always tolerated the Forevermore Kingdom, but we've never liked them. The only reason they haven't attacked us is because we have a bigger army."

"What will happen to them?"

"We will take the country easily," Katherine said. "If King Arson doesn't surrender the Forevermore Kingdom to us during his trial, we will take it by force."

"If?" Caitlin asked. "You can control what the man thinks, so..."

Katherine smiled. "Should I use the obliteration device to make him give it over? Then it will be peaceful transfer of power. We will take the kingdom and the Reid family will be exiled. Or should I have the royal family killed and take the country by force?"

"I'd go for the peaceful option. If you start a war, the other countries might join in."

"You're a smart girl," Katherine said.

"When is the trial?"

"Two days from now," Katherine said. "And a week from now, Prince Reagan will be crowned king and I will be his right hand."

"Have you ever thought about becoming queen?" Caitlin asked.

"I have no desire to be queen," Katherine said. "I'm perfectly happy with the position that I am in. I have all the power I need in this role."

Caitlin nodded.

"What about you, child? Are you happy with your new position?" Katherine asked her.

"Yes, I'm happy...."

"But I sense that something is bothering you," Katherine said.

"It's nothing big."

"Tell me anyway."

"I think it's just the little things Dylan says to me. They bother me sometimes."

"Like what?"

"He wants me to leave with him. He thinks I will have a better life away from Sky Castle."

Katherine's face twisted. "Being in love makes one very selfish. He just wants you for himself. That's fine." She used her napkin to brush some biscuit crumbs from her lips. "But it never lasts. I trust you already know that."

Caitlin nodded. "I do."

"Love only yourself and you'll never get hurt," Katherine told her. "What else has he been saying?" She started playing with her napkin, folding it once, twice, and then smoothing the folds with her thumb and forefinger.

"He doesn't like the obliteration device and what it does to people's minds."

Katherine sat up straighter and looked squarely at Caitlin. "How much does he know? How much does he know of what has been happening down in the tunnels?"

Caitlin swallowed. She had forgotten that Katherine

didn't know that Dylan knew everything. "I told him most of it..." Caitlin confessed weakly.

Katherine looked at her with a blank face.

"I don't mean to upset you."

"I'm just surprised," Katherine said. "Who else did you tell?"

"No one."

"Caitlin, you shouldn't be telling people about the device. They won't understand that it's being used for the greater good. Its existence should be top secret."

She nodded. "But I trust Dylan."

"Men can't be trusted. It's only a matter of time before he leaves the castle and goes back to being a hunter."

"He's changed."

"People don't change."

"Have you used the obliteration device on everyone who knows about it?" Caitlin asked and she thought about how empty the tunnels were.

"Almost everyone," Katherine said. "With the exception of a few people who I trust and need—people such as yourself."

Caitlin swallowed and shifted forward, tensing. "Will you use it on Dylan?"

Katherine looked at her and hesitated. "No."

"Good," Caitlin said, relaxing back in her chair.

They enjoyed the rest of the morning together. They drank tea and ate and laughed as if they were the best of friends.

CHAPTER 52

THE NEXT THREE days were eventful. The Reid family confessed to murdering King Leonard. They made an official announcement to surrender the Forevermore Kingdom and were subsequently given the more lenient sentence of permanent exile. Had the Reids contested the court's ruling, they would have all been beheaded.

Caitlin watched them walk away in shame, leaving with nothing but the clothes on their bodies. Katherine gave orders that they were not to be harmed. No one dared to defy her.

Caitlin was sitting on the castle wall, watching the Reid family make their way toward the big gates that led to the road down the mountain.

"She did it...." Dylan's voice made Caitlin jump. He had silently climbed up on the wall behind her.

She turned to look at him. His eyes followed the Reid family to the gates. Eugenie was clinging to her mother's hand. "Who did what?" Caitlin asked.

"For years, King Leonard wanted to take the Forevermore Kingdom for himself. And now Lady Katherine has done it."

Caitlin looked down at the royals. Was she supposed to feel sorry for them? She didn't. "She did it in a peaceful way," she said, her tone defensive.

Dylan sat down next to Caitlin and let his feet dangle off the castle wall. He looked sympathetically at the exiled royals.

"If they'd had the chance, they would have done the same to us," Caitlin said.

"You don't know that," Dylan mumbled.

They sat in silence for a while and felt the sun bake their skin. Caitlin looked at Dylan before she decided to tell him the news. "Katherine is taking a portion of the army to the Forevermore Kingdom, to go and claim it."

"Why am I not surprised."

She decided to ignore his scornful remark. "She's leaving tomorrow morning."

"How efficient of her."

"She asked me to go with her," Caitlin said, a note of irritation creeping into her tone.

Dylan paused. "And do you want to?"

Caitlin nodded. "I will go with her."

Dylan clamped his mouth shut, although she knew

he wanted to object and argue with her. Instead, he sat on the wall with her, silent for a long time.

"What will you do when I am gone?" she asked, breaking the stillness.

"I might start looking at different schools," Dylan said, eyes focused on the far horizon.

"Close by?"

"I promised not to leave without you," he said, turning his blue eyes to her. "So yes."

"That's good," she said with a smile, relieved that they were back on a more pleasant, easygoing footing.

They spent the day together and had fun. That night Dylan walked her to her room as always. He lingered in the doorway.

"What?" she asked.

"I don't want to say goodbye yet," he confessed.

"Well, we are leaving at first light tomorrow," she said.

"I will come and say goodbye then," he told her.

"You promise?"

"I promise."

He pulled her into a hug that lasted much longer than it should have. When he let go, she realized she didn't want him to leave. But she said nothing and watched as he left the room and closed the door behind him.

Caitlin felt lonely. She threw herself down on her bed and wiggled out of her boots, kicking them with a grunt of satisfaction at the spot where Dylan had repeated his promise. She saw that her bags had been packed by the servants earlier and now sat ready for her by the door.

She had nothing more to do so she closed her eyes, not bothering to change out of her comfortable linen shift dress. Sleep came much easier than she thought it would.

Dylan lingered in the hallway. He didn't want to leave her so early, but she needed her rest. He knew that if he stayed, they would have been awake talking the whole night and she would have been exhausted the next day. Traveling when tired wasn't fun—Dylan knew this better than anyone. So instead, he walked down the hallway and then outside toward his own room.

The night air was chilly, but Dylan didn't get cold easily. He looked up at the sky. Black clouds loomed over the castle grounds. He wondered if it would rain again. Everything outside was quiet and still except for the wind rustling through the trees and the sound of his feet crunching on the gravel. Soft chatter drifted out of some of the houses he passed.

Then he felt the hairs on the back of his neck rise and he slowed his pace. He turned to look behind him, but there was no one there. He couldn't shake the feeling that he was being followed. He shook his head. It was ridiculous to think that someone was following him. Why would anyone want to do that?

It got darker as he neared the inn. Most of the lights were out. Two girls walked past him. They giggled and looked up at him through their long eyelashes, but he didn't stop to talk to them. He reached one of the walls where he knew a tunnel entrance was located. It was down an alley that was dark and deserted.

A banging sound to his right startled him and he spun around. A black cat had knocked over an empty barrel.

He turned back to the alley. There was no one there. He wasn't usually a paranoid or anxious person. *Why does something feel off?*

He walked back to the inn. As he mounted the front porch steps and was about to push open the door, he glimpsed a figure to his right. The figure was only there for a second before disappearing into the night. *Is someone following me?*

He walked toward the spot where the figure had stood. Perhaps the figure had come out of the tunnels.

He spied the figure just around the corner and sprinted quickly after him. Dylan reached out and grabbed him, slamming him against the wall.

"I don't have any money!" the man cried out.

"What?" Dylan asked confused. Then he realized that the man had mistaken him for a robber.

The man looked underfed and stared at Dylan with wide, scared eyes, so Dylan let him go and took a step back. The man had dropped the bundle of firewood and kindling that he was carrying and nervously raised his hands up as if to ward off further attack when the light from the inn caught the gleam of a ring on his left hand.

Then the man touched his shoulder and Dylan wondered if he had hurt him. "I am sorry," Dylan said.

The man didn't respond. He looked jumpy and Dylan thought he might run. So he moved slowly and deliberately in order not to scare the man any further and bent down to pick up the firewood. He handed them to the man who hesitantly took them. "I really am sorry," Dylan apologized again before letting him go on his way.

Dylan went to his room in the inn. He felt like an idiot. He slammed his door shut and locked it. He sat on his bed with his head in his hands for a while. Then he got up and walked to the window. He looked outside. The streets were empty. He closed the curtains and took off his clothes and changed into his nightshirt. He climbed into bed and lay there.

It took him a long time to fall asleep because he replayed the fight between Flynn and Caitlin in his mind. She was so young, yet she fought better than anyone Dylan had ever seen. He wondered what she was capable of and hoped he wouldn't find out. If only he could take her away from the castle... Slowly, Dylan's thoughts turned into dreams.

He awoke suddenly to a draft coming through his doorway. The door had been pushed wide open. He noticed a solid shape, a dense shadow to the right of the doorway, just inside his room. As the figure moved into the moonlight, Dylan saw a scar slowly take form on his face. Then the man lunged forward as Dylan jumped to one side and punched him in the stomach.

Dylan heard a groan and was about to hit him again but didn't realize that another man lurked on the other side of his bed. This man picked up the lamp on the bedside table and swung it at Dylan's head. The lamp shattered and Dylan's world went black.

A servant woke Caitlin before the sun came up. She got dressed and had something small to eat. Her luggage was taken from her room by the servants who carried them to the horse-drawn carriages.

Caitlin made her way to the stables early. She enjoyed the fresh morning air. Her riding trousers felt like a second skin and she noticed some men's heads turning as she walked. She didn't give them a second glance and went straight to her horse's stable. She much preferred riding on horseback over traveling inside a carriage, no matter how luxurious it was.

She waited patiently for Dylan, hoping he would arrive soon so that they could spend a little more time together. She would miss him.

As she saddled her horse, a task she preferred doing herself, she wondered how long they would be away. It was a long journey. Maybe they would have to stay there for a few months to get everything in order.

The first sun rays lit up the sky. Where was Dylan? It was unlike him to be late.

"Good morning," Katherine said. She looked different. She was wearing black trousers with boots and spurs. She wore gloves so that her soft hands wouldn't get blistered from holding the reins. Apparently, she too preferred horseback over a fancy carriage.

"Good morning," Caitlin responded. "I would have thought that you would ride in the carriage."

"I enjoy riding, although the horses never like me," she smiled in a catlike way. "If I had more free time, I would be doing it more often."

"Aren't you scared of falling?" Caitlin thought about how Rafe had to hold on to the saddle horn so that his horse didn't buck him off.

"I like the challenge," Katherine responded.

Caitlin had finished saddling her horse and now

gathered the reins. The horse sniffed the air and took a step away from Katherine.

Katherine didn't attempt to pet it. She just looked at it and then back to Caitlin. "Let's get going," she said.

Caitlin looked in the direction of Dylan's inn. She didn't say anything.

"What's wrong?" Katherine asked. "It looks like you've forgotten something."

"It's nothing," Caitlin said and then she mounted her horse.

"You're welcome to ride up front with me," Katherine said.

"Thank you."

Caitlin watched Katherine walk toward the horse that had been saddled for her. A groom held its reins and tried to calm it with soothing noises, but the horse still moved around nervously as she mounted. It tossed its head as Katherine took the reins from the groom and almost reared up as Katherine turned it toward the stable doors.

They were leaving. Caitlin rode at the front of the entourage beside Katherine and kept looking back over her shoulder. The horses trotted along briskly.

"What is it?" Katherine asked when Caitlin kept looking back.

"Dylan," Caitlin confessed. "He didn't come to say goodbye."

"Maybe he overslept," Katherine suggested.

"That's not like him."

"There's no point in going back now," Katherine said. "We have a long road ahead of us."

Katherine urged her horse to a canter while Caitlin held hers to a trot before pulling off to the side of the road and slowing to a halt. They had reached the big gates. The entourage began to make their way down the Whispering Mountains, but Caitlin's horse remained still, obedient to her command.

Caitlin watched as first their entourage of servants and then the army filed past. Katherine had personally selected every soldier in her retinue. No one would fight such a big army. It was an impressive display of power.

She noticed Katherine looking back at her. Their eyes met and Katherine motioned for her to come forward.

Something didn't feel right. Caitlin shook her head at Katherine before turning her horse and then sinking her heels into its side, urging it to a gallop—back through the castle gates, back toward the inn.

CHAPTER 53

CAITLIN DISMOUNTED IN front of the inn, tied her horse's reins to a tree, and rushed inside.

"Have you seen Dylan this morning?" she asked the innkeeper.

"I have not," the innkeeper replied. He looked like she had woken him up when she burst through the door. He rubbed his eyes and yawned.

Caitlin made her way to Dylan's room. When she saw that the door was wide open, she knew that something was terribly wrong. She walked inside. The bed was unmade and there was a broken lamp on the floor.

Someone had come in and taken him by force. Who could it be? Caitlin panicked. She had no idea where to start looking for him. He didn't have any enemies in the castle that she knew about. Who would want to hurt him? Was he hurt? Was he alive?

Caitlin felt her body shaking. The pain of losing Gerald, Daisy, Maggie, and Rafe stabbed her heart like a dagger. There was no way that she would lose Dylan too.

She paced around the room. She didn't know that many people. Who could she ask for help? She thought of running to Katherine first, but Katherine was leading their army to the Forevermore Kingdom. She wouldn't have time for this.

Evelyn. She was probably getting ready to teach class. Caitlin rushed to her room and banged on the door.

But it wasn't Evelyn who opened the door. It was a man Caitlin hadn't seen before.

"Hello, I'm Riley," he said when she just stared at him awkwardly. "Can I help you?"

It took Caitlin a moment to realize that he was Evelyn's husband. She was about to say something when Evelyn appeared in the doorway.

"Caitlin!" she exclaimed. "It's good to see you!"

"Can we talk?" Caitlin said curtly. Then she added, "Please."

"Come in," Evelyn said.

Caitlin stormed into the room. Riley stood by the door. "I'll give you a moment," he said. And he left.

"What's going on?" Evelyn asked.

"Dylan is missing," she said. "I can't find him any-where and someone broke into his room last night and I found a broken lamp and I don't know what to do."

"Okay, slow down," Evelyn said. "When was the last time you saw him?"

"Last night. He walked me to my room."

"Do you know of anyone who would want to hurt him?"

"No..."

"Do you know of anyone who would want to hurt you and use him to do that?"

"No..."

Evelyn thought for a moment. "A lot of people have disappeared, never to be seen again.... Many of my students..."

Caitlin realized what she was saying.

"If only we knew where they were being taken."

"Evelyn!" Caitlin exclaimed. "What's the fastest way into the tunnels?"

"I have an entrance right here in my room."

"Show me!"

Evelyn did just that. Caitlin thanked her but didn't give an explanation. She made her way down and into the dark as Evelyn closed the trapdoor behind her.

Caitlin slowed to a halt and stood still to allow her eyes to adjust to the dark. Then she sprinted in the direction of the MOP.

Dylan woke up.

His head hurt like hell and the world was blurry. He had to blink several times so that he could see normally. He found himself inside a cage. A cap of woven wires was strapped to his head. His hands were bound, as were his feet. He bolted up to a seated position and kicked at the cage with all his strength. The frame rattled but didn't give way. He wasn't strong enough.

"Ah, you are awake."

Dylan turned to the voice. It came from Healer Dan.

"What are you doing to me?" Dylan asked.

"I've not done anything—yet," Healer Dan said. "I couldn't do anything while you were sleeping. I don't know why Brutus and Scarface had to knock you out. My orders were to bring you here unharmed."

"Well, here I am," Dylan said. "Which is where, exactly? The obliteration device? Why?"

"You know too much.... People shouldn't know too much. And you are trying to convince Caitlin to leave. She needs to be focused."

"What?" Dylan didn't understand.

"But that's enough talking," Healer Dan said, ignoring him. "This won't hurt a bit." He started flicking switches.

Caitlin pushed past the patronizer. She opened the metal door and ran inside—straight to the room with the obliteration device. The doors were closed but she didn't slow down. She slammed into them and they flew off their hinges.

Her eyes met Dylan's. He was kicking against the cage that contained him. Caitlin ran toward the cage.

"Stop!" yelled Healer Dan.

She didn't even look at the healer. She pulled against the cage with the rage of a hell horse and tore through the bars. She tore a hole big enough to free Dylan who did his best to wiggle and crawl his way to the opening, with both hands and feet still tied up. Caitlin ripped the wire cap off his head and was about to untie his bindings when she felt a hand grabbing her arm.

She didn't need to look at him. She simply turned her shoulders, straightened her elbow letting loose her arm, and slammed him in the chest with her fist.

Healer Dan gasped and fell back. Caitlin ripped Dylan's bonds off so he could climb out of the cage.

"I should have killed you when the king ordered it!" Healer Dan spat out once he regained his breath.

But Caitlin heard nothing but the blood rushing through her veins and the angry drumming of her heart. She lunged at him and snapped his neck before Dylan could stop her. The healer fell to the ground like a puppet whose strings had been cut.

Dylan rubbed his wrists as Caitlin looked at the obliteration device. Suddenly, she hated it. She remembered how she had used it on herself. She remembered the pain that shot through her head from the now mangled wire cap that lay on the floor. She thought of what the device had done to her family. She thought of the power that it gave Katherine.

"What happened?" she asked Dylan.

"Two men grabbed me in the middle of the night," Dylan confessed with red cheeks. "I only just woke up."

There was a sound at the door and Caitlin rushed toward it. She was much too fast for Dylan to keep up. She grabbed the two men at the door by their shirts and yanked them into the room. They fell forward. She recognized Scarface and grabbed his hair and then slammed his face into a counter. Then she flipped him over and gouged her nails into his neck. They had become as hard and sharp as a hell horse's hooves.

Dylan attacked Brutus. He slammed his fist into Brutus's jaw. Then he grabbed a metal bar that Caitlin had torn off the cage and held it to his neck.

"Please don't kill me!" Scarface begged Caitlin.

"I was hoping I would find you again," Caitlin said and remembered how they had stolen Maggie.

"Please... please don't kill me...." Scarface repeated.

"We will tell you everything we know—please!" Brutus cried.

CHAPTER 54

"WHY DID YOU take me?" Dylan asked the two henchmen.

"We were told to bring you here to have your mind obliterated by Healer Dan," Brutus said.

"Then we were to take you away from the castle before you woke," squeaked Scarface, his voice pitched higher because of Caitlin's continued grip on his throat.

"Yes, we were ordered to take you to a village far from Sky Castle, to the house of the healer's friend," continued Brutus. "We were told to pretend to be your travel companions so that—"

"Yes, yes, fine. But you have also been stealing a lot of people lately, like my sister Maggie," Caitlin interrupted, impatient to learn the big picture. "Why?"

"We made a deal," Brutus said. "Both of us have Magic. We said we would help with the MOP if our secret was kept and we were protected." He shot a look at Scarface who tried to nod but couldn't because of Caitlin's grip on his neck.

"You actually made a deal with Campbell? He seemed to hate Magic folk so much—I didn't think he was capable of striking that kind of arrangement," Caitlin said.

"Campbell? Of course not!" Brutus said. "That man hated this place and everything that was done here at the MOP. He wanted to tear it up from day one. He only worked here because he was scared that things would get out of control."

"But didn't he build this place?"

"No, he didn't..." Brutus said.

"Then who did?" Caitlin asked.

Brutus remained silent and darted a glance at Scarface who swallowed before saying, "Lady Katherine did."

Caitlin pressed her nails in a little deeper. "You're lying."

"We're not—I swear!" Brutus said, helping his friend. "She told us she would protect us if we worked for her and brought her Magic folk to experiment on. She was the one operating this whole place. She got permission and support from the king to do this."

Caitlin thought back to when she followed Dylan and the king. She could still hear the king's words: "I *was advised to build a weapon. A weapon so strong and scary that it would stop a war before the war could even begin. It was a stupid idea to create this monster. I should have listened to my own advice."*

He was advised.... Who was his adviser?

Caitlin released Scarface who then gasped and wheezed. "So Katherine was the one who had me made into a weapon..." she realized, her eyes widening.

"Yes, you and all of the other kids who died. When that program failed, she started focusing on the MOP," Brutus said. "We've been working with the king's right hand almost since the first experiments began. We knew that you escaped and then obliterated yourself."

"And although that wasn't part of her plan, Lady Katherine thought that sending someone as strong as me to River Town would be the ultimate test of the obliteration device," said Caitlin as she started to piece together the puzzle of her life. "She must have sent Campbell, or at least approved his going to River Town so that he could watch me and report back to her."

"We thought Campbell would kill you because he feared you. We even heard that he'd hired the services of an assassin," Brutus said.

"Black Blade..." Caitlin confirmed. "But Katherine didn't want me dead...." she said softly, more to herself.

"It *would be a shame to see you dead after every-thing you've been through*," Katherine had said. Caitlin had thought she was talking about River Town being destroyed when she was actually talking about Caitlin's childhood. She was the only experiment that survived everything. Because Divan had gone mad.

Everything made sense now. Katherine wanted the Forevermore Kingdom. She wanted it without going to war. She had the ultimate weapons: the obliteration device and Caitlin.

All she had to do was win Caitlin to her side. Katherine knew that Caitlin had the same natural instincts as a hell horse. She knew Caitlin would be fiercely loyal so she had to win her loyalty. And she did.

First, she warned Caitlin that Campbell wanted her dead, which he did. Then she had him executed in front of Caitlin. Caitlin had thought that Katherine was trying to protect her. But Katherine had actually executed Campbell so that he couldn't tell Caitlin the truth. She remembered that Katherine had gagged him on his march to the executioner's block. He couldn't even speak his final words, let alone tell Caitlin the truth—that Katherine was at the root of everything.

Katherine had won Caitlin's trust when she revealed her secret, that she herself was a shifter and that she was helping all the Magic folk. Caitlin thought she was doing it because she cared, while actually Katherine had just wanted to develop a cure for Craybies so that she herself wouldn't get sick.

"So Katherine was the one who ordered you to take Dylan..." Caitlin said.

"Yes," Brutus said. "She wanted to erase his mind like they did to all those kids."

"All of the kids?" Caitlin asked. "But you took them back to their families, didn't you?"

"Huh?" Scarface said. "How would we do that? We can't even remember where most of them came from —there were so many."

"But Katherine said they would go home. What did you do with them?"

"We killed them," Scarface said.

"Yes, and buried them in the tunnels," Brutus added.

Caitlin was speechless for a few heartbeats. "A *lot of people have disappeared and never came back*," Evelyn had told her.

"So why go through all that effort with Dylan? Why not just kill him like all the rest?"

Brutus and Scarface looked at each other and shrugged. "We don't ask questions. We just do as we're told," Brutus spoke for the two of them.

Scarface added with a shiver, "Yes, to question the king's right hand would mean a seat at the obliteration device."

At last breaking his silence, Dylan said to Caitlin: "Katherine didn't think you were strong enough to handle the death of another person you love or care about. She probably thought it would tear you apart."

Then it hit Caitlin: "When I first arrived at Sky Castle, Katherine tried to convince me to leave. She kept bringing up my family. I think she wanted to figure out if I really loved them.... She realized I did when I made it obvious by staying with them. And then she saw me kissing Rafe.... I didn't remember how to be a weapon. I'd forgotten I even knew how to fight. And then the emotional trauma of Divan's death triggered the return of my memories, and my skills. And she knew all this. She also knew that more pain would bring back even more memories. And if I lost the people I loved, I would grow closer to her...." Caitlin swallowed and thought for a moment before continuing.

"The day my family was killed, Rafe was supposed to be there with them. Katherine had heard him say that he was going there. The only reason he wasn't in the house, the only reason he is alive today, is because my father had chased him away. Something Katherine hadn't planned on. At first, I thought someone had recognized him and told the king. Then the king sent his men...."

Caitlin remembered how unfairly she had treated Rafe. She remembered blaming her family's deaths on him. But it was all Katherine.

"You've been played like a puppet," Scarface sneered. "She ordered your family's deaths as well as Rafe's." Spittle sprayed out from the gap between his teeth.

Caitlin squeezed her eyes shut in denial. She had never felt more betrayed. Her emotions took over. Scarface thought he was safe. He though she had let him go. He could never have seen it coming. She used her nails and sliced through his neck in one fluid motion. His blood splattered all over her and he sank to the ground while clutching his neck.

"Caitlin!" Dylan cried.

She didn't listen to him.

"Caitlin! Think about what you are doing!" Dylan cried. He was smart enough to not get in her way.

Caitlin started flipping switches, activating the obliteration device. Then she spun around and kicked Brutus. He fell into the machine. Sparks flew as he was electrified and the entire device caught fire.

"Let's get out of here!" Dylan cried as he yanked Caitlin away from the machine.

They ran and the whole thing exploded, the blast catapulting them forward into the tunnels. Then the tunnels started caving in.

Caitlin and Dylan made it out just in time.

"So what now?" Dylan asked as they both gasped for breath and shook their clothes free of dirt.

"Now I'm going to talk to Katherine." With that, Caitlin marched out of what was left of the tunnels with Dylan at her heels, scrambling to keep up.

Caitlin somehow had to get Katherine to confess. A part of her knew it was true. Another part of her wished that it wasn't.

If it was true, then she had slaughtered so many innocent people—not to mention killing the king—for crimes they didn't commit. If it was true, she had aided Katherine in all of this destruction and she was as bad as the evil cat lady.

Caitlin bit her lip. She should have known that

Katherine was the mastermind behind everything. Katherine had even told her so. "*I know about everything that happens behind the castle walls.*"

CHAPTER 55

DYLAN AND CAITLIN both knew that it wasn't a good time to confront Katherine. Not when she was leading an army to overthrow another kingdom. But Dylan also knew that Caitlin lacked the patience to wait for the right opportunity.

"I need to do this alone," she told Dylan.

No surprise there, Dylan thought but said aloud, "I will wait close by."

Then Caitlin fetched her horse and galloped after the army. She caught up with them and rode to the front of the army. Her horse fell in step beside Lady Katherine's mare.

"I thought you weren't coming anymore," Katherine stated with a tight jaw.

"Of course I'm coming with you," Caitlin said casually. "I just really wanted to say goodbye to Dylan."

"And did you?" Katherine asked innocently.

"I didn't," Caitlin lied. "I went to his inn but he wasn't there."

"That's a shame." Katherine didn't sound sympathetic at all.

"It just shows me that I am not a priority for him." Now she had Katherine's attention. She continued lying easily. "He told me last night that he didn't want to stay at Sky Castle without me. So I saw this coming."

"I didn't think he would leave," Katherine said.

I didn't say anything about him leaving, Caitlin thought.

They were riding with a good distance between them and the soldiers behind them. The soldiers were also talking and therefore weren't focusing on Katherine and Caitlin. So no one could hear what the two were saying.

"How are you feeling about his sudden departure?" Katherine asked in a concerned tone.

"I'm not feeling much anymore," Caitlin confessed. "Ever since my memories returned, I don't seem to get easily attached to people. I guess I was only programmed to love certain people."

"Are you talking about your family?"

"Yes, but they were never truly my family."

"And Rafe?"

"I loved him in a way, but he still left. He never loved me."

"You haven't spoken about these people in a long time...."

"Because before now I didn't trust you completely, and I didn't understand you either. I thought you might be scared of me if I told you that I knew the truth."

"What truth?"

"That you created the MOP after getting the king's permission—that you in fact were the one who created me. And that you killed the Wilde family."

Katherine's face was blank. "Who told you that?"

"It doesn't matter," Caitlin lied easily. "What matters is that I now understand why you did it. You did it all to help me—so that I could remember who I was and so that I could be the best weapon in the world."

Katherine met her eyes. She was still not speaking.

"So I guess I want to say thank you, for making me such a strong person." Caitlin was running out of words. She let silence take over their conversation for a little bit.

Just when she thought Katherine wasn't going to say anything, she heard a tiny exhale and then: "I thought you'd never understand."

That was all the confession Caitlin needed. *So it was true. Katherine had been behind everything all along. She had used, abused, and betrayed me. She killed almost everyone I loved.*

Caitlin allowed herself several slow, deep breaths and let her eyes wander over the distant view. From their vantage point, on a road edging a sheer cliff, the Silver Kingdom sprawled before them below, rich in its forests, rivers, animals, and productive villages. And to all this wealth would now be added the riches of the Forevermore Kingdom.

Katherine's eyes fell on Caitlin's necklace—the one Maggie had made for her—the one with the two wooden girls on it—and the blood drained from her face. "If they don't matter, why are you still wearing that?"

Caitlin met her eyes. "They will always matter."

Then like a predator, Caitlin pounced. She jumped from her saddle and slammed her body into Katherine's. Katherine slid off the side of her saddle and they both went tumbling over the cliff.

The wind rushed past Caitlin's ears. She didn't hear the soldiers screaming after them. The men wouldn't risk their lives trying to climb down the cliff after them —they would have to look for a safer way down.

Caitlin landed on her stomach and felt her breath leave her body. It hurt! She rolled over onto her back and found it hard to breathe.

Katherine landed gracefully on her feet—the way a cat would.

"You are a brilliant liar," Katherine told Caitlin.

"I'm not nearly as good as you," Caitlin said. She got to her feet with a hand still on her stomach. "How could you do this to me?"

"All I ever did was help you."

"All you ever did was help yourself!" Caitlin retorted. "You never cared about me. You never thought about what was best for me."

"It is all about the bigger picture." Katherine rolled

her eyes. "I grew up in a poor shifter family, but we were happy during the days of Magic. Until Leonard decided to overthrow the Witch King and kill Magic folk. My entire family was slaughtered by his soldiers. But I survived. I was too weak to protect them, and I decided that I would never be that weak again. So I befriended Leonard, I even saved his life and gained his trust. I admit I wanted to kill him for what he did to my family. But I decided the best revenge was pulling his strings, turning him into my puppet instead. I've become the most powerful shifter in the kingdom—and you can be by my side. Having all this power will ensure that no one ever hurts you again. Can't you see? We can rule the world. Yes, some minor obstacles stand the way, but we can overcome them."

"My family wasn't an obstacle."

"They weren't your family! They only loved you because I told them to!"

"I'm not just a weapon! I'm a person capable of love."

"But people aren't capable of loving you," Katherine said in an icy voice. "Just look at yourself. You're a killing machine. You weren't designed to live a normal life. People will always be scared of you."

"You're wrong! Rafe loved me."

Katherine laughed. "Then why did he leave you?"

"You must have obliterated him!"

"No, sweetheart. I did not."

Caitlin felt the tears in her eyes. She knew that that was the truth.

"I never took anything from you, because you never had anything."

Caitlin clenched her fists.

"But you can have everything you want if you just join me. It's that simple. It's that easy."

"I think this is the first time that I've ever seen you scared," Caitlin smiled.

Katherine made a scoffing sound but Caitlin could tell that she was trembling.

"Did you tell your guards to make my family suffer before they murdered them?"

"No."

"I think that's a lie," Caitlin said.

Katherine stood with her back to the cliff. A ledge above hid her from the soldiers who were trying to find a way down to them.

Caitlin walked confidently toward her. Katherine knew she could not win this fight. She backed all the way up against the cliff wall.

"If you kill me, you will be a fugitive for the rest of your life."

"Do you think I care?" Caitlin asked. "You took away everything that was important to me. I have nothing left to live for."

Caitlin slashed out and Katherine ducked. Her nails scraped the cliff. Katherine tried to run but Caitlin grabbed a handful of hair and pulled her back.

Then Katherine shifted. Her clothes fell to the ground. The cat was small and impossible to hold. She broke free of Caitlin's grasp and scrambled over the rocks. Caitlin followed—as if she was the cat and Katherine the mouse—but Katherine was faster and more agile, jumping from one rock to the next.

There was a small ledge jutting out from another cliff. Katherine reached it before Caitlin had time to stop her.

"NO!" Caitlin cried in frustration as she watched her enemy make her way safely to the other side.

There Katherine shifted back into human form and looked at Caitlin. She smiled, clearly pleased with herself. She'd gotten away. Caitlin couldn't reach her—she was too big to cross the cliff. "Goodbye, Caitlin," Katherine said. "I so wished that you had joined me."

"No chance of that now, lady," Caitlin said.

Caitlin sensed his presence before he even appeared. At first, they heard the heavy footsteps coming from behind Katherine. Slowly the lady turned and looked into blood-red eyes.

The hell horse had never left Sky Castle. Its nature required it to stay with its herd—its family—and Caitlin was the closest thing to that. So unbeknownst to Caitlin, it had never left her and continued to watch over her.

Katherine stood frozen in place. She was trapped. There was no way up, not even for a cat. To her left was the ledge that led back to Caitlin and to her right was a steep cliff that presented no footholds. In front of her was the hell horse that she had starved for years and years.

"Enjoy your feast," Caitlin said to the hell horse, "and thank you, my friend."

Then she watched as it ripped Lady Katherine apart piece by piece, eating her alive. Her screams made Caitlin smile.

CHAPTER 56

THE SOLDIERS FOUND rope and helped Caitlin up. She pretended to be in shock. Sobbing and seemingly inconsolable, she explained that her horse had stumbled on a loose stone, lost its balance, and bumped hard into Katherine's horse, unseating them both and causing them to fall over the cliff. Since Katherine and Caitlin had ridden far enough ahead of the army, no one had seen the accident and they all believed her.

Caitlin sold it. She was uncontrollably shaking and intermittently hiccupping and gulping down air. Tears streamed down her face and snot stopped up her nose. Everyone thought she was crying over Katherine, when in truth she was crying over who she had become.

They made their way back to Sky Castle and she separated from the army. She didn't know where to find Dylan, but she felt the need to be alone. So she went to the only place she could think of: Rafe's tower.

She was tired and hurting when she climbed the stairs. She climbed them slowly, one step at a time. When she reached the top, the sun was high in the sky. Its rays shone on her face and into her green eyes making her squint. She took a seat on a ledge, rested her back against one of the four pillars supporting the tower's roof, and looked down the cliffs over the castle grounds. There she sat for hours and hours.

What am I? What kind of monster have I become? Dylan should have killed me all those years ago when he found me on the battlefield. If she had known then what she knew now... the person—the weapon—she would become... the lives she would take... the people she would grow to love and then lose... all those needless deaths, all because of her. *He should have killed me then.*

She was only six years old. She had run away from the castle for the first time, scared and confused when she accidently stumbled into a battle and realized that her life was in danger. Then her hell horse instincts kicked in and the world blurred by. She didn't hear the soldiers' dying screams; she didn't hear the shifters' dying pleas. She painted the ground red, and when all was done, she crawled away into a little ball.

She remembered lying on the battlefield, alone and scared until she heard someone walking toward her. She felt him stop next to her and imagined him being one of the big soldiers—one she had failed to kill. She

411

lay as still as she possibly could and kept her eyes closed.

Maybe he'll think I'm dead and leave, she remembered thinking hopefully.

But the man lingered, and she remembered wondering just how big he was. Could she snatch out, grab his ankle, and make him fall? Maybe that could buy her time to run. But she wouldn't kill him—she didn't want to kill him. She hadn't wanted to kill anyone. But she had been so scared by all the fighting around her.

She remembered feeling relief when the man had turned away. She waited a few seconds before jumping to her feet and rushing to the cover of the nearby trees. She remembered her surprise when she finally saw the person who had spared her life. He was not a big, scary man at all but a small blond boy, only slightly older than herself. She remembered the sword that was way too big for him, remembered him dragging it behind him as he walked away. Had he attacked her, she knew she could have easily killed him too. Young and small as she was, he was no match for her.

Caitlin's heart grew heavy and her breath became slow and labored. She hung her head and slumped her shoulders. Then she raised her hands to study them. Deceptively slender, capable, and lethal—a killing machine.

Her eyes wandered down, down the high stone ledge from where she sat—the cold stones of the pillar at her back pushing her forward—down the sheer cliffs of Sky Castle, down to the rocky terrain far, far below.

Feeling alone and hopeless and lost, she slowly stood up and leaned forward. It was so high....

Would it just be easier to jump?

Then she couldn't hurt anymore. Then she wouldn't be lost anymore.

All I have to do is take one small step forward....

"Don't you dare," Dylan said as he climbed up the last few steps to the top of the tower.

"W-what?" she asked, startled into wobbling. She regained her balance and then gave a short, bitter laugh. Then she straightened, her body rigid, and didn't turn around as she barked, "You don't want me to kill myself? Maybe you'd rather do the honors? Why not finish the job you couldn't do ten years ago? It'll be so much easier this time.... Just give a little push, why don't you?" Her voice was raspy and harsh.

He gently reached for her and she let him touch her arm—all the fight suddenly gone from her. "I forgive you," was all he said.

Caitlin took a deep breath and turned to look at her friend. She looked long and deep into his steady blue eyes. "Ah! You're so good at that," she said at last, her voice tinged with bitterness. "But I can't forgive the people who did me wrong."

"Caitlin, it's important to be able to forgive people for the things they do wrong, for the ways they hurt you. But that can only happen if you can manage to forgive yourself."

She let her head drop and took a deep breath in and

413

out before she stepped away from the ledge. When she turned to face him, he pulled her into a hug. She allowed it and then mumbled into his shoulder, "I have to let it all go, don't I?"

"That's your choice," Dylan answered. "You have to find a way to let go of the past and look forward to the future."

She remained quiet for a long while. His arms remained securely around her and the rough fabric of his shirt scratched at her cheek. Then she lifted her face to look into his calm blue eyes, and said softly, "Dylan, take me away from this place."

He gently but firmly took her hand and led her to the staircase. But she stopped before starting their descent. Dylan threw her a questioning look, which she answered wordlessly. Then Dylan simply nodded before walking down a couple of steps, just enough to give her the privacy that she needed.

Caitlin's eyes lingered on him before she turned around and then reached up to gently remove the necklace that Maggie had made her. She slowly walked back to the ledge and she stared at the two carved wooden figures of sisters. Then she drew a deep breath in, closed her eyes, and dropped the necklace into the abyss. "I'm letting you go," she whispered, and the wind carried her words away.

She let go of Maggie. She let go of Gerald and Daisy. She let go of Rafe. She let go of the pain.

She would never forget them and would keep them

alive inside her, deep within her heart where they would never be lost and would always comfort her. And she felt her heart grow warm, felt it begin to open—open to receiving whatever the world would have to offer—and then through her tears, she smiled.

"So, where are we going?" she called to Dylan who had witnessed everything and was eager to start down the staircase and away from Sky Castle.

"I thought we could go to some towns, find the shifters who need to be cured," his bright, eager voice called back to her.

"Brilliant idea," she said, watching his straight and strong back as he skipped down the spiral stairs.

At the top of the stairwell, she paused and smiled, thinking of the boy who had the compassion to spare her life when she was a little girl. She smiled at the realization that he had grown to be a man who would always keep his word. And that knowledge made her heart open fully as she hurried to catch up to him.

The former hunter paused at the sound of the girl's quick, light footsteps. He smiled and knew that she would always be there for him.

THE STORY CONCLUDES IN BOOK 3
OF THE SILVER KINGDOM

Acknowledgments

I started this book thinking I would write only one, then it split into two, and now I am considering writing book 3....

Should I start writing book 3, then you, Grandma Edith, will be the first to know. I've dedicated this book to you because you always inspire me. I'd like to thank you for listening to me brainstorm the plot, the twists and turns, while we drink tea. I hope you enjoy reading this book as much as you enjoyed listening to me telling you the story.

A big shout-out to all of my friends who so eagerly helped me create a song and music video to go with the series. Christopher, thank you so much for your hard work and dedication and for filming such a stunning video. Readers, you can find Christopher at (www.youtube.com/christopherdevilliers).

Pierre, thank you so much for adding music to my lyrics and for singing. You are incredibly talented and I look forward to listening to your music in the future. I wish you could have been on the set with us! Readers, you can find Pierre on Instagram (@Pierrestemmet).

Zander, through all the ups and downs, you are still here and for that I thank you. Your sense of humor and positive attitude made filming so much fun! And you look exactly how I picture Dylan. Readers, you can find Zander on Instagram (@zander0cronje).

Franco, thank you so much for participating in the video and giving me the chance to admire your acting skills. You played the perfect Rafe! Readers, you can find Franco on Instagram (@frann_man).

I would like to thank everyone at Aionios Books for helping me turn my dream of becoming a published author into reality. I appreciate all of your hard work and effort and I'm so proud of the end result.

JP, thank you for my beautiful author photo!

Thank you to all the readers! Without you, all of this would mean nothing.

About the Author

Mermaid. Heroine. Actress. Assassin. Princess. Dragon rider.

Tayla Jean Grossberg was all of these things as a child—she had overactive imagination. She grew up on a game ranch in South Africa, among animals such as leopards, buffalo, zebras, and giraffes.

She expanded her horizons by traveling to America and Europe. Her experiences, the people she meets, the places she visits, and the animals she loves inspire her to write novels. Now Tayla spends her time reading, writing, and continuing her crazy adventures.

The only thing she can't do is reach the top shelf.

You can connect with Tayla on social media:
- Instagram (@tayla.jean.grossberg)
- TikTok (@taylajeangrossberg)

She'd love to hear from you!

BOOKS OF THE SILVER KINGDOM:

AIONIOSBOOKS.COM